You Matter

Also by Jazzy Mitchell

Musings of a Madwoman

Lost Treasures

You Matter

Jazzy Mitchell

Desert Palm Press

You Matter

By Jazzy Mitchell

©2019 Jazzy Mitchell

ISBN (trade) 9781948327343
ISBN (epub) 9781948327350
ISBN (pdf) 9781948327367

Desert Palm Press
1961 Main Street, Suite 220
Watsonville, California 95076
www.desertpalmpress.com

Editor: Kellie Doherty (https://editreviseperfect.weebly.com/_
Cover Design: Michelle Brodeur (https://mich-bro.myportfolio.com/)

Printed in the United States of America
First Edition May 2019

Acknowledgments

Thanks to my family, friends, and colleagues—all helped me push through my blocks and listen to my characters' tales. In particular, thanks to my wife and our three children. They've taught me how to be present in my life so I don't miss the good stuff.

Thanks also go to Desert Palm Press—Lee, Mich, and Kellie for their expert work with getting this book in publishable shape. And to those who read the rough versions, David, Sara, and Ashley, your feedback made a difference. Many thanks go to Eileen T. for being my medical consultant and to Kelly P. for being my Massachusetts criminal law expert—you both helped me sound like I know what I'm talking about.

Dedication

To all those people who believe they don't make a difference. To all those people who melt into the background. To all those people who feel lonely in a crowded room. Your smile may be the balm to a hurting heart. Your words may be what lift up a heavy soul. Your actions may be the reason someone keeps trying.

You may not see it, understand it, or believe it, but to others, you matter.

Chapter One

IT DOESN'T MATTER WHO or why or how. Chrissy Kramer doesn't try to figure out any of those oh-so-important factors. She needs to act instead of waiting and thinking and hoping. Because there's no time. There's no time, and she has to save them. Ben and Reggie.

The gunman stormed off the elevator on the fortieth floor of Hawk, Esposito & Associates, the law firm with some of the best attorneys in Boston. She saw him with the rifle and the ammunition belt and the resolute expression. She knows he won't listen. Won't talk. Won't reason. He's on a mission, and she can't let it happen.

It's not that she's particularly brave or has a hero complex or wants to risk her life. Or die. No, she doesn't want to die. But she'll make an exception this time. She won't hide under a desk or behind a wall or in a supply closet. She won't hope for someone else to step up. No one else is willing or has as much to lose.

Of all of them, everyone in this building, she's the most expendable. She's the most fucked-up. She's the one no one wanted. Thrown out of her home when she became pregnant while a senior in high school, a single parent with a beautiful boy named Ben—*No, not a boy. A teenager now.* Chrissy knows her worth. It wasn't until her son, but he's in danger now.

This is all her fault, after all. Ben shouldn't even be here. She'd allowed him to visit after school for months, taking advantage of Reggie's unexpected indulgence and selfishly wanting him near. Coming out of the restroom, though, she saw Frank Hogan striding down the hallway, shooting each person he saw, ignoring the screams and whimpers. He's a disgruntled former client. Someone who lost everything, even though Reggie fought hard for him in court. Chrissy recognizes his hopelessness, despair, disregard for anything other than his endgame—killing Reggie Esposito. The one who lost him everything. He has no money, no home, no family. No reason to live.

Chrissy worked on his file. Remembers the weariness on Reggie's face, the second-guessing and the endless research. A pro bono case. A white knight's crusade. But the knight came back from the fight bloodied and bruised, and now the knight must be saved.

The floor is a labyrinth of hallways and offices. Chrissy uses that to her advantage by running down a parallel hallway to get to Reggie's office before Hogan arrives. She pulls Ben out of his seat, startling him since he has his headphones on and is engrossed in a book. As he squawks in surprise, she opens the door to Reggie's office and shoves him inside. Music blares from the headphones as they slide off his head and fall to the ground. His eyes widen when he hears the screams.

"What's going on?" Ben steps forward, and Chrissy holds her hands up to stop him. "Mom?" His voice shakes.

She takes in the moment, regret resting heavy on her chest, taking her breath away. So many things she should have done differently. Her eyes travel around the well-known office, Reggie's personality on full display. The ornate cherry-wood desk, matching bookcase filled with legal books, and two water-color paintings of flowers she's never seen in person—all speak of Reggie's sophistication. She shakes her head to dislodge the thoughts. *I don't have time for this.*

Searching every inch of Ben's body with her eyes, Chrissy mutters, "It'll be all right."

An agonized shout rends the air, and Chrissy glances toward the front office, half-expecting Hogan to have his weapon trained on them. He isn't there, yet, but she's out of time. She presses her lips together. *I won't let him get past me.*

Reggie rises, eyes widening as more screams fill the air, and Chrissy says in a voice that brooks no argument, "Get under your desk, and don't move. Ben, go with her."

Chrissy throws her son's backpack behind the desk and takes one last look at her son, at Reggie, one more long, heart-wrenching look. "Don't come out unless I tell you to or the police do. Call 911. I love you." Her voice cracks, and she cannot keep herself from looking at Reggie's beautiful face, stalling for one more precious moment to make sure her message is received by both.

Expressive, umber eyes well up as they ask questions Chrissy has no time to address. She studies the antique desk as they duck under it, remembering how she tried to move it one time. Even when she pushed with all her strength, it hadn't budged. Reggie's father used it for years before it became Reggie's. Chrissy hopes it will keep them safe if Hogan gets past her.

She flicks the lights off, closes the office door, and slides into her seat at the receptionist's desk. The L-shaped configuration and dark wood may look like it can shield her if she hides behind it, but she knows how flimsy the manufactured wood is. It's where she sits everyday as Reggie's paralegal and has for the last eighteen months. She loves her job, loves impressing her boss, loves her boss. But she can't think about that now.

Hogan turns the corner and stalks toward her, not stopping until he's standing on the other side of her desk with the semiautomatic rifle leveled at her. "Where is she? Where's that bitch?"

Raising her hands, Chrissy shows him she's not a threat. "She's in court."

"Don't lie to me." His eyes are bloodshot and wild, jumping from Chrissy's face to behind her. He looks like he slept in his clothes, black stone-washed jeans with a wide swath of dirt smeared across his thighs and a navy T-shirt with a hole near his bellybutton. Nausea rolls through Chrissy when she realizes the dirt is dried blood.

"I want that cunt Esposito. She ruined my life." Spittle hits the desk, and Chrissy flinches. He wiggles the rifle in her face. "Tell me where she is."

A pregnant pause blankets them, and Chrissy take a deep, calming breath, not surprised when it does nothing to keep her heart from beating a mile a minute. "I don't know."

She rises. "Look, you seem upset. Let me get you some coffee, and we can talk about it. You like it with cream and two sugars, right? I remember from when you were here last. You know, Reggie's been researching ways to appeal your case. I can go over it with you. Help you."

She steps to her right, standing in front of Reggie's office door, even as he swivels to keep the rifle trained at her heart. Never in a million years would she have guessed she'd be seconds away from being shot by a madman. She's shaking like a leaf, and with every moment that passes, she becomes more afraid he'll shoot her and step over her dead body to get to Ben and Reggie. She doubts Hogan has one ounce of humanity left, certainly not enough to take pity on a young man who still has an entire life to live. No, if he sees Ben, he'll shoot.

"I don't want your help." His voice sounds like a foot dragging through gravel.

This is it. This is my last chance to protect them. Roaring, Chrissy lunges, tackling the man's knees. She hears a crack, a scream, and shots so loud Chrissy can't make sense of the other noises around her. Glass shatters, voices shout. *That's Ben's voice. He sounds scared. And Reggie's. She's calling for me. They need to be quiet. Hogan can't know they're here.*

Hogan falls down, she bounces against the ground, hanging on to his legs even as his fists rain down on her back and blood splatters against her skin. She scrabbles up Hogan's body, pulls the rifle away, and strikes his chin with the butt of the weapon. Pain radiates through her, but she doesn't know why. *Am I shot? Am I going to die? Did he hear them?* She shifts to get a better look at him and screeches, a sharp pain racing through her torso. Her left side is burning, and she can't focus on where the pain originates. All she knows is she's hurt. Against her wishes, her body sags, and she rests against him, even as bile rises in her throat. She hates being this close to him. Although he's not moving, Chrissy holds the rifle across his chest.

Pounding. That's what she hears. The pounding of her heart. Of her head. Of her blood. It overtakes her. Consumes her. Blackness flitters along the edges of her vision, and the sounds converge, as the pain intensifies. She can taste the pain, thick and pungent.

As arms pull her off the unconscious man, she hears Reggie's worried voice and her son's cries, and she knows she's protected the two people she loves most in this unfair world. She's glad about that, glad she can hear their voices.

The rough rub of the carpet against her arms redirects Chrissy's attention. She tries to sit up and shrieks, the white-hot pain lancing through her body, slicing through her mind. Tears pour down her cheeks. Panting, her eyes slip closed, and she concentrates on not moving.

"Christina, you're going to be all right." Soft fingers stroke through her hair and cup her cheek.

Chrissy works hard to open her eyes. Devices beep and urgent voices float around her, as she struggles to remain conscious. Hands move her, hurt her, and she cries out again.

"Christina, don't you dare leave me. You fight. Dammit, you have to fight." Reggie's voice splinters across Chrissy's consciousness. She tries to keep her eyes open, tries to speak, but she's tired. Tired and cold. Her body trembles, and she grits her teeth. Waves of pain flow though her like a relentless tide.

"It doesn't matter," Chrissy mumbles, having trouble focusing on Reggie's worried face. "I don't..." She falls silent.

And it's okay. Not that she's hurt, but that they're not. She closes

4

her eyes, ready to let it all go. But before the pain overwhelms her, before the cold envelops her, before the blackness cloaks her, she hears Reggie utter four incredible, life-changing words.

"You matter to me."

Jazzy Mitchell

BEFORE

Jazzy Mitchell

Chapter Two

SIX MONTHS EARLIER

SITTING AT HER DESK, typing away, Chrissy's surprised when her cell phone rings. It's Ben, and he knows not to call while she's working unless it's urgent. Normally, he texts her once he gets home. Her stomach knots up, jumping to all the terrible things that might have spurred her son to call. It's less than an hour before school lets out for the day.

"Ben? What's wrong?" Chrissy uses a soft voice, not wanting to attract attention. Reggie Esposito, senior partner of Hawk, Esposito & Associates, is in her office, an intense look of concentration pulling down her brows while she sits at her desk reviewing a case file. Although Chrissy can take personal phone calls, she prefers to avoid them when anyone is close enough to hear.

She stares at the computer monitor, although she doesn't attempt to continue working on the cover letter. It's for a court filing, and she's used the same template countless times. All she has to do is print it.

"Mom, I'm in study. Billy wasn't in English class today. Stacey said he's out sick." Ben's voice holds an apology.

"Okay. Okay." Chrissy's foot bounces, her thoughts whirling. It's the middle of June, and he has one more week of school before summer break. Although he stays at home alone until she finishes work, she doesn't want him taking the subway by himself. He normally takes it with Billy and his mom, who live down the street. "I'll come get you." She'll have to take the rest of the day off. It's okay, though. He comes first.

"I can take the T home. It's only three stops."

"Three stops but two different lines. No. I don't want you taking it by yourself." Although the Boston subway system is old hat for Ben, it tends to be busy this time of day, and he's never taken it alone.

"Mom, I'm thirteen not three."

Chrissy smiles. Lately, it's his response any time she expresses concern. "Don't remind me. For now, I'll come get you."

Glancing to the right side of her desk she stifles a sigh. She has three thick files that need to be organized. Reggie has a tendency to throw all correspondence—whether they're emails, transcribed notes, or court documents—inside them without bothering to affix them. Chrissy has to file them from newest to oldest—court documents on the left and all other paperwork on the right—using the prong fasteners.

"But, Mom, I've taken the subway for years. I know all the stops. I promise I'll go straight home and lock the door."

"No, sweetie. We'll talk about this later. I promise. Stay there." Her eyes trace the glistening rocks featured in a framed photograph hanging across from her. One of her first duties as Reggie's paralegal was to choose a picture she wouldn't mind seeing every single workday. Whenever she needs a moment to regroup, her eyes latch on to the ocean scene. After she hears his reluctant agreement, Chrissy disconnects the call and rises, slipping her vintage flip cell phone in her pants pocket. Ben keeps telling her to get a newer model, but it works fine, and it's more important for him to have a newer phone in case he needs to contact her. Like today. She knows she's overprotective. Ben's street-smart and cautious. She'll have to pull back on her mama-bear routine soon. *But not today.*

With a sigh, Chrissy smooths down her mint-colored pantsuit and straightens her gold rope chain over her robin-blue blouse. Ben claims the outfit makes her pale blue eyes pop, particularly with her shoulder-length, sand-colored curls. Chrissy thinks she looks like a character in *Miami Vice*. It wouldn't surprise her if Don Johnson strolled over to her and asked for his clothes back. Still, she has to admit the colors do showcase her eyes. Nodding, Chrissy approaches her boss.

Reggie is staring straight at her, chocolate eyes alert. Her office has a gorgeous view of the Boston Commons, but it hardly registers when Reggie's in the room. She's wearing a pale-yellow dress with a sweetheart neckline, and her matching four-inch high heels are lined up next to the desk. Chrissy often forgets Reggie is shorter since she wears heels every day. Her chestnut locks crowd her face, and Chrissy has the irrational urge to tuck them behind her ears.

"Problem?"

"My son. He usually takes the T with a friend, but Billy's not in school today. I'm sorry, but I'll have to leave early to pick him up."

"Of course. You can take the rest of the day off. Or," Reggie says, raising a finger while leaning back in her chair and crossing her legs, "you can bring him here, and we'll count your time retrieving him as a break since we both know you never take any."

Chrissy's mouth drops open. "Really?" Watching one of Reggie's sculptured eyebrows rise, Chrissy grimaces. Reggie never says anything she doesn't mean. "Thank you. I'll be as quick as I can."

She wouldn't categorize Reggie as a hard-ass, but she doesn't suffer fools gladly. She expects professionalism at all times. Chrissy's worked in Reggie's division for a year, and during that time she's witnessed several acerbic tirades regarding how colleagues dress on casual Fridays. Grabbing her purse, Chrissy makes her way out of the building while recalling one memorable diatribe. Reggie had said, "You would think others would know casual Friday does not mean dress-as-if-you're-getting-sloshed Friday. Honestly, we're running a business, and business casual does not mean roll-out-of-bed attire. Thank God you got the memo, at least." Chrissy remembers preening at the back-handed compliment, but right now she worries about how Reggie might view her with having her personal life intrude on the workday.

It's not professional to run a personal errand outside of my lunch hour, but it's the first time I've had to since I started working for her. If anything, Chrissy tends to overwork herself. Although it took a while for Chrissy to notice, Reggie makes sure Chrissy has time to eat lunch, and she often urges her to leave work as soon as five rolls around.

The four stops outbound to the Prudential are quick, and Chrissy makes the short walk to Titus Sparrow Park. It's a straight shot on the Green Line to reach his school, Boston Science Academy, tucked away on the edge of Rutland Square. Several students are indulging in a pick-up game at the basketball court, while groups of chatting teens sit under maple trees in the park, the dense green leaves providing shade. It's a beautiful sunny day with a slight breeze, and Chrissy wishes she could be one of those carefree students. The brick edifice exudes a gravitas borne of age and history. It's a large building, sectioned off by an enclosed hallway connecting the kindergarten through eighth grade school to the high school.

The school boasts famous alumni who've donated money, time, and mentoring to the fortunate students attending. Ben is one of the lucky recipients of such generosity. Chrissy met the school guidance counselor while taking a criminal law class at the community college three years ago. Delilah was taking the class as an elective for her master's degree and offered to help Ben not only enroll in the private school but also secure a scholarship for him. It was an unexpected kindness and changed their lives.

Walking toward the front entrance, Chrissy spots Ben slouched on the school steps, speaking to one of his friends—*Leroy*—who's a tall kid, already taller than her, and lanky. Chrissy's about five feet seven inches, and she can't help but think Ben will bypass her within the next few years.

She watches her son's body language change when she gets closer. He stands up, hands gesticulating and mouth moving fast. He's dressed in his school uniform of navy slacks, white Oxford button-down shirt, and matching navy blazer with the school's coat of arms across his left breast pocket. His red and white striped tie hangs from his belt. There's a shadow of a mustache on his upper lip. His shaggy, ash brown hair flops over his eyes, as he says goodbye to Leroy and jumps down the school steps to greet her.

"Thanks for coming, Mom. Did you get in trouble?"

"No, honey. As a matter of fact, we're going back to work. Reggie said you can stay in the office, and that way I'll be able to finish my work." She leads the way to the Prudential stop, Ben's loping gait keeping pace with her short, quick steps.

"Cool. Hey, do you think I can hang out with Leroy on Friday? He has some new game he wants to show me, and he wants me to sleep over."

Chrissy swipes her subway pass, and they make their way to the platform. She glances at the digital screen to see how long until the next car arrives. One minute. "Sure. I'll contact his parents tonight." She loves how easily he makes friends. His social calendar is more crowded than hers. As soon as the doors open, they make their way on the train and claim seats.

Once settled, Ben says, "You know, you can come, too. His parents are nice."

Biting the inside of her cheek, Chrissy sighs. He's always trying to look out for her. "That's all right. By the time Friday night rolls around, I'm exhausted. I'd rather get into my favorite sweats and relax."

"You mean sit in front of the boob tube with a tub of Ben & Jerry's."

Chrissy dons an expression of mock outrage, and she slaps his arm. "Such sass. Here I thought I was raising a sweet boy. What happened to him?"

Ben chuckles. "I'm still your sweet boy. If I weren't, that ice cream would be long gone."

"Not if you wanna live to the ripe old age of fourteen."

They emerge from the subway station. Chrissy smiles. "You can sit in the chair across from my desk and study for your finals. No talking to me or anyone else, no wandering, and no games until you're finished. The good news is we can pick up pizza from your favorite place on the way home."

"Don't worry about me. Quiet as a mouse." He sports an endearing smile and a sparkle in his light brown eyes.

They make it back to the office in record time, and as soon as they're seated, Chrissy focuses on her work. She finishes up the cover letter and turns her attention to the files on her desk. Reggie had added a fourth one for her to clean up. Ben does as asked. It's quiet and comfortable, reminding her of endless nights at the kitchen table when she studied for her paralegal degree and he finished his homework. Not so long ago, but in some ways a lifetime ago. The only sounds breaking the silence are those she makes while shuffling papers and typing information into the office schedule. The clacking of the keys sounds too loud, and Chrissy slows down her typing enough to prevent it from sounding like a military march.

"Hello." Chrissy looks up to see Reggie focused on Ben, who also looks up.

"Hi. I'm Ben." He smiles while standing and shakes Reggie's hand. Chrissy and Ben have worked on him not having a limp-fish handshake. She's told him several times how important first impressions are. "Thank you for letting me hang out here."

Chrissy smiles, proud of how mature her son is.

"It's a pleasure to meet you, Ben. I'm Reggie Esposito. You're welcome to hang out here anytime." Chrissy's lips quirk when she hears the emphasis on the words "hang out." She doesn't remember Reggie ever uttering slang.

"Thank you." Ben sits down, and when Reggie turns her attention to Chrissy, he returns his focus to his homework. The rest of the afternoon flies by, and when five o'clock arrives, Chrissy gathers her belongings so they can leave.

They say their goodbyes to Reggie, still hard at work. The hairs on the back of Chrissy's neck rise. Glancing behind her, she sees Reggie watching, an inscrutable expression on her face. Chrissy smiles and waves, both quick and choppy, before speeding to the elevator. *So busted.*

They make their way to the subway. It's much more crowded, the noise of various conversations blending in with a street musician plucking at guitar strings and singing off-key. The distinctive smell of urine pervades the air, and Chrissy scrunches up her nose. Once the subway car arrives, they shuffle inside with the crowd and plop down on a bench. Ben dons his headphones to listen to music while Chrissy grabs a copy of *The Boston Herald* she finds on a neighboring seat. The front cover displays a picture of a corrupt politician, the sensationalistic title proclaiming what an upstanding guy he is. *No surprise there. What a hack paper.* Hearing their Hynes Convention Center stop announced, Chrissy throws the paper back on the seat and rises, Ben next to her. When they emerge from the subway terminal, Chrissy has to blink several times to adjust to the sun's brightness, a contrast to the dark, underground station. The sun feels wonderful. It was a hard winter, and she looks forward to spending more time outdoors now that it's getting warmer.

They eat at the pizzeria instead of taking their food home. It's a small place with only a half-dozen tables available for patrons. They place their order at the tall counter before picking out a table near the window to people-watch. Once their order's ready, they dig in.

"I like her." Ben chews a slice of cheese pizza. It only costs ten bucks for two huge, cheesy slices with crunchy crusts—the size of half a pizza. That's enough to fill her growing boy. It's a bonus that she enjoys the food at Nicky's, too. Ben's eyes are bright, and his smirk warns Chrissy of where this is going.

"Me, too." She shoulder-bumps him.

"Is she single?"

"Ben." Her voice holds a warning she knows he'll ignore. "She's my boss."

He delivers one of his specialty looks—puppy-dog eyes. *I need to be clear.* Otherwise, it won't be safe to allow him in the law firm again, not with his mile-long mischievous streak.

"You're right. She's beautiful and intelligent, but she's also my employer. You know how hard I worked to get into that firm. I like working there. I can see myself working there for a long time." She fixes him with a serious look. "I won't be able to work there if I make a pass at her. Even a casual date invitation could get me sacked. Or, on the off chance she's interested, she'd be a fool not to consider the ramifications of becoming involved with her employee, someone in her division. We're not equals at work, and if a romance went bad, sexual harassment could become an issue."

"You've thought about this."

"Since the day we met, so please drop it. The only relationship Reggie and I can share while I work for her is a professional one. Besides, she's seeing that guy, Ashford."

Scrunching up his face, Ben scoffs. She's mentioned him in passing a few times. Okay, maybe she's ranted a bit. He's a personal injury lawyer and rather smarmy. His ill-fitting suits and hardboiled charm grate on Chrissy's nerves. Last week he showed up with a bouquet of daisies and an apologetic smile. *Daisies.*

"Still?"

"Still."

Nodding, Ben snags another piece of pizza. "Maybe you can see if there are any openings in another division."

Chrissy peers at Ben, but he's staring out the window with an affected nonchalance. Chrissy groans. Reluctant to admit she has watched the job boards for months, she presses her lips together and taps her fingers on her knee. She settles with humming in a noncommittal way before changing the subject.

"How about I cut your hair tonight?"

"Yeah. Okay. Thanks, Mom."

"Sure thing."

He finishes his second slice. "So, can we talk about my taking the T?"

Although she wants to shut down the conversation, she knows it's not the best way to handle her fear for his safety. "Yep. Let's hear it."

"How about starting tomorrow I take the T right after school to the law firm, and I can study there? It's only for a week, and once I'm out of school, I'll be working for Parks and Rec. Reggie said I'm welcome, and I'll be on my best behavior. Promise."

Chrissy thinks about it. It's a good solution, a way to give him some independence, and it will be a good trial for his taking the T home from school during the next school year. If she's being honest with herself, he's old enough to be commuting home without supervision. He's never given her any reason to distrust him.

"Okay. We'll try it." At his triumphant smile she shakes a finger. "While you're at my work, you'll need to be on your best behavior."

"Best behavior, I promise."

"That means no matchmaking. No hinting about dating. No inviting her to come anywhere with us. Not only could it get me in trouble, it could make Reggie uncomfortable around me."

"Mom, I'd never embarrass you that way."

"Good."

"If I invite her to anything, it'll be up to you whether you want to go, too."

Rolling her eyes, Chrissy drops her head in her hands. "What did I ever do to deserve such a sarcastic boy?" His chuckle fills her heart.

After finishing their food, they walk to the corner of Commonwealth and Mass Ave. Their apartment is in a building converted in the early 1980s into ten condominiums. Walking up the stairs to the third floor, Chrissy resists the automatic self-castigation she feels every time she gets out of breath. *Thirty-two is not old.* Ben takes off his shoes at the door, and Chrissy looks around the immediate area while removing her off-white leather flats. The front door opens up to the kitchen. One wall is the original brick, while the rest of the kitchen is painted soft yellow. Linoleum floors and light-colored wooden cabinets give the kitchen an airy feel. To the left are the refrigerator and a door leading to Ben's bedroom.

Chrissy walks through the kitchen and into the living room, picking up stray articles of clothing and placing them in the hamper. When they bring their clothes to the basement each Saturday morning, she finds half of the socks missing if she hasn't completed a thorough sweep through the apartment beforehand. A welcome breeze is coming through the three bay windows, the traffic noise fading away as she walks into her bedroom. When she looks at the light green walls, she imagines sipping mint juleps at an outdoor café, something she's never done. *I bet Reggie has.* A large burgundy armoire is against the far wall, and her bed is to the left of the door. To the right two large windows face the street.

Placing her purse on the end of her bed, Chrissy changes into jeans and a T-shirt before returning to the living room. Ben is set up at the dining table behind the couch near the windows. He's decided to review his English notes for tomorrow's final exam. As she sits down next to him with her laptop, Chrissy sighs. Her boy is getting older, and she needs to figure out what she wants in her life. *Be honest.* Staring at the computer, Chrissy knows exactly what she wants. Or rather, who. But she doesn't have a chance of ever gaining Reggie's love. That woman is too good for her in countless ways.

"I think Reggie likes you, too," Ben says, not looking up from his notes. "Don't lose hope."

Shaking her head, Chrissy can't help but smile. "Thanks, sweetie."

Chapter Three

"MOM, ARE YOU READY?"

Staring at her reflection, Chrissy applies red lip gloss. She tightens the elastic band in her hair and uses a bit more spray to secure the bun. Her hair will probably fall out if the breeze picks up, but it looks neat. She likes the way her cheekbones and eyes are more prominent when she wears her hair up, and she's hoping Reggie will appreciate her efforts. *Fat chance.* Chrissy wears a red satin sleeveless blouse and black linen slacks with black flats. Not the fanciest outfit, but her casual business attire is limited. She grabs her black cardigan sweater and meets Ben at the door.

"Ready. Don't worry, though. We have plenty of time."

"I know, but this way we won't have to rush."

Ben isn't fooling Chrissy. Contrary to his blasé attitude, his constant questions—when are they leaving, who else is going, and how long will take to get to the harbor—are indications of his building excitement. In the past they went to the Hatch Shell to watch the fireworks, but this year they're attending the law firm's Harborfest Cruise. Last year she'd been working for the firm for a mere few weeks before the annual cruise, and she's heard from several colleagues how fun it is. The clincher was hearing how it's family-friendly.

They amble down the street toward the subway stop, and Ben asks, "So, Reggie's going?"

Chrissy sighs. "You know she is. You asked her last week. Remember?"

"I thought something might've come up."

"Even she takes breaks." A thrill races down her spine as she remembers how Reggie asked her yesterday whether they still planned to attend. She's doing her best not to read into it, but her traitorous heart leaps each time Reggie asks a personal question.

"Is what's-his-face going to be there?"

Chrissy can't help chuckling. "God, I hope not."

"It doesn't matter, Mom." Ben claps a hand on her arm and

squeezes before they walk through the subway turnstile, swiping their CharlieCards. They make their way down the stairs to the lower platform. "Remember how she reacted when he came by last Friday? I think she's over him."

The sound of a train entering the station saves her from responding, so Chrissy flashes a quick grin and takes a position close to where the doors will open. She sets herself up the way she used to while playing basketball, ready to box out anyone who tries to get past her. Several people press into her, and she grunts while maintaining her footing. The whoosh of the subway blows warm air at Chrissy, and perspiration erupts on the back of her neck. The humidity makes her feel as if she's standing in a sauna.

As soon as the subway doors open, Chrissy's pushed forward. Since she's only able to snag one seat, Chrissy holds on to a pole above Ben's head while he sits between two college kids. Everyone is in good spirits, their loud conversations swirling around her. She's glad it's starting to cool down. A packed subway car and sweating commuters are a combination she hates. They hop off at the Aquarium stop since Rowe's Wharf isn't far and they've decided to walk along the harbor. The police are interspersed with wandering revelers, providing directions to those who ask. Chrissy's stomach rumbles. She missed lunch. *I'm so glad the cruise will include dinner.* Although she normally isn't comfortable attending these types of events, Reggie brought it up in front of Ben.

"Christina, are you and Ben planning to attend the Harborfest Cruise to watch the fireworks?"

Glancing up from the correspondence she's sorting, Chrissy crinkles her eyebrows. She'd heard of the event, but it sells out quickly.

"I don't have tickets."

"Well, today's your lucky day then." Reggie holds two up, a small smile on her face. "I happen to have two extra ones."

"I couldn't take those from you. Don't they cost money?" She flashes a quick glance across her desk. Ben's head is tilted to the side, hands still on his tablet. He's listening instead of playing his video game. Looking back at Reggie, she sees her thoughtful expression. Chrissy's stomach starts to hurt. She doesn't like revealing how limited her finances are, not wanting to receive handouts from people. She does the best she can for Ben, and he understands she can't always budget extras like Red Sox tickets and harbor cruises.

"All partners receive several tickets each year. I'd rather they not go

to waste. Ben, what do you think? Have you ever been on a harbor cruise?"

"No. It sounds cool." Ben's eyes are bright, and he's practically vibrating in his seat.

"Are you sure you don't need them for someone else?" Chrissy can see she isn't going to win this battle, not with Ben wanting to go. In truth, Chrissy wants to go, too.

"Yes. So, I'll see you both there?"

Chrissy takes them, smiling. "If you're sure. Thank you, Reggie."

"You're welcome."

Chrissy doesn't bother chastising Ben when he pumps his fist. If she could, she'd do it, too.

The cruise ship is huge. It looks sleek with its white fiberglass and tinted windows, like a Hollywood star donning sunglasses. Last night Chrissy studied the ship's layout online. Knowing what to expect helps calm Chrissy's nerves. She's afraid she'll stick out like a sore thumb, that with one look everyone will know she's never attended a social event like this one. They'll be having dinner on the second floor before making their way to the top deck for the fireworks. She blows out a breath, practically bouncing as each step brings them closer to the ship.

At least she'll know a few people attending, like Cathy Freedman, an estate-planning attorney she met last year, and her husband, David. Chrissy crinkles her nose. Estate-planning seems like boring work, but she can imagine why Cathy's successful working with people while they create wills and trusts and documents needed to protect a family and its legacy. The first time she met Cathy, she felt as if she were wrapped in a warm blanket. Cathy projects a caring demeanor, and Chrissy can tell she's sincere. Her ability to make others comfortable is one of her best qualities. As they draw near the boat, Chrissy hears her name called. Looking around, she spies Cathy and David. The couple met while attending a continuing education seminar together, and they married two years later. Chrissy waves at them, leading Ben through the crowd to a small gathering of employees at the dock. She leans in to deliver hugs before introducing them to Ben.

"It's great to meet you, Ben. I think you'll have fun tonight. We'll have an unobstructed view of the fireworks from the top deck," David says.

"That sounds cool. Mom told me the firm does this every year."

"They do. It's one of my favorite functions, second only to the

Christmas party," Cathy says while she gathers her long, brunette hair and ties it back with a hair clip.

"Right. The food is the best."

"Oh, you and your stomach." Cathy pretends to whack David in the belly, and he bends over as if winded. He straightens up a moment later sporting a wide grin, his gray eyes filled with mirth. He has a boy-next-door air about him with his straw-colored hair and trim build.

They are ridiculously cute. Not long after Chrissy started working at the firm, she ended up sharing a table with Cathy during her lunch break, and over time it became a regular occurrence. David joins them when he isn't in court.

"We'll have to introduce you to our nephew, Todd, when he visits next," Cathy says. "He's about your age. They live in Rhode Island, and we take turns visiting each other. I think you'll like him."

"That sounds fun. Thanks," Ben says.

Chrissy smiles. He's so agreeable. She wishes she was like that when she was his age. Perhaps if she'd had some self-confidence, life might have turned out much differently.

"As a matter of fact, we're going down next week to visit. If you want, I can pass along your contact information so you can start talking," David says.

When Ben looks at Chrissy for permission, she nods. She trusts them. Sensing movement behind her, Chrissy turns to see the line beginning to move toward the ramp. "Looks like we can go onboard."

"Oh, good. The sooner we're onboard, the sooner we eat," David jokes.

"There you go about food again," Cathy teases, her soft brown eyes sparkling, a blush on her slightly round face. Chrissy doesn't try to hold back her chuckle. They make their way up the gangplank and have their tickets scanned before finding seats for their dinner.

"You know this ship holds over four hundred people," Cathy says. "It sells out every year. I'm glad you were able to get tickets."

Confused, Chrissy tilts her head, her mind racing. Reggie handed her the tickets without answering her about whether they cost anything. She saw a price printed on them, but she assumed law firm partners received some for free. Chrissy fights her natural inclination to pull out the tickets and look at the price. *Later.*

"I'm glad we're here. I've heard how fun it is, and with David's ringing endorsement of the food, well, this is the place to be."

Glancing at Ben, she sees his lips turned down, eyebrows pulled together. *Worried about money again.* Placing her hand on top of his, she smiles when he looks up. He shakes off his thoughts and shoots a grin at her. Squeezing his hand, she lets go. He's too young to be thinking about making ends meet. She's making enough to afford their monthly expenses. The last thing she wants is for him to offer his summer job money to pay bills. She won't take it. His first pay check is next week, and she wants him to enjoy the result of his hard work.

"Let me get the first round. Honey, you want a glass of wine?" David asks.

"Red, please. Chrissy, do you want a glass of wine?"

"That sounds great. Ben, why don't you go with David to help carry the drinks?"

"Sure." As they walk away, Chrissy hears Ben asking about Todd. Once they're out of sight, she turns her attention back to Cathy, who's smiling at her.

"He's such a handsome young man. And polite. No wonder Reggie's taken a shine to him," Cathy says.

"Oh, thank you. He likes Reggie, too. I love how they've hit it off. I think she misses him being underfoot now that he started working at the park."

"Is that full-time?"

"Well, he had training last week, but after the holiday he'll be working four days a week in the mornings."

"Perfect. He can come to the office afterward," a well-known voice says. Chrissy doesn't attempt to hold back her smile while swiveling. Her eyes widen when Reggie's outfit registers. A sheer silk button-down blouse, one side navy blue with white stars and the other side red and white stripes, is tucked into tailored red slacks. The white camisole under the shirt makes Chrissy lightheaded. Ashford is at Reggie's elbow, jarring her back to earth.

Chrissy tries her best to keep her smile pleasant. "I wouldn't want him to intrude, but thank you for the offer."

"Don't be silly. He's quiet and respectful. I don't mind."

Ashford pulls out a chair for Reggie next to Cathy, but Reggie ignores him, sitting in the chair next to Chrissy. Reggie stifles a snort, looking down. She really needs to quell these inappropriate feelings for her boss. They're selfish and destructive. A foot nudges hers, and she shoots a quick glance at her friend, seeing the amused look on Cathy's face.

"Here we go," David says, placing drinks in front of Cathy and

Chrissy. Ben sits down on the other side of Chrissy, drink in hand.

"What did you get?" Chrissy asks, eying the red fizzy concoction.

"It's a Raspberry Frost Soda. Try it." Ben offers the glass, and Chrissy takes a sip, humming her approval.

"That's good." She licks her lips while glancing at Reggie and stops when their eyes connect. Something about her intense dark eyes darting to Chrissy's mouth makes her heart speed up.

"So, Ben, tell me about your summer job," Cathy says. *Cathy's such a good person.* Although unassuming, she's the one who always bridges the silence.

Ben has no problem talking about his first job, and Chrissy sits back in her chair, allowing her thoughts to wander while sipping her red wine. Reggie's engaging with the rest of the table, and Chrissy relaxes into the sound of her voice, its woodwind tones a sumptuous symphony of sound. If only she could block out Ashford's discordant squawking, the outing would be perfect.

Once dinner is finished, they make their way to the top deck. Chrissy leans against the railing, watching the waves. She enjoys how the wispy clouds turn brilliant orange, red, and purple as the sun sets. Ben is to her left talking to David about a videogame he played at Leroy's last week, and Chrissy wonders whether the Freedmans might accept a dinner invitation to their home. Ben likes them, and she feels they could become more than work friends. A hand on her arm draws her out of her thoughts, where she's surprised to see Reggie leaning against the railing, a concerned look on her face.

"You've been awfully quiet tonight. Is everything all right?"

Chrissy stares at her clasped hands. The truth is she's not sure whether she should bring up the cruise tickets. She sneaked a look at them during dinner, and they were a hundred bucks apiece. "This is the first time Ben's been on a harbor cruise, or any boat, really. He's enjoying himself." Chrissy looks up at Reggie. "Thank you for the tickets." She holds her gaze, only realizing Reggie hasn't released her arm when she squeezes it before letting go.

"I wanted you both to experience this. Even if that meant leading you to believe the tickets were free." Reggie shrugs.

Chrissy looks away, gritting her teeth. She struggles to thank Reggie, but the words stick in her throat. Her pride insists she find a way to pay for the tickets, but she knows Reggie was trying to do something nice for her. Still, she doesn't want Reggie to think she needs handouts. She stares at the horizon, pressing her thumbs together while she processes Reggie's words.

Reggie sighs. "Please, don't be upset with me. I had the best intentions."

Chrissy's surprised to see the distress in Reggie's eyes. Seeking to reassure her, Chrissy reaches out to cover Reggie's hand, her eyes widening when she realizes what she's doing. She fights the urge to pull her hand back. "I know. My pride's a little dented. I don't want to be a charity case."

"No, Christina. That's the last thing I think when I look at you. Truly." Her hand covers Chrissy's, and it burns.

God, I can drown in her eyes.

"I admire you. You work hard and never complain. I know you've made sacrifices while working for the firm. Not that it's any of my business, of course." Reggie withdraws her hand, her eyes sliding away.

"It was thoughtful of you, and I'm thankful." Chrissy turns to catch Reggie's eyes. "There's no need for subterfuge, though. I'd rather you be straight with me."

A smirk disrupts the pensive look on Reggie's face. "Really?"

Heat engulfs Chrissy with a suddenness that makes her eyes water. She bites her upper lip while staring at the deck. *Does she know how I feel? Shit!*

"Right. I'd rather you tell me the truth," Chrissy tries again, and with a fluttering heart she looks back into warm eyes.

"Good to know." They gaze at each other, Chrissy's heart beating a million miles a minute, when Ben interrupts them.

"We're going to sit down at the table David got. You coming?"

With a quick glance at Reggie and a tilt of her head, they make their way to the table. As soon as they're seated, David says, "I'm going to get some more drinks. Chrissy, another glass of red wine?"

"Please. Let me give you some money—"

"Actually, I believe it's my turn to pay," Reggie cuts in, handing over several twenty dollar bills. "I'll have a glass of red wine, too."

"You've got it." David takes the money and leaves to get drinks for everyone, Ben with him. Ashford is nowhere to be seen, much to Chrissy's relief.

"And here I've been calling you Christina since day one."

It takes Chrissy a moment to figure out what Reggie means. "Oh. Um, well, I use my full name for work-related things like signing documents. I guess I didn't think about it. With Cathy and David, our interactions are mostly during our breaks. And I like how you say my name," she adds in a soft voice, half-afraid of Reggie's response. She needn't have worried, if the pleased look Reggie sports is anything to go by. "What about you?" Chrissy hurries to ask. "Is Reggie short for anything?"

"It's my middle name. Dad fought my mother about it for months. He wanted to give me every opportunity to get ahead, and part of that meant giving me a name that could be misconstrued as male. He planned for my law career long before I did." Reggie has a faraway look in her eyes, fingers ripping apart a napkin into thin strips.

Chrissy wonders what it would feel like to have a father who loves her that much. "Sounds like he loves you unconditionally. I worry about Ben not having a male influence."

"David always wanted a son. You'll want to watch him. He might try to steal Ben now that he's met him."

Chuckling Chrissy agrees. "They do seem to have hit it off. Ben's always had an easy time getting along with others."

"You've raised a great young man. He's lucky to have you." Reggie's firm tone of voice captivates Chrissy. "I haven't known Ben for a long time, but we've interacted enough to convince me you've done everything in your power to provide him with a loving home. That's more than many children receive in a two-parent home. You're a wonderful mother."

Overwhelmed, Chrissy swallows down her instinctive objections. In her mind, she'll never be able to provide Ben with all he deserves. That won't stop her from trying. "Thank you. It's always been the two of us against the world. I haven't spoken to my parents since I was pregnant with Ben, and I have no siblings. Sometimes I feel like I'm not offering him enough." She casts a furtive look around the table to make sure no one's listening to their conversation. Cathy's talking to a few colleagues at the next table, and the other two people at the table are in a world of their own. Looking over at David weaving through the crowd, Ben behind him, Chrissy grins. "I think that's why he's soaking up the attention he's receiving from David."

"I take it since he doesn't have a male influence, his father isn't in the picture."

"No. He wanted nothing to do with a child. We were so young, and he was planning to go to college out of state. I have no idea what he's doing nowadays, and I'd rather he not come back into our lives. If Ben ever wants to meet him, though, I won't stand in his way." She doesn't mention how her heart will break if Ben decides to find his dad. *That selfish dirtbag doesn't deserve to have Ben in his life.*

"You really are too good to be true."

Chrissy shakes her head. "You think that because you only spend time with me at work, where I try to present my best side."

"I have a feeling I'd like all your sides." Reggie smirks.

Chrissy flushes. *Is she flirting with me? Come on, Chrissy. Play it cool. Flirting is harmless.* She looks away while clearing her throat. She realizes she's bouncing her leg as if she's tapping in time to Tchaikovsky's *1812 Overture* and places her hand on her knee, reminding herself Reggie is her boss.

"I can tell you from experience having a family is a mixed blessing. I have two older sisters, and all they do is meddle. It's their chief purpose in my life. And my mom, ugh. She keeps reminding me how she's not getting any younger and expects me to produce a grandchild."

Chrissy's eyebrows rise. She doesn't want to think about Reggie producing a child. "And your dad?"

"He died a little over a year ago, shortly before you joined the firm." A sad look shades Reggie's eyes. "I was a daddy's girl, I'll admit. I miss him."

"I'm sorry. I didn't mean to pry."

"You're not." A small smile graces her lips. "When I was young, he used to complain about our house being overrun by females, but he loved it. He would bring us trinkets from his travels abroad, always excited to see our reactions."

"What type of work did he do?"

"He was in international law, looking out for the interests of large, global companies. He was the original Esposito of Hawk, Esposito & Associates. I came to the firm through good, old-fashioned nepotism."

This surprises Chrissy. "I'm sure that doesn't matter to anyone, not with your record. I mean, your reputation is impeccable." Red blooms on Reggie's cheeks. *She's beautiful.*

"You'd be surprised what matters to people, particularly those on the partner track."

"Then they don't know you."

"And you do?"

The penetrating look in Reggie's eyes gives Chrissy pause. "I think it will take much longer than a mere year working for you to know you." She wishes she could tell her how she wants to spend time with her outside of work. This cruise is her first opportunity, and what Chrissy's seen has whetted her appetite.

"I've been working at the firm for fifteen years, and I realized long ago some people will never change their opinion."

"Good thing you aren't the type of person to care about what others think."

"I wish that were true."

Chrissy leans in. "Tell me who's talking crap about you, and I'll have a word with them."

A rolling chuckle transforms her. Her eyes brighten, and face flushes. "My savior." Reggie's voice conveys affection, and Chrissy's helpless to control her broad smile, delighted by Reggie's response. "Before you know it, Ben will be graduating high school and making his way into the world. You ready for him to go to the prom?"

Watching Ben walk toward them, slow and steady while he holds two glasses of wine, Chrissy wonders if she'll ever be ready to let Ben go. "It's a scary thought for me. Once he's an adult he'll have so many options, ones I didn't. I won't be able to guide him." She barks out a laugh. "God, I never even got to go to my prom. Or Senior Week. Or graduation."

"You didn't?" The shock in Reggie's voice causes Chrissy's heart to sink.

"No. My school district has a policy of forcing pregnant students to enroll in online classes. I actually finished high school before my graduating class. They mailed me my diploma." She peers at Reggie, wondering what she thinks about these admissions.

A burst of bright-blue color rends the air, and screaming fireworks follow. Ben tugs on Chrissy's arm with excitement, and she leans back in her chair, cheering when more pops of color paint the sky. A hand squeezing her arm redirects her focus to Reggie, who delivers a soft smile, one that settles Chrissy's nerves. Another percussion of another round of fireworks competes for her attention, but she doesn't look up until Reggie breaks their stare. Truth be told, if she had her choice, Chrissy would continue to stare at what she's realized is much more captivating. Reggie's smile.

Chapter Four

AFTER RECHECKING HER WORK one more time, Chrissy emails the finished memorandum to Reggie for review. A few months ago, Reggie began relying on her more with preparing court filings, and she loves it. Loves learning more about the legal system and the practical aspects not taught in paralegal school. Loves earning Reggie's compliments when she does a good job.

It's taken her all week to write the memorandum about whether responsibility attaches to a landlord when he fixes a leaking gas boiler instead of hiring a company to deal with the problem. She researched the assumption of risk tenants take by not raising any objections, how common it is for landlords to repair property themselves instead of hiring professionals, the duty of care landlords have to their tenants, and any resulting liability, whether it be monetary, emotional, physical, or some combination. Reggie met the defendant, Frank Hogan, while volunteering as a Lawyer for the Day at the Boston Municipal Court. The negligence action is coming up for a pretrial hearing in a little over a month, but Reggie isn't confident she'll be able to help him.

If anyone can help him, it's Reggie. Sometimes Chrissy watches her in court while taking notes. Always respectful to the person on the stand, her straightforward style gets to the crux of the matter, often eliciting the truth in a way the judge or jury can follow. Not that Reggie's always warm and fuzzy. She can be quite ruthless in court. If she makes a witness cry, or a heart break, or a person betray another, that's all part of the job.

And it's damn sexy. Nearly as sexy as the way she struts into the courtroom, head held high and high heels clicking. Chrissy wants to do whatever she can to help Reggie prepare, even if that means hours of research. The gleam of appreciation she sees in Reggie's eyes provide all the incentive she needs.

Chrissy knows she's failed to get rid of her attraction for her boss. *Not like I have a shot in hell.* Since the harbor cruise, she's noticed a shift. More personal conversations. More smiles. More thoughtful gestures. Gathering up her belongings, Chrissy logs off the firm's secure server and rises from the desk. She can hardly believe Ben starts school next week. *I can't believe how fast the years have passed. Next month he'll turn fourteen.*

"Done for the day?" Reggie asks, reading glasses perched on her nose, when Chrissy stands in the doorway to her office.

This woman is alluring without trying. "Yes. I'm picking Ben up from his friend's house. Are you staying for much longer?"

"Not much longer. Ben starts back to school next week, doesn't he?" Reggie sits back in her chair, crossing her legs and showing some skin through the slit of her tight skirt.

"Sure does. Ninth grade. It's crazy." Chrissy shakes her head to clear her thoughts of Ben's age. Of Reggie's toned legs.

"I have a little something for him." A blush emerges on Reggie's cheeks.

"You didn't have to." Chrissy steps closer to Reggie's desk to receive it.

"It's nothing." She waves her hand, but the expression in her eyes negates her words. She opens a side drawer and retrieves a gift bag, handing it to Chrissy.

"Thank you, Reggie. I'm sure he'll be thrilled." Chrissy wants to look in the bag, but she tightens her grip on it.

"You should look at it. Make sure it's okay." A hesitant look crosses Reggie's face. It's different. Charming.

The gift is in a black rectangular box and Chrissy gives Reggie a reassuring smile. She can't imagine Ben not liking whatever he receives from her. In the box is a pewter sports pendant of a basketball player about to dunk the ball in the hoop. Above the design are the words, 'Guardian Angel,' and underneath the player are the words, 'Protect Me.' Turning it over, she sees engraved, 'Never give up on your dreams, Ben.'

"Ben told me one time, you're his guardian angel." Reggie shifts to lean on her forearms against the desk. "He said you always make him feel safe, invincible, like the superheroes he reads about in those comic books. He's worried once he starts school he won't be around enough to protect you. He views it as his responsibility. I told him you'd never want to hold him back. I thought this might help, symbolize how you're always with him while he's reaching for the sky. Remind him you want him to live his life and fulfill his dreams."

Chrissy stares at the necklace, eyes narrowing as she runs her thumb over the front of it. Although Reggie's only known him for two months, they've gotten close. *I wonder when they had this conversation.*

"Christina," Reggie says, a hint of pleading in her voice. "Did I overstep? Is this inappropriate?"

"No." She looks up, knowing Reggie will see tears in her eyes. "It's thoughtful. I knew you two hit it off, and I'm happy about that. He'll love it."

A black cord is attached to the pendant, long enough for him to tuck it under his shirt. Chrissy is touched by Reggie's effort. The space between them vibrates, the silence full.

"He told you he wants to try out for basketball?"

"Yes. He's afraid he's too short."

"Yeah. He's fast, though, and he doesn't know how to give up on something once he sets his heart on it."

"Sounds like a Kramer trait."

Chrissy chuckles. "If it's something I think I have a chance at, then I can be pretty persistent."

"I see. So, if you think it's an impossible goal, you don't try?"

Forehead crinkling, Chrissy wonders whether this is an idle question or something more. The glimmer in Reggie's eyes makes her pause. "Not necessarily, but I might take more time to gather my courage. I mean, it took me years before I took the plunge of going to paralegal school. Before I did, I visited court and sat in the gallery, watching different proceedings. I memorized lists of courts, their jurisdictions, and different types of lawsuits. I even watched court procedurals on tv. Stupid, huh?"

"On the contrary. It reinforces my belief of how fortunate I am to have you here."

Biting her lower lip, Chrissy shrugs away the compliment. "Thank you, Reggie. For the gift. He'll cherish this. I know it." She wants to hug Reggie. She gets a dangerous idea and tries to ignore it. But Reggie has gotten Ben a gift, and she's talking to her like a friend instead of a boss, and Chrissy aches to learn more about her. *Don't do it.* "You know, we're eating out in the North End." *You're fucking crazy.* "Why don't you join us for dinner, and you can give this to him yourself?" *She's going to say no and ignore you for weeks if she doesn't find a way to fire you.* Chrissy sees the conflict on Reggie's face. "You haven't seen him at all this week since he's been finishing up his summer job, and he'd love to see you." *You're a moron. This is ridiculous. She doesn't want to spend time with you.*

Chrissy ignores the voice in her head screaming at her. A work-related event is one thing. Inviting her to spend time outside the office is a bad idea. Their recent exchanges probably mean nothing more than Reggie relaxing more around her. *I'm so stupid.*

Another thought crosses her mind—*maybe she has other plans, perhaps with Ashford.* "Unless you have other plans? It's Labor Day weekend, after all. Are you going away with Ashford?" Chrissy winces at her tone of voice, disapproving despite her best intentions. She watches Reggie, afraid her question is too personal. She's about to apologize when Reggie answers.

"No. No plans. It didn't work out with him."

"Oh. Are you all right?" She does her best to smother the surge of joy singing through her veins. She doesn't feel bad about the breakup, not by a long shot, but she doesn't want Reggie to be in pain.

"Well, I ended the relationship." Reggie shrugs.

"Maybe it's me, but whenever my relationships have ended, regardless of who broke it off, I always find myself grieving a bit. I tend to dwell on the good times, the things I liked about the person, the little things. I question myself, wondering whether I could have tried harder, done things differently."

"Self-reflection is a noble trait, but could you really think of something to miss for that last guy you dated? What was his name? Dick?" Reggie teases with twinkling eyes.

"Drew," Chrissy says, as her cheeks flush." I'll have you know he taught me how to wear eyeliner the right way," Chrissy jokes, glad to hear Reggie's chuckle.

"Ah, yes. I can imagine. He's certainly metrosexual."

"No kidding. He knows the best places to get manicures. All right, then. You absolutely must go with us. It will get your mind off what's-his-name, and Ben loves spending time with you."

"And do you, Ms Kramer?"

"And me," Chrissy confirms after a loaded pause, ignoring the formal address. Reggie's teasing her. She didn't start calling Chrissy by her first name until after the three-month trial period ended. Chrissy grins, and when Reggie nods, it broadens into a smile. *I hope this will become a more common occurrence.*

"Give me five minutes. I can drive us, so that will save some time."

With a nod, Chrissy returns to her desk and sits down. She sends a text to Ben to let him know Reggie's joining them. The string of emojis he sends make her laugh. She hears Reggie step out from her office and spins in her chair. "Ready?"

Reggie flicks off her light. "Sure am." Chrissy falls into step with Reggie, and they stop in front of the elevator, waiting for a car to arrive. "Which restaurant are we going to?"

"It's on Hanover. We like three of them, so we go to whichever has seats available. Do you have a favorite place you'd like to go to? We're always looking for good restaurants."

"I do know one I think you'll both like. It's called Gino's." Reggie removes her cell phone from a side pocket of her purse and after a moment of scrolling, she calls someone. "Hi. This is Reggie Esposito. I'd like a table for three at six tonight."

The elevator opens, and Chrissy enters, holding it open while Reggie finishes her call. With a smile, Reggie disconnects and enters the car. "All set. You're going to love this place. I represented them a few years ago, and I have an open invitation to eat there anytime."

"Wow. If I'd known that, I would've invited you out a long time ago," Chrissy jokes. Her face heats up when she realizes what she's said. "I mean..." The elevator dings and the doors open to the parking garage.

"If I'd known that, I would have mentioned it a long time ago." Reggie struts out of the elevator while Chrissy stands motionless. "Coming?" Chrissy hears the amusement in Reggie's voice and hurries to catch up.

They stop at a silver Mercedes-Benz, and Chrissy whistles through her teeth. "Nice ride."

She doesn't know much about cars, but this one screams wealth. It reminds her how out of reach Reggie is. They live in different worlds, and no matter how attracted she is to her boss, this is a good reminder of how hopeless it is to harbor romantic feelings for her. *This isn't a date, and you're a shithead if you think she'll ever want one with you. Get it together, Kramer. Take what you can get.*

"Thank you. Hop in."

Once they're settled, Chrissy gives Reggie the address where Ben is, and Reggie starts the car. "I was never one for fancy cars, but my parents taught me that for better or worse, sometimes you have to look the part. Once I became a partner, I got the fancy car, the brownstone, and the vacation home." She shrugs, pulling the car out of the parking lot. "I can't say I don't like them, but I never thought of myself as materialistic."

"Still, if you have the money, why not enjoy the finer things in life?"

"Well, I will admit I love shopping for clothes." She chuckles.

Chrissy looks out the window, noting the pedestrians filling the sidewalks, talking and laughing. She wants to ask Reggie silly questions like where she shops, what size she wears, and what designers she prefers. Maybe if they were close friends she could. "You like going to stores and trying on tons of clothes?"

"Yup. I'm one of those odd women, I know. It's better than ordering clothes online, though. With my body shape," Reggie waves her hand from head to her lap, "it's better for me to try on the clothes to make sure they fit right. Otherwise, I end up returning things. Especially blouses."

That's because you have beautiful breasts, Chrissy doesn't say. She swallows, her throat dry. When that doesn't work, she clears her throat. Reggie purses her lips, eyes shining. *Shit! Great. She can read minds.*

"I'm surprised you don't have a personal shopper."

"No, thank you. No need to throw money away. Bad enough I have to bring clothes to a tailor for altering." Reggie stops at a red light and looks over. "I get the impression you think I have a lot more money than I do."

"Oh, I have no real frame of reference." Chrissy looks down at her lap, wringing her hands. She flattens her palms on her thighs and looks up. "We've come a long way, but living in the city is expensive. Ben earned a scholarship for his school, and I imagine he'll have to do the same for college. Of course, I'll give whatever I can…"

A hand on her knee stops Chrissy from saying more. "You raised Ben to be a fine young man. He's smart and hard-working. Money can't buy those attributes. He has all he needs, and that's you."

"Thank you." Chrissy looks out the window once more, blinking several times. Her leg is on fire, and it's the hardest thing in the world to keep it still. Reggie squeezes her knee. Chrissy dares to look over and is met with a gentle smile. She loses her breath, but she keeps their eyes connected until Reggie must watch the road. She doesn't remove her hand until she pulls over at the address Chrissy provides.

Chrissy texts Ben, and a few seconds later the phone chimes. "He's on his way down." Chrissy opens her window so Ben will see her. Once he approaches, she waves. Ben gets in the back, already talking.

"Hi, Reggie. Nice car. I'm starving. Are we going to the North End?"

Chrissy grins. "Hello, Ben. Great to see you. Yes, I'm fine. Work was good. Thanks for asking." Chuckles fill the car.

"Sorry, Mom."

"I hope you don't mind, Ben, but I'm bringing you to one of my favorite restaurants in the North End."

"Cool. Mom, have we gone there before?"

"Nope. It's called Gino's."

"The best Italian you'll ever eat." Reggie pulls into a parking garage off of the waterfront. "I hope you don't mind walking from here."

"Not at all. It's a nice night."

They walk up the hill to the North End and follow the road until it intersects with Hanover Street. It's a warm summer evening. The sun won't set for at least another hour, and its warmth makes it unnecessary to wear anything over her short-sleeve blouse. She brought her sweater in case it cools off while they're at dinner, but she doubts she'll need it. The streets are crowded. Several cars are double-parked. She's glad they didn't attempt to navigate the congested one-way streets.

Chrissy tries to shake off her nervousness. At least Ben can serve as a buffer. She keeps reminding herself not to take Reggie's hand as they make the short trek to the restaurant. It's not a date, no matter how much she wishes otherwise.

Once they arrive at Gino's, a restaurant they've seen but never tried, a middle-aged, dark-haired, stout fellow smiles. "Bella, you look stunning. Too thin, though. You don't come here enough." He leans in and delivers air-kisses on both of Reggie's cheeks. "And who are your friends?"

"Christina and Ben, meet Bruno. He owns this fine establishment. It's their first time here."

"Well, then, let's get you settled. You have two choices: a table near the front windows or upstairs."

"Upstairs, please."

Chrissy looks around the restaurant, noticing several hanging pots filled with colorful flowers. On the walls are murals of Venice, Pisa, and Rome. The tables are packed into the small space, but no one minds how little room is between them. She can smell marinara, and her stomach growls.

With a nod Bruno leads them to a circular metal staircase. It's surrounded by brick, and toward the top a large sign warns customers to watch their step. Once they reach the top, Chrissy sees several tables filled with couples. Bruno stops before an empty table next to a railing on the edge of the rooftop. White fairy lights illuminate the area, wrapped like ivy around the black metal fencing. Thick white linen tablecloths cover the tables, cutlery, cloth napkins, and lit candles creating a cozy atmosphere.

They sit, and Chrissy watches the stream of people meandering down the street below them. They have a fabulous view of the Tobin Bridge. She looks forward to the sun setting, as the purple lights of the bridge will be visible.

A server hurries over to take their drink order. "Would you like a glass of red?" Reggie asks Chrissy.

"Yes. That sounds great."

"We'll have a half carafe of the house red."

"I'm fine with water," Ben says to the server.

"Please bring over a black napkin for me," Reggie says before the server turns away.

Glancing at the white one in her hand, Chrissy asks, "Do I need one, too?"

"I'm wearing a black skirt, and the white napkin can leave white lint on it. Since you're wearing a light-colored dress, you don't need to worry about that."

Nodding, Chrissy takes her napkin and places it on her lap while raising an eyebrow at Ben. He takes the hint and places one in his lap, too.

He looks at Reggie, a wide smile on his face. "This is awesome. Thanks for bringing us here."

"You're welcome. I wanted to give you this."

Chrissy watches Ben open the present, and she smiles when his eyes widen.

"Wow. This is great." Much as Chrissy had, he rubs his thumb over the engraving, his brows puckered. When he reads the words on the back of the pendant, he grins. "Thank you. It's perfect." He lifts it from its box and fastens it around his neck. "I really like it."

"I'm glad. I hope you'll invite me to some of your basketball games."

"If I get on the team."

"Positive thinking, kid. You'll make it."

The server returns with their drinks, pouring the wine before telling them what the specials are.

"I think I've eaten everything on the menu at one time or another. You can't go wrong."

"I'll get the fettuccini Alfredo with chicken, and a small Caesar salad." Chrissy closes her menu and hands it over to the server.

"I'll have the chicken parmesan, and a small Caesar salad," Ben says.

"I'll have the chicken Marsala, and a garden salad with the house dressing."

Soon after their server leaves, another server arrives with several appetizers. "With the owner's compliments."

Chrissy's mouth waters. Before them are dishes filled with shrimp cocktail, fried calamari, and bruschetta.

"Dig in." Reggie takes a piece of bruschetta. She moans while biting it, and Chrissy shivers at how erotic she sounds.

By the time their dishes are cleared, Chrissy's stuffed. As Reggie promised, the food was delicious.

"I hope you have enough room for dessert."

"I don't know." Chrissy pats her stomach. "As it is, I'm bringing home half my meal."

"Mom, you've said it yourself. We have two stomachs. One's for food, and the other's for dessert."

Chrissy's face flushes. "I'm guessing that means you want dessert."

"Ah, come on. We can share a dessert." Reggie pats Chrissy's arm. "Do you like tiramisu?"

"Love it." Chrissy knows a losing battle when she sees it. She promises herself to run an extra mile the next morning. And to drag her traitorous boy with her.

"What about you, Ben?"

"I think I'll get the chocolate-dipped cannoli."

"That's one of my favorites. You'll love it."

When their desserts arrive, Reggie scoops up a large bite of the tiramisu and holds it close to Chrissy's mouth. "You get to have the first bite."

Chrissy reaches out and wraps her fingers around Reggie's hand to steady the fork before leaning in. She shoots a look at Ben, nearly choking at the shit-eating grin he has. Reggie looks at her with a slight smile. *Here I am romanticizing this as if Reggie's hand-feeding me chocolates in bed. Leave it to me to make this awkward.* The dessert melts in her mouth, and the explosion of flavors causes her to close her eyes and moan. When she opens them, she sees Reggie's lips part and cheeks flush. Chrissy thinks she's never looked more enticing.

"You weren't kidding," Chrissy says in a soft voice. "It tastes like heaven."

Reggie clears her throat before breaking their gaze and taking the other fork to scoop up a bite for herself. Ben's excited chatter about how tasty the cannoli is lightens the moment, and Chrissy picks up the discarded fork to snag another piece.

"We'll have to come here again, Mom. The food's awesome."

Chrissy has to agree, although she knows it's more than the food that's made the night special. "Definitely."

"I'm glad you came with us, Reggie. Maybe next time we can bring you to one of our favorite places."

Chrissy jumps on the opportunity to spend more time with her outside of the office. "Right. We know the best place for most types of food. Chinese, Mexican, Italian, although this restaurant is serious competition for the one we usually frequent, Greek, Polish."

"Wow. You must eat out often."

Ducking her head, Chrissy mutters, "I'm not much of a cook."

"Nah, Mom. You're great, but we're both busy. During the week, it's hard to find time to cook. I get it. Plus, you cook on the weekends."

Chrissy loves how Ben tries to reassure her. She doesn't point out how weekend meals are simple. "I don't know how I got so lucky with you."

"I understand. I tend to cook on the weekends, too. I freeze some of it for weeknight meals." Reggie waves at the server, who hurries over. "I think we're all set."

Realizing their night is coming to a close, a weight settles on Chrissy's chest. Bruno hurries over, a large smile on his face. "How was your dinner?"

"Great," Chrissy says. "I love the fettuccini sauce. And the tiramisu is the best I've ever tasted." She glances at Reggie and bites her lower lip when she sees the smirk on her face.

"Good. Good. You'll come back, no? Any friend of Reggie's is a friend of ours. Ask for me."

"Thank you. We will."

"Hopefully with Reggie," Ben adds, and when Chrissy shoots him a warning look, he smiles.

To her surprise, Reggie agrees. "We'll come back soon. Thank you, Bruno."

Reggie insists on driving them home. "That's us." Chrissy points toward their apartment. She turns toward Reggie once she parks the car. *This is not a date.* "I'm glad you came with us."

The soft look in her eyes captures Chrissy's attention. "I'm glad you invited me."

Ben opens his door. "Goodnight, Reggie. Thanks for the gift." He pats the pendant.

Reggie nods. "You're welcome. Enjoy your last few days of the summer. Once school settles down, I hope you'll start coming by the firm again. You're always welcome."

"I will." Ben clambers out of the car, waving after he closes the door.

"Have a nice weekend. I'll see you on Monday." Chrissy smiles and opens her door.

"You, too."

It's the hardest thing in the world to get out of the car. Before she closes the door, Chrissy looks in one more time. "Sweet dreams, Reggie." Chrissy knows who will be in her dreams that night. And she can't wait.

Chapter Five

"HI, REGGIE," BEN SAYS, slinging his backpack from his shoulder onto the floor. His smile is bright and easy. Chrissy looks up from the file she's reviewing and as Reggie leans her hip on the desk, inches from her hand, Chrissy bites back a gasp. Reggie's backside is on full display, thanks to the perfect cut of her slacks. Tearing her eyes away from the alluring sight, Chrissy is embarrassed to see Ben's knowing look.

"Good afternoon, Ben. How's school?"

"Not bad. My Spanish class is going to a matinee showing of *Don Quixote* tomorrow."

"Ah, yes. Tilting at windmills. Like what I'm doing for this case." Reggie gestures toward the file splayed across Chrissy's desk.

"What do you mean?"

"I offered to defend someone, and I'm realizing how futile my efforts are."

"Did the person do something wrong?"

Reggie shrugs. "The plaintiffs believe he did. Your mom's been helping me with the case. Enough of that, though. Tell me more about school."

Ben bends over to rummage through his backpack. "We have to pick a place to work for our shadow program. It runs from the first week in October to the week before Thanksgiving. We get out of school at noon once a week and go to the place we're shadowing." He pulls out a piece a paper before straightening his lanky frame.

Chrissy shakes her head. He's at least two inches taller than a month ago.

"That sounds fun. Do you get to choose the place from a list the school gives you?" Reggie asks.

"They do give us a list," Ben says, sitting down, "but we're not limited by it. We can go wherever we choose as long as someone signs off to be a mentor and fills out an evaluation at the end." Ben wants to shadow Reggie, Chrissy knows, and she told him he'd have to ask.

"What are the mentor's responsibilities?" Reggie leans forward, focused entirely on Ben.

"Well, nothing more than allowing the student to tag along each week and explain things. At the end of the program, students turn in a report on what they learned. There's a matrix on what to cover." He shrugs. "I know it's a lot to ask, but I'd like to have you as my mentor, if it's not too much trouble."

Reggie raises her eyebrows. "Don't feel you have to say yes," Chrissy rushes to say.

"No, no. I don't feel pressured. I'm surprised. I didn't realize you're interested in the law."

"I've watched Mom while she learned about it, and while being here this summer, I saw how some of this works. I'd like to watch you in court and get more information on the process. I mean, Mom talks about what happens here in general terms, but I'd like to see examples."

"What day each week would it be?"

"Wednesday." Chrissy can hear the barely-contained excitement in Ben's voice. He can tell Reggie is about to say yes, not that it should come as a surprise. He's wrapped Reggie around his little finger.

A hand on her shoulder redirects her attention to Reggie. "Are you okay with it?"

"Yes. We've talked about it. I can't think of anyone better to mentor him." Chrissy grins.

Reggie squeezes her shoulder. "Looks like I'll be your mentor then."

"Great. I have the form right here." Ben passes the paper to her.

Reggie's eyes flitter over the form, and she grabs a pen from Chrissy's desk to sign it with a flourish before handing it back.

"Thanks, Reggie."

"Sure. I think I even have a pre-trial hearing coming up on this case. That will be an interesting one for you to see."

"I can't wait. Oh, I wanted to tell you I have basketball tryouts next week."

"Let me know what happens. I'm rooting for you," Reggie says.

"I will."

***

Three weeks later, Reggie and Ben enter the office, and Chrissy asks, "How'd it go?" Reggie's sigh says it all. "That good, huh?" Reggie runs a hand through her glossy chestnut hair, mussing it in a way that makes Chrissy's hands twitch.

"We're not going to win, and Frank refuses to settle. He made a costly mistake, deciding to repair the furnace himself. His insurance won't cover his tenant's losses, and it turns out they're fighting him on even covering the cost of repairs. On top of that, the mortgage company is foreclosing on the property and suing him for the difference between the amount they'll receive for selling it and the amount he'll still owe for the loan. He'd taken out an equity line a few years ago to replace the roof and pay off some credit cards."

"I'm sorry. Is there anything I can do?" Chrissy follows them into Reggie's office. Ben takes a seat in front of the desk while Reggie hangs her coat in the small closet to the right of the office door.

"Not unless you can convince him to settle."

"I would if I could," Chrissy says, frowning. She hates when Reggie's upset.

"The best I can hope for is to mitigate his liability as much as possible. He's lucky the DA isn't pressing charges against him for criminal negligence." Reggie slumps into her chair, a pensive look on her face.

Helplessness gnaws at Chrissy. She sits in the other visitor chair. "How much are we talking about?"

"If he doesn't settle, he may be responsible for up to three hundred thousand. And if he settles, he's still looking at about fifty-six thousand."

Shit! He's screwed either way. "That's tough. He must be pretty upset."

"He yelled at the insurance lawyer. Reggie had to calm him down," Ben says while loosening his school tie. "So, what happens next with the case?" He takes out his notebook and jots down some words.

"Trial. It's set for the second week in December. I'll have to prep him for questioning." Reggie grimaces. "He isn't the most sympathetic person. I'm afraid his testimony will hurt him."

"Does he have to testify?" Ben asks, pen poised over the notebook page.

"It's a bad idea for him not to. Christina, you'll need to contact him to schedule a meeting for next week, say Tuesday or Wednesday afternoon. I want to go over discovery with him."

"Sure." Chrissy had organized the file with the discovery documents last week. It was the first time she created requests for interrogatories and production of documents all by herself, and she's proud of herself. She also subpoenaed the police report, insurance claims, and fire report. The last step is scheduling depositions of their client and his tenants. The documents they have paint a clear picture of their client's negligence. On top of that, Hogan is always abrupt when they speak on the phone. Chrissy hasn't met him, but she knows this guy is bad news. Even though she dreads talking to him, she will to help Reggie.

"I thought I saw you with Reggie," David says, walking into the office. He claps Ben on the shoulder. "Visiting your mom?"

"I'm shadowing Reggie once a week for school credit."

"I bet you're learning a lot," David says. "Todd's coming to visit this weekend since he has Monday off. I thought you might like to come over. You, too, Chrissy. We were thinking you could come over tomorrow afternoon and stay for dinner. What do you think?"

Glancing at Ben, amusement ripples through Chrissy as he nods his head several times, a beseeching look in his eyes. "I think that will be fun. Can I bring anything?"

"Just yourself. Reggie, how about you? We'd love for you to join us."

Chrissy watches Reggie cross her arms. "Yeah, Reggie. It will be fun."

Reggie stares at her for a minute, eyes jumping back and forth. Whatever she sees must be enough. "Sure. I haven't been to your home in too long."

"That's our fault. We'll make sure to have your favorite wine on hand," David says with a charming smile.

"Well, that seals the deal."

"Wonderful. Let me write down our address for you, Chrissy." David grabs a piece of paper and a pen.

"I can give you both a ride."

Chrissy looks over at Reggie. "Are you sure?" She frowns when Reggie avoids her gaze.

"I'll be out doing errands, anyway." Reggie studies her nails before looking at David. "And I know where you live."

There's a slight edge to Reggie's voice, and Chrissy's mouth twitches. A quick look at David reveals an amused grin on his face. Although she has a great poker face, it's obvious Reggie's not being entirely truthful about her plans. Chrissy melts a little, knowing Reggie's going out of her way for them. "Oh, well, in that case, thank you."

David turns around, obstructing Chrissy's view of Reggie, and waggles his eyebrows. "Here you go. See you then."

Rolling her eyes, Chrissy takes the paper with his address and phone number and pockets it. "Thanks."

David looks over her head. "A man is outside. Do you have an appointment?"

Ben turns around to get a look. "That's your client from today. He looks upset."

"Christina, please send him in. Ben, it's probably best if you go with your mom while I talk to him."

"And that's my cue." David walks out of the office, and Chrissy hears him tell the client they'll be right with him.

Chrissy and Ben move to the receptionist area, and Chrissy greets the man. "Hello, I'm Attorney Esposito's paralegal. Please have a seat, and she'll be right with you, Mr. Hogan. Would you like some coffee?"

"Yeah. Cream and two sugars." He shifts from foot to foot. "I know I don't have an appointment, but I need to talk to her." His focus moves to Ben. "Weren't you at court today?"

"Yes. I'm doing a school project where I shadow Attorney Esposito."

"I'll be right back." Chrissy walks down the hall and turns into the break room. She's relieved to see a new pot of coffee, and she pours a cup for Mr. Hogan and for Reggie, adding cream and sugar to both. When she gets back to the office, Mr. Hogan is already seated in Reggie's office.

"Here you go, Mr. Hogan," Chrissy says, breezing in to place his cup on a coaster near the edge of the desk. She places the second cup on another coaster, close to Reggie. "Is there anything else you need?"

"No, thank you, Christina."

With a nod, Chrissy returns to her desk, keeping Reggie's door open. Ben sits in one of the visitor chairs, concentrating on his homework. It's nearly five o'clock, but Chrissy feels uncomfortable leaving Reggie alone with her client. Something about the guy makes her nervous. He looks like the typical working-class guy. He is about 5'8" with dark hair and hazel eyes. Not particularly muscular, but not overweight either. It's the way he carries himself. He's like a pressure-cooker, and Chrissy's afraid he will blame the results of his case on Reggie.

Logging on to the server, Chrissy pulls up a file and starts crafting a motion. She listens to the murmurs drifting out from Reggie's office while she works, leg bouncing. She keeps making typing mistakes, and she hits the delete button enough times and with enough force that Ben looks up at her, his eyebrows raised. She shrugs. *Calm down, Kramer. She can handle him.* Reggie's doing most of the talking, her voice soothing Chrissy's nerves. Reggie sounds caring and calm, as she explains the results of today's court appearance and the next steps for the case.

"What am I supposed to do?" Mr. Hogan's voice rises. "I made a mistake. People make mistakes all the time. And now you're telling me the insurance won't cover repairs?"

His shout has Chrissy standing up and moving toward the doorway. Her eyes connect with Reggie, who shakes her head. Although uneasy, Chrissy sits back down. Reggie's speaking again, her voice too soft for Chrissy to understand the words.

"Mom," Ben whispers. "Is she all right?"

Chrissy nods but replies in a quiet voice. "I think he's upset with how the hearing went. Reggie's good at calming people down. And we can stick around until he leaves."

"Okay." Ben goes back to his homework, and twenty minutes pass in relative quiet. Many have left early to start their long weekend. A raised voice breaks the silence again.

"I don't want to settle! How am I supposed to pay that amount of money?"

Chrissy can see Mr. Hogan pacing back and forth, his face red and eyes wild. Reggie remains in her seat, her eyes trained on him, while she keeps talking. He returns to his seat and sits forward, elbows on his knees and hands bracketing his head. When Reggie finishes talking, he sits up and shakes his head before rising once more. "Let me think about it," he says as he leaves the office.

Quick to look busy, Chrissy says as he passes, "Have a good night, Mr. Hogan."

"Yeah, thanks," he mutters, turning into the hallway and stamping away.

"He's kind of scary," Ben whispers.

"He's upset." Reggie's leaning against her doorframe, arms crossed and shoulders rounded. She looks like she's hugging herself. She straightens up a moment later and glances at her watch. "You two need a ride home?"

Chrissy's conflicted. They were planning on stopping for pizza, and she wants to invite Reggie, but they're going to spend time with her tomorrow. She fears that might be too much time together. *Or maybe*

I'm the one who's afraid. Every time we spend time outside of work, I find something more to like about her.

"We're stopping somewhere to eat," Ben says. Chrissy doesn't know whether to thank him or punish him for answering before she does. "We can be persuaded to go to Gino's again," he says with a smile. "Or wherever."

When Reggie's eyes find Chrissy, she raises her eyebrows, and Chrissy's not sure what to say. She settles with smiling and tilting her head.

"I wish I could. I'll have to take a rain check. I'm having dinner with my mother and sisters."

"How many sisters do you have?" Ben asks while stuffing his homework in his backpack.

"Two. Any time you want to feel what it's like to have siblings, you can borrow them. They think they know much better than I do how I should live my life."

Ben chuckles. "Sounds like extra parents to me."

"For that, you don't get any dessert tonight." Chrissy smiles at Ben's groan. She pulls on her coat and turns to Reggie. "Thanks for the offer, but we'll take the T. We'll see you tomorrow."

"Yes." Reggie straightens up. "I'll pick you up at two. Have a good night."

"You, too."

***

A knock on her door the next day has Chrissy stopping mid-step. Her eyes fly to the microwave clock, and she swears under her breath.

"I heard that," Ben says. "It must be Reggie."

Chrissy sighs. She took too much time fretting over what to wear before settling on a red Boston University sweatshirt, dark blue jeans, and black loafers.

"You look good, Mom."

"Thanks, kid." Chrissy opens the door and stares. The woman is gorgeous in casual wear. The way those jeans hug her curves is a sin. And her blouse does nothing to hide the shape of breasts. Noticing Reggie's expectant look, Chrissy moves aside. "Hi, Reggie. You didn't have to come up to get us."

"I lucked out with a parking spot in front." Reggie enters, eyes sweeping around the apartment with interest.

"That is lucky. Maybe you should play the lottery. Come in for a sec." Chrissy takes a few moments while closing the door to regain her equilibrium. She inhales a deep breath before turning away from the door.

"So, this is our kitchen. In here's the living room," Chrissy hears Ben say while walking toward the back of the apartment. "My room's here." He opens the door and stands aside while Reggie steps in. Chrissy hurries into her room, taking a quick look around to make sure nothing too personal is visible. She picks up her jacket and purse and turns to them when they reach her room.

"This is my room." Chrissy steps aside, ducking her head. She watches Reggie walk over to the windows and look out before making a slow tour of the room.

"It feels like you." Reggie gazes at her with a soft smile.

"How so?"

"It's calm." Reggie waves her hand around. "Everything has its place. Not many trinkets or keepsakes, so what you do have must be important to you." Reggie stalls before the dresser and hums when she picks up a few pictures resting on top of it. They're from the Harborfest.

Remembering who's in them, Chrissy nibbles on her lower lip, shifting from foot to foot.

"These are great pictures."

"Cathy took them. She gave me copies last week. I was going to frame them." Chrissy stops, realizing what she's admitted. Three pictures, one with Chrissy and Ben, another with Chrissy and Reggie, and the third of the three of them. The one of Chrissy and Reggie makes her breathless each time she sees it. They're leaning against the railing, and with the way the sun hits them, you can't see their expressions. Their bodies are turned toward each other, heads close together while they talk.

"I'll have to ask her for copies." Reggie's staring at the picture of the two of them, and Chrissy's nerves begin to settle. Once Reggie places them back on her dresser, she smiles. "Sorry for being so nosey."

Knowing she would love to explore Reggie's home if given the chance, Chrissy lets go of her reticence. "It's okay. Ready to go?"

"Oh, yes. After last night, I could use good wine and good friends."

"Well, that sounds ominous." Chrissy chuckles. She locks up the apartment before following Ben and Reggie downstairs to the car. Ben fills up the twenty-minute drive talking about junior varsity. He's excited to be on the team, and he promises to give Reggie a copy of his game schedule. They reach Cathy and David's home in Cambridge by driving over the Mass. Ave. Bridge and a few blocks east of Harvard Yard. Their home is on a quiet side street.

Reggie parks in front of a two-story brick façade. David comes outside and hands Reggie a parking permit to place in her windshield. He's wearing tan khakis and a blue cable-knit sweater. They follow him up a few concrete steps and through double wooden doors into a hall. To the right is a welcoming parlor. The crème-colored walls, detailed white moldings, and pine hardwood floors create an airy quality. Chrissy steps into the room to study the detailed Victorian marble mantelpiece. The craftsmanship is breathtaking. To either side are built-in shelves, stuffed with books and knickknacks. To the right are three bay windows looking out onto the street.

"Let me give you the five-cent tour." David smiles.

Nodding, Chrissy follows along, taking note of how comfortable their home feels. The dining room has the typical square wooden table and chairs situated on a light-colored area rug, but this room also has a fireplace with different-sized white candles arranged in it instead of wood. The room flows into the kitchen, where Cathy stands cutting some vegetables behind the kitchen's center-island. She looks like the perfect mom with the pink, flowery apron on over a long-sleeved red cotton shirt and jeans. Chrissy can't help but wonder why they never had children. Cathy's talking to Todd, her eyes shining with laughter.

"Todd, I want you to meet our friends. This is Reggie and Chrissy. They both work at the firm. And this is Chrissy's son, Ben." Todd's a few inches shorter than Ben with short blond hair and light green eyes. He has an easy smile, and Chrissy likes him immediately.

Todd smiles at everyone before turning to Ben. "Hi. Do you want to go downstairs? I have some cool games we can play on my tablet." Chrissy nods when Ben looks at her for permission, watching them scamper away, already talking about the various superheroes they like. Chrissy and Reggie settle at the dining room table, glasses of wine and plates of snacks littering the rectangular spruce wood. David leans back against the island, a glass of wine in his hand.

"The latest gossip is how you dumped Ashford," David says, a gleam in his eye.

Cathy stops cutting a cucumber and looks up with a saddened expression. "Aw, I thought he would be perfect for you."

Reggie scowls, leaning back in her chair and crossing her arms. "That's why I'm never listening to you again when it comes to my love life."

Chrissy takes a long sip of her wine, doing her best to seem politely interested instead of starved for information regarding Reggie's romantic life. David refills her glass, winking at her.

"Well, there are plenty of other fish in the sea—"

"No, thank you," Reggie interrupts Cathy. "I don't need anyone's help."

"But, Reggie, I know the perfect person—"

"I'm sure you do, but I can choose who I'm interested in, thank you very much."

"Sounds like you have someone in mind," David chimes in.

Chrissy studies Reggie, noticing the blush kissing her cheeks. A wave of jealousy rips through her, and the sweet wine tastes sour in her mouth. She wonders whether she's been imagining the subtle flirtations they've shared over the last few months. Perhaps it was all wishful thinking. She crosses her legs and plays with the stem of her wine glass, eyes focused on it.

"I assure you that you'll be the last to know. God, you're worse than my mother and sisters, and that's saying something."

"That bad?" Cathy frowns.

Reggie sighs. "They mean well. I think. They want me to be happy and settle down and have a family." She waves her hand. "I keep telling them when the timing's right, it will happen."

"Or you might not recognize the love of your life sitting in front of you and need your friends to help you," Cathy says.

From the way Reggie rolls her eyes and her face darkens, Chrissy gets the feeling they've had this conversation many times. *How long have they been friends?*

David grins. "I don't know, Cathy. Remember when you fixed her up with Timmy?"

Chrissy can't help but chuckle with the others when Reggie lets out an exaggerated groan. When she chances a look at Reggie, she looks like she's in pain. "That bad?" She grins when Reggie drops her head in her hands.

Cathy keeps cutting the vegetables, glancing up. "How was I supposed to know he really wanted a meeting with your father, and the fact you have to reach back that far, David, proves most of the men I've paired Reggie with weren't that bad."

"Women, too," David says with a sly smile. Chrissy tucks away that important piece of information to think about later while ignoring the sliver of ice that winds its way down her spine.

"Oh, right. How could I forget? There's a woman I see at the gym I bet you'd like."

Another bolt of jealousy jolts Chrissy, and her hands begin to tremble. She stands up, her sudden action stopping Reggie from uttering a retort. "Where's the bathroom?"

"I'll show you," David says, a guilty look in his eyes. Chrissy turns to follow, not willing to listen to any more of Cathy's attempts to play matchmaker. With her feelings growing each day, Chrissy can't stomach the thought of Reggie dating anyone beside herself.

"Cathy means well." David's voice lowers as they walk down a hallway toward the back of the house.

"How long have you both been friends with Reggie?"

"I went to law school with her. Cathy met her through one of the annual firm events, and when she came onboard a few years later, it was natural for all of us to spend more time together. Anyway, here we are." He squeezes her shoulder. "Reggie's a good person, and I've seen the way she acts around you. Be patient. You're special, and she knows it."

Feeling her face heat up, Chrissy mutters, "That's nice of you to say, but she's my boss."

"True." He leans in. "But that doesn't always have to be the case. It's a large law firm. Lots of opportunities to transfer into another division." With a bright smile he walks down the hall, whistling.

Closing the bathroom door, Chrissy sits on the lip of the marble tub, taking some deep breaths. "This is ridiculous. How could I ever believe she's interested in me? This is probably why she was always so professional with me in the past. She must have picked up my interest and not wanted to encourage me." Chrissy rubs her forehead. "I need to get a grip."

A knock on the door makes Chrissy gasp. She wonders whether anyone heard her talking to herself. Ben is constantly teasing her about her penchant for talking things out. "I'll be right out."

"Take your time. I just wanted to make sure you're all right," Reggie says.

Chrissy stands up and moves to the sink, staring at herself in the mirror, eyes wide. *Well, shit. How long was I gone?*

"Christina? Can I come in?"

"Um, yeah. Sure," Chrissy squeaks out. Reggie enters and shuts the door behind her. "Sorry. Now you know why I'm so bad at making friends. I find I need time to myself to process things."

Reggie leans against the tub and crosses her legs at the ankle. "I was afraid all that boring talk about my love life ran you off."

"What? No. No, no, no. That's...well, you've obviously been friends with them for a long time. I can understand if they made you feel uncomfortable talking about that in front of me, though. I mean, you're my boss, and I'm sure you don't want me hearing about your private life like that."

Reggie gives a slow nod. "Normally, that would be true. I am a private person. I was hoping, however, that we've gone beyond the boundary of boss and employee."

"I think we have, and I'm happy about that. I like spending time with you, and so does Ben." Chrissy leans back against the sink, crossing her arms. "I guess I'm not really sure how to navigate this."

"You seemed to become uncomfortable when David mentioned I've dated women in the past. Does that bother you?"

Chrissy's mouth becomes dry, afraid Reggie has guessed her feelings. About to deny caring about her preferences, Chrissy stops when she sees the vulnerable look in Reggie's eyes. Chrissy joins her at the tub, her hip kissing Reggie's side. She takes a deep breath. "Would it bother you to know I prefer dating women?"

A relieved smile overtakes Reggie's face. "No."

"Good, because that's my answer, too."

"Right." Reggie slaps her hands on her thighs before straightening up. "We should probably get back before they send out a search party."

"And here I thought you were the search party." Chrissy follows Reggie to the door, stopping short when Reggie turns around. Chrissy gasps, their noses nearly touching. She steps back.

Reggie chuckles. "Sorry. I just, I hope you know I enjoy spending time with you and Ben. If you ever feel uncomfortable around me for any reason, will you promise to talk to me about it? Please?"

"Yes. Of course. Same here. I like where our relationship is going, but it's scary for me. I don't trust a lot of people."

"I'll do my best to make sure you don't regret it." Reggie runs her hand down Chrissy's arm before turning and opening the door.

Chrissy follows the hypnotic sway of Reggie's hips and vows to do the same.

Chapter Six

CHRISSY STEPS OUT OF the elevator and shivers. It's a wicked, cold day, well below freezing, and she needed to take care of some errands during her lunch hour. She places her takeout food on her desk and unwraps her threadbare, useless scarf from around her neck. Peering in Reggie's office, she sees her on the phone and waves to let her know she's back. Shucking her black winter leather coat, which also serves as her spring and autumn coat, Chrissy pulls off her black knit beanie with the Bruins logo on it, patting down her unruly curls. Once her outerwear is stashed in the closet, Chrissy settles at her desk to eat.

Tomorrow is Halloween, and Chrissy is trying to decide whether to go to David and Cathy's costume party. Ben will be spending the night at Leroy's house, so she has no reason not to go other than good old nerves. They've assured her she'll love their friends and enticed her with the promise of Reggie attending.

Sensing movement, Chrissy turns in her chair to greet Reggie. "Do you need anything, Reggie?"

"Yes. How are you doing on the Bartlett Answers to Interrogatories?" Reggie leans against the filing cabinet, a slight smile on her face. Since they went to the Freedmans' house six weeks ago, they've eased into a comfortable camaraderie, and Reggie is more relaxed around her.

"Nearly done. I should be able to get the draft to you today." Chrissy wakes up her computer screen by shaking the mouse before she logs on. She pulls up the requested document. "I only have five more to answer." Reggie moves closer to look, her breath caressing Chrissy's cheek.

"Great. Thank you," Reggie murmurs, her lips brushing Chrissy's ear.

Biting down on a gasp, Chrissy barely stops herself from turning so their lips can meet. Gentle fingers glide through her hair, and Reggie straightens.

"Your hair has static electricity."

"Oh. Thanks." She loves the shy look overtaking Reggie's face, at odds with her usual confident demeanor.

"Are you going over to David and Cathy's tomorrow night?"

"I'm thinking about it." The understatement of the year. She has two costumes to choose from, and the decision of which one she'll wear hinges on whether Reggie will be there. "You?"

"I'll be there. Cathy will never let me live it down if I dare miss it. Want a ride there?"

Chrissy's eyebrows rise. "That sounds great. What time are you planning to go?"

"Around seven." Reggie pauses and lifts her chin, eyes searching Chrissy's. "Would you like to have dinner beforehand? We can go back to Gino's or somewhere else if you prefer."

Is this a date? Is she asking me out? Even if she isn't, her answer's the same. "I've been dying to go back to Gino's." Chrissy's wide smile is mirrored by Reggie's.

"I'll pick you up at five, and we can change at your house before going to the party, unless you want to wear your costume to dinner?" Chrissy chuckles at the gentle teasing and shakes her head. Reggie shrugs. "I didn't think so."

"What's your costume?"

"You'll have to wait to find out." Reggie smirks.

For the rest of the afternoon, Chrissy leaves Post-it notes on Reggie's desk with outrageous guesses of her Halloween costume. The theme is Broadway musical characters. Not having any real reason to disturb her, Chrissy's excuses for entering Reggie's space are equally outrageous. By the end of the day, Reggie doesn't even try to hold back her smug look each time Chrissy approaches her.

"So, you're not a cat, a pirate, or an ogre. Won't you at least give me a hint?" Chrissy leans against Reggie's desk, arms loosely crossed. Reggie leans back in her chair, eyes sparkling.

"I'm enjoying your guesses. The last one." Reggie lifts a Post-it off the edge of her desk and hums, twisting a piece of hair around her finger. "You think I could be Belle?"

"Hell, yes. Or Elsa or Velma or Jasmine or Mary Poppins. It doesn't matter what you wear." Chrissy bites the inside of her cheek, holding back the words she wants to say. How beautiful Reggie is. Elegant. Classy. Everything she can never hope to be.

"I think you'd do much more justice to Elsa than I could."

"Nah. I'd do a better job as Olaf. Or Sven."

Reggie's cackle takes them both by surprise. Reggie claps both hands over her mouth, eyes wide. Chrissy lets loose a guffaw, thrilled she was able to break through Reggie's professional façade. She wants to be the cause of Reggie's laugh again.

Reluctant to leave once the workday ends, Chrissy takes her time clearing her desk. When she sees Ashford approach, she frowns. *Why is he sniffing around?* She doesn't want him anywhere near Reggie, who's on the phone anyway. Ashford stops at her desk. "She's on the phone with a client. Can I help you with something?"

"Do you know if she's going to the costume party tomorrow?"

Chrissy clenches her fists on her lap and sits up. She can hear Reggie setting up an appointment with whoever's on the other line. "You were invited?"

Ashford barks out a laugh. "Of course. I've been friends with Cathy for years. She's the one who set me and Reggie up."

Although she cannot hear Reggie talking on the phone any longer, Chrissy dares to say, "You do realize you're no longer together."

"That's a small misunderstanding. One I intend to rectify tomorrow. So, is she going?"

"Yes, but not with you." Reggie's hand on her shoulder comforts Chrissy, and although she knows she's being petty and unprofessional and way out of line, she bares her teeth in a poor approximation of a smile at Ashford.

"Can't we talk about this?"

"There's nothing to discuss." Fatigue shines through Reggie's voice, and Chrissy wonders whether that's due to the subject matter or the long workweek.

"I've made it clear I'm no longer interested. If you keep persisting, I'll have to lodge a complaint with HR, and I really don't want to do that. You're a good guy, and you deserve to be with someone who can give you what you want."

"That's the thing. I was being selfish. I realize that now." Ashford shifts from foot to foot, hands extended toward Reggie. Chrissy wants to slap them away. "Give me another chance."

This guy's a piece of work. He can't take no for an answer. Chrissy's insanely curious about why their relationship ended. Reggie's hand remains on her shoulder, anchoring Chrissy to her chair.

"I've moved on. I suggest you do, too." Reggie squeezes Chrissy's shoulder. "I'll be ready to leave in five minutes. Ben invited me to join the two of you for pizza, if you have no objection."

"Of course not." Chrissy decides Ben's meddling is a godsend, as Reggie returns to her office.

"Ben?" Ashford echoes, his face a mask of confusion. "Is he your boyfriend?"

Chrissy scoffs. "No way." She smiles. "Have a good night." After a pronounced silence, he leaves her desk, and Chrissy exhales loudly. *What an ass.*

"Ready?"

Logging off the computer with a few keystrokes, Chrissy retrieves her belongings in record time and jumps up from her chair. "Ready."

"Sorry about that. I expected him to give up by now." They step into the elevator, moving to the side as others join them. The Friday night rush is in full effect, and Chrissy tries not to squirm when she realizes her arm is against the side of Reggie's breast.

Once they exit to the parking garage, Chrissy dares to voice her opinion. "Well, I can't blame him. You're quite the catch. Too bad for him he was such a blockhead that he didn't realize it sooner." Chrissy looks over to see Reggie duck her head. The garage is shadowed, but she swears Reggie's cheeks have turned a rosy tint.

"Thank you." Reggie offers a sincere smile before pulling out her keys to unlock the car. "Ben didn't tell me where you normally get pizza. He only said you were going to pick it up on the way home."

"Right. Let me make sure he already ordered." Chrissy shoots a text over to Ben, making sure to mention a little heads up would have been appreciated. His smiley emoticons couch the pizza order, and their regular order of pepperoni pizza takes center stage with the addition of a white pizza with sweet Italian sausage. "Seems like we're all set. You can take the route toward my apartment. It's just down the street from there. Are you sure you don't have other plans? I feel like I'm monopolizing your time."

They stop at a red light and Reggie glances over at her. "I don't have other plans. Ben texted me a few minutes before I took that last phone call, and I was coming out to confirm with you when I realized Ashford was taking up space. I hope he didn't bother you too much."

Chrissy shakes her head, wanting to put Reggie at ease. "He didn't. Actually, I feel bad for the guy. That said, I hope he gives up hounding you."

"I was assuming Ben had checked with you about pizza."

"Reggie, you're always welcome to spend time with us. I know it's a bit tricky with work and everything, but we like spending time with you."

"As do I." A comfortable silence fills the car, and it isn't until they find parking and step into the pizzeria that Reggie speaks again. "Let me pay."

"Absolutely not. You were invited to share pizza with us, not pay for it."

"But—"

"No buts. Just accept it." She holds Reggie's glare, watching it soften until she grins and nods. Once they get to the apartment, Ben opens the door with a wide smile. Chrissy scowls at him, pretending to punch him in the stomach. He catches her fist and laughs.

"You should be thanking me," he whispers before turning to Reggie. "Hi, Reggie. Glad you could come."

"Me, too." Although she's only been to the apartment once before, she doesn't hesitate to remove her coat and hand it to Ben. "Where are the cups?"

"Cabinet closest to the fridge." Chrissy grabs some plates and utensils, placing them next to the pizza boxes on the counter. She loads each plate with a piece and brings Ben's and Reggie's to the table before returning to retrieve hers and the silverware.

"I've got the napkins," Ben says while grabbing one of the cups, now filled with water.

"Oh, there's a bottle of wine in the lower cabinet," Chrissy says when Reggie sits down. "Shall I open it?"

"Maybe later."

Ben tells Reggie about the results of his latest test, and before Chrissy realizes it, the pizzas become a fond memory and she's rising to uncork her most expensive bottle of red wine. She'd received it from Cathy and David for a birthday present, and when she looked it up online, she'd nearly passed out at the price. Pouring two glasses, as Ben and Reggie clean up the area, Chrissy feels giddy. She likes having Reggie in her space. Likes watching her interact with Ben. Likes spending time with her outside of work. Likes her.

When Reggie catches her eye, raising an eyebrow, Chrissy smiles. Maybe she should feel embarrassed at being caught staring, but she can't find it in her to care. "Come sit on the couch." Ben follows and commandeers a nearby chair, content to pull out an Avengers graphic book, long legs crossed at the ankle.

"Are you coming to David and Cathy's tomorrow night?" Reggie asks, sitting on the couch and curling up her legs beneath her. Chrissy hands her one of the glasses of wine before settling in the other corner of the couch.

Ben looks up. "No. I'm going to my friend's house. Leroy's having a party. I'm going as Spiderman."

"That sounds fun, probably better than a bunch of adults dressed up as Broadway musical characters."

Ben chuckles. "Mom has an awesome costume. What are you dressing up as?"

Reggie narrows her eyes at Chrissy. "Did you put him up to this?"

Chrissy raises her hands in mock-defense. "No way. I didn't do anything."

"Your mom's been trying to guess my costume all afternoon. If you tell me her costume, I'll tell you mine."

"Don't you dare," Chrissy warns Ben.

With a shrug, Ben says, "Sorry. I have to live with her."

Reggie makes a show of snapping her fingers and grimacing. "It was worth a try."

"So, what are you doing for Thanksgiving? Spending it with your family?" Ben asks.

"Yes. I go to my mom's house, as do my two sisters, their spouses and children. She lives in Chestnut Hill." Chrissy wonders what that feels like, spending the day in a noisy house filled with relatives. Growing up, Chrissy learned to be quiet and on her best behavior when people visited. Everyone was much older, and she found herself counting the minutes until the meal was over so she could hide in her room.

"That sounds cool. Does she cook everything?"

"She cooks the turkey and a few side dishes. We bring other side dishes and dessert. What about you two?"

"Oh, nothing too elaborate. Usually we order the food and pick it up. Then all we have to do is heat it up. But I do make a great apple pie."

"Mom does make the best apple pie. And usually on the holidays we go see a movie afterward."

"It's tradition," Chrissy adds. "You'd be surprised how many people go to the movies on the holidays."

"You'll have to save me a piece of pie."

"I suppose I could be persuaded." Chrissy doesn't mean to make it sound suggestive. Reggie looks intrigued, though, so she swallows back any apologies and waits.

"Really?" Reggie taps her lips with her index finger. "I'll have to think about how best to entice you into letting me taste a piece."

Gulping down the rest of her wine, Chrissy leans over to refill it. Reggie's emphasis on her words causes Chrissy's heart to speed up. With how regularly that happens, she's surprised she hasn't suffered a heart attack. "Shall I top you off?" she asks, holding up the bottle.

"I think I'd like that." A sly smile crosses Reggie's face as she extends her glass, and Chrissy takes a deep breath before pouring wine in it. She's thankful her hand doesn't shake. It takes a moment for her mind to catch up to what she offered, and when it clicks, her face floods with heat. She bends toward the coffee table and takes her time filling up her glass and placing the half-full bottle down, hoping her blush will fade. *What the hell are you doing? Be persuaded? Top her off? Christ! She could easily accuse me of sexual harassment.* Swallowing several times while ducking her head, Chrissy's grateful Ben picks up the conversation.

"Are your mom and sisters attorneys, too?" he asks.

"No. Only my dad was. My mom teaches English literature at Northeastern. My oldest sister, Maria, is an architect with Blackman Design Group, and Tracy is an art curator for the Museum of Fine Arts."

"Are you artistic, too?" Chrissy asks.

"Unfortunately, no. I appreciate art, but I didn't develop any such skills."

A thousand cheesy compliments cross Chrissy's mind. *You create art everyday just by being you. Beauty begets beauty. You're a living masterpiece.* "It's never too late to learn, if that's what you want to do. Look at me. I didn't enroll for the paralegal degree until a few years ago."

Reggie hums while leaning against the couch arm, both hands wrapped around her wine glass. Her eyes become unfocused as she taps the side of her glass with one finger. "It's funny. In many ways, I feel like every milestone in my life was predetermined. College. Law school. My firm. All that was laid out for me by my father."

"Your father may have set the stage, but you're the star. You prove your talent every day."

"Perhaps, but so do countless other attorneys."

Chrissy has to smile, even though the thought of Reggie believing she's no one special upsets her. She takes Reggie' hand and squeezes. "No, Reggie. You make a difference. You matter." Reggie's eyes start to moisten, and Chrissy changes the subject. "Now if only you'd admit you're dressing as Elphaba tomorrow night..." Reggie's laughter is music to Chrissy's ears.

***

"Ready for your big date?" Ben plunks down on Chrissy's bed while she adds some mascara to her pale eyelashes.

"I wish." Chrissy steps back from the mirror to study her face. "Good enough."

"You wish you were ready or wish it was a date?"

"Both." She hears a text alert and glances at the clock. "That's probably her." Ben's in his Spiderman costume. "That looks good. Is it comfortable?"

"Yup. Look—I can even dance." He starts doing the floss, and Chrissy laughs.

"Everyone will love it. Maybe even that girl you have a crush on."

"Mom," Ben squawks. He stands with his hands on his hips and an outraged expression on his face, holding the pose for all of five seconds before he giggles. "Have fun. I hope she likes your costume."

"Me, too." Chrissy shuts off the bedroom light and walks toward the door while donning her coat. "Be good tonight. Text me when you get there, so I know you're safe."

"I will. Love you."

"Love you too, kid." Chrissy gives him a quick hug before opening the door and rushing down the stairs. When she gets to Reggie's car, she slides in the front seat. "Hi." She fastens the seatbelt.

"Hi, yourself." Reggie eases into traffic, and Chrissy smiles. It's hard for her not to get carried away with romantic notions when they had such a great evening yesterday, and now they're going to dinner and a party. "How was your day?"

"Lazy. Well, except for my morning run. I dragged Ben out of bed for that, but once we got back home, we were in slow motion for the rest of the day." Chrissy chuckles. "We even took a nap since we knew we'd be up late tonight." She doesn't usually take naps, but she wants to be at her best while they spend time together.

"I didn't know you jog. I never got into it."

"Well, you must do something. You're in great shape." Chrissy sees Reggie raise an eyebrow and hurries on. "Do you go to a gym?"

"I use the one at work. I prefer using the machines and some free weights. I have a personal trainer who changes my routine every few months." She parks the car in a nearby parking garage, and they walk to the restaurant.

"Damn, it's cold tonight." Chrissy shivers, placing her hands in her coat pockets and hunching over.

"That coat's too thin. You need to dig out your winter coat." Reggie loops her arm through Chrissy's, and they walk together at a brisk pace. Reggie's warmth seeps through her left side wherever they touch. *At least I'm warm now.*

As soon as they reach Gino's, they're led to a table next to the front window. Bruno comes over moments later. "Bella! You look beautiful. This cold weather brings out your rosy cheeks. And your friend is back. Welcome. Welcome. Where is your boy?"

"He's going to a Halloween party tonight. He was disappointed to miss having dinner here."

"Ah, another time. Enjoy your dinner. If you need anything, let me know."

Soon they're sharing a half carafe of red wine while making guesses on what David and Cathy will be wearing for costumes. "They always wear couple costumes." Reggie stops talking to eat some of her Caesar salad.

"I'm thinking they'll wear something from a Disney musical. Hopefully, not *Tarzan.*"

Reggie snickers. "Agreed. They're not that daring. It will be something cute like *South Pacific* or *Oklahoma.*"

Chrissy finishes her salad. "My guess is *Aladdin* or *My Fair Lady.*"

Reggie shakes her head. "Cathy would never wear such a revealing outfit for *Aladdin. My Fair Lady*'s a good guess." When Chrissy's phone chimes, Reggie waves her hand. "Go ahead. It might be Ben."

Pulling out her cell, Chrissy laughs when she sees the text and passes it over. On it is a picture of Ben in his Spiderman costume, crouched with arms extended as if he's about to shoot a web. Reggie stares at the image with a soft smile before handing it back. "He's such a good kid."

"Yeah. I lucked out." Their server arrives with their entrees, and Chrissy does her best not to shove too much in her mouth at one time. The food is as delicious as she remembers. Chrissy chose the chicken piccata this time, while Reggie is having baked eggplant.

"I'm surprised you never had kids. You're great with Ben." Chrissy looks up from her meal, gauging how her words are received. She doesn't want to make Reggie uncomfortable, but she's curious.

"I thought about it, but my relationships were never strong enough for me to want to become a mother, and I didn't want to do it alone. Honestly, I don't know how you do it." Reggie looks down at her plate, pushing around a piece of eggplant.

"I muddle through." When Reggie looks up, Chrissy leans forward as if she's about to reveal a secret. "And I do exactly the opposite of what my parents did."

"Ah. The age-old 'I'll never be like my parents' attitude. In this case, it worked."

"What about you? You've told me you followed in your dad's footsteps. How was it growing up in a two-parent household with two older sisters?"

"All the normal things you hear...my sisters were annoyed by me, and I'm a disappointment to my mother. She's worse every time I see her. Always telling me I'm such a workaholic that I'll never settle down. My sisters and I are close, so at least they defend me when Mom becomes too vocal about my life choices." Reggie pops a piece of eggplant in her mouth, thoughtful as she chews. "She was pretty unhappy when I told her I broke up with Ashford. I don't want to be with him, though. It doesn't help that whenever a relationship fails with a man, she wonders aloud whether it's because I'm also attracted to women." Reggie shakes her head. "I've told her a million times it's the person I'm attracted to, not the sex."

"I get it. I've dated men and women over the years, and I can't tell you how thankful I am that Ben has no problem with it. But," Chrissy raises a finger and tries to look as solemn as possible, "I must admit to being attracted to the sex, too." She wiggles her eyebrows. "Sex is important." Reggie's laughter lights her up, and Chrissy basks in the warmth created. She can't believe she's said something so outrageous, but the way Reggie treats her makes her want to be daring.

Bruno comes over as they get ready to leave, a bag in his hand. "For you and your boy. He likes cannolis, yes? I give you three to have later."

"Thank you, Bruno. He'll be ecstatic." Chrissy smiles and takes the bag.

They make their way back to Chrissy's apartment in record time, and her nerves come back with a vengeance. "I'll change in my room. You can use the bathroom."

Once in the privacy of her bedroom, Chrissy strips and retrieves her costume. She's taking a leap of faith people will like it. She steps into the yellow bellbottoms, the three-tiered green and white ruffles from knee to ankle standing out against its brightness. She slides her hands through the matching shirt and ties the green laces in front. From elbow to wrist the material is loose and billowy with the same green and white pattern as on the pants. She tucks in the shirt and attaches a wide white belt, clipping the oval silver buckle closed. After donning silver platform shoes, Chrissy takes a look in the mirror and laughs. Her costume is from *Mamma Mia*'s Donna and the Dynamos. When she saw it online, she knew she had to wear it. It's skintight, but jogging for so many years has paid off. A knock on the door has her reaching for the knob. She opens it and stares.

Reggie wears a Cleopatra outfit which outlines her curvy figure. The sleeveless black velvet dress has a thigh-high slit on each side of the skirt, and a deep V-neckline edged with gold sequins. She wears a metallic collar and matching belt. On her head is a gold diadem. Her eyes pop out with the smoky eye shadow. Blush emphasizes her cheekbones and her lips—*Jesus!*—they look ripe for the kissing. Long, gold dangly earrings and gold sandals complete the look.

After an extended silence, Reggie steps forward, placing a hand on Chrissy's shoulder and gently pushing her back. "Oh, sorry." Chrissy pivots away while taking a deep breath.

"That's quite all right. You weren't kidding about jogging." Reggie walks around Chrissy slowly, her eyes roaming. "I've never seen you wear anything quite so form-fitting."

Chrissy shifts from one foot to the other, insecure now that Reggie's studying every inch of her. "Does it look bad?"

"Are you kidding? You look gorgeous." Hearing a breathless quality to her voice, Chrissy studies Reggie, wondering whether she means it. Reggie's chest and face are flushed, eyes dark, hands clasped together in front of her. Chrissy has to force herself not to stare at Reggie's nipples, which are erect enough to see through her costume.

"And you look sexy as hell, as you well know, since I just made a fool of myself." Chrissy chuckles, shaking her head at how obvious she is. "You make a pretty good queen. No doubt everyone will be fawning all over you. And, hey, I kind of look like a court jester."

"As long as you're my court jester," Reggie says before walking out of the room. She looks back over her shoulder, a smirk on those dark red lips. "Ready to go?"

Blinking several times, Chrissy shuts off the light and hurries to follow. She fears tonight is going to test her ability to hide her feelings from anyone who sees her near Reggie. They get in the car and after a few minutes of silence, they ease into a conversation about work. "Any progress with the Hogan case?"

Reggie's sigh is answer enough. "No. He won't settle. Says he did nothing wrong. And now it sounds like he's having marital problems. They're staying at his in-laws to save money for a rental deposit. His wife is working overtime to supplement their income since they're no longer receiving rental payments, and with the holidays around the corner, I'm afraid he might not be able to handle the pressure."

"What do you mean?"

"He seems angrier and more desperate each time we speak. I don't know how else to help him other than to do my best to limit his liability."

"I'm sorry. I wish I could help." Chrissy reaches over to cover Reggie's hand where it rests on the center console between their seats. She squeezes it and starts to pull away, but Reggie turns her hand over and interlaces their fingers. *Holy shit! She's holding my hand. Is this a normal friend thing? Is this a signal that we're more than friends? What should I do?* Chrissy sits still, staring straight ahead as she attempts to regulate her breathing. Her heartbeats are so loud in her ears, she nearly misses Reggie's next statement.

"Thank you," Reggie says, her voice soft. "You help more than you think."

Their hands remain clasped throughout the ride, and Chrissy wishes they were driving farther than to Cambridge. Like to Los Angeles. When Reggie lets go to park the car once they reach the Freedmans' house, Chrissy immediately misses the warmth of her hand. The best she can do is shove her own in her coat pockets and follow Reggie into the party, hoping she'll get to hold Reggie's hand again. Soon.

Chapter Seven

PADDING OVER TO BEN'S bedroom, Chrissy taps on the door, waiting a few moments before opening it. "Rise and shine. Are you coming with me for a jog?" It's only six in the morning, but he's used to her waking him up this early during the week. She flicks the light on and looks over to see whether the lump in the bed is moving. It's not. "Ben?" She pulls the blankets back so she can see his face. It's flushed. Feeling his forehead, Chrissy frowns. He's warm. "Ben?"

He struggles to open his eyes. They're red and watery. "Mom, I don't feel good."

"I can tell. What's wrong?"

"My throat hurts. And I'm all stuffed up. It's hard to breathe."

"That doesn't sound good. You're staying home. Let me make some phone calls." The fact that he doesn't argue confirms he feels awful. Chrissy detours to the bathroom to wash her hands before getting her phone from her bedroom. She calls the school first to report his absence. After leaving a message on their automated service, Chrissy calls his doctor, leaving a message. She's afraid he might have the flu and wants to check on medicine dosages. With a sigh, she resigns herself to missing work. She leaves a message with the call service at the firm before sending a text message to Reggie. Modern technology is great, but it doesn't cut down on the number of phone calls she has to make when Ben's sick.

She returns to his room with a glass of water, a roll of toilet paper, and the thermometer. Her heart hurts when she hears his sniffling. "Let's prop you up a bit." She helps him sit up, watching him do an impression of loose spaghetti by slumping forward, and she arranges a few pillows behind him. He sits back, and she uses her fingers to brush his hair away from his eyes. He looks a mess.

"Thanks. That helps." He delivers a wan smile that breaks Chrissy's heart.

"Good. Let's take your temperature so I can tell your doctor whether you have a fever when she calls back. Keep it under your tongue until it beeps." Chrissy sits on the bed near his hip, thinking about what needs to happen next. She doesn't like to give Ben medicine unless it's essential. She'd rather he fight the infection naturally. Hearing the beep, Chrissy reads the results. "Hm. One-oh-one. That's not too high. It means your body's fighting it." She hands him the glass of water and watches him drink from it before she gets up. "Are you hungry?"

"Not really."

"Okay. Why don't you go back to sleep. After I speak to your doctor, I'll run out to get some things to help you."

"Aren't you going to work?" Ben twists the blanket between his fingers, not looking up.

Chrissy smiles at how worried he looks. "No, sweetie. I have ten sick days a year, and I only used two of them last year. It's not a big deal to take the day off."

"Okay." He pulls the blanket up over his shoulder and closes his eyes. "Thanks, Mom."

Pulling the door closed, Chrissy makes her way to the kitchen and washes her hands before putting water in a pan to boil. She sits at the table, staring into space. It's a week before Thanksgiving, and the meteorologist has forecast snow for today. Commuting during the winter months can be challenging. Although she loves snow, it's not fun when she has to walk through slush and watch out for black ice. The water rolls and she turns off the stove, gathering what she needs to make tea. She's not hungry, but she makes toast, munching on it. Ben starts coughing and she winces in sympathy. Her phone rings after she finishes her small breakfast. It's the doctor's office.

"Hello. This is Chrissy."

"Hi. This is Doctor Jameson. I'm returning your call about your son."

"Yes. Thank you for calling back so quickly. He has a fever of a hundred and one, is coughing, has a stuffy head, and his throat hurts."

"How was he yesterday?"

"He was fine. A lot more energy. His eyes were clear, and he wasn't coughing."

"Sounds like he may have the flu. It comes on quickly. You can give him some acetaminophen or ibuprofen for the fever and body aches to make him more comfortable. Lots of fluids and rest will help him. A hot shower may help clear his sinuses. Cough drops and chamomile tea will help his throat. If he's coughing so much he can't rest, you may want to consider giving him antihistamines. Try to get him to eat. Call me if his fever spikes or he seems to be getting worse after a few days."

Chrissy jots down what she says. "Okay. Thank you."

Chrissy pokes her head in Ben's room. He's asleep, mouth open and drool dripping down his chin. Chrissy grabs her keys and locks the door on her way out. Instead of her usual morning run, she keeps her head down against the wind gusts and walks to the drug store in record time. Grabbing orange juice, tissues, cough drops, mint tea, and a box of antihistamines, she decides to see how he's feeling later before buying more food. Once she returns home, she puts everything away before checking on Ben again. He's still asleep.

At a bit after eight, Chrissy's phone rings. Her heart speeds up when Reggie's name flashes across the screen. "Hello?"

"I just got your text that Ben's sick."

"Yeah. The doctor thinks he has the flu. He's sleeping, poor thing."

"Are you all right?"

Chrissy's eyebrows shoot up. "I'm fine. I hardly ever get sick."

Reggie hums. "Right. Come to think of it, I don't remember you ever calling in sick. Well, don't worry about anything here. I have a temp covering for you. Take tomorrow off, too."

Grimacing, Chrissy tries not to feel distressed over being so easily replaced. She shakes her head, irritated with herself. She has no right to feel hurt. It's a job, not a relationship. Reggie is being generous, something many bosses aren't.

"Hey. I'd rather have you here. You know that, right?" Reggie's soft voice assuages Chrissy's insecurities.

"Yeah. Thanks, Reggie. I hope your day goes smoothly."

"Thanks. I have the last Hogan deposition this morning. We go to trial in a few weeks."

"Oh, that sucks. I can probably come in for a few hours. I suspect Ben will be sleeping all day." *I don't trust that guy. Ben won't mind if I go in for a few hours.*

"No way. I'll let you know how it goes."

"Oh. All right."

"I'll talk to you later. Tell Ben I hope he feels better."

"I will. Bye." After they hang up, Chrissy sits at the kitchen table, staring at the phone. Although they haven't spent any time outside of work since the Halloween party, they're working toward something. Reggie touches her all the time, little brushes of her fingers on her arm, her shoulder, her back. Nothing unprofessional. It's more to make a connection, and Chrissy's reassured each time.

It's hard for Chrissy to hold back from kissing Reggie, particularly after a night of dreaming about it. Not spending time together is the best deterrent she has, but she knows when given the opportunity, she'll jump at the chance of being with Reggie outside of work again. Each day Chrissy's becoming more certain Reggie returns her feelings, and each day she looks at the job postings, hoping to find an opening she can transfer to.

Hearing Ben stir, Chrissy pushes aside her musings and pokes her head in his room. "How are you feeling?"

"Gross," Ben says, groaning as he rubs his eyes.

"I want you to take a hot shower. It will help you breathe. I'll change your bed sheets and make you some breakfast."

"I don't want—"

"I know. I know. But you need to keep hydrated. Some tea will soothe your throat, and toast will keep your stomach satisfied. I won't force you to have more than that until later. Deal?"

"Deal."

Chrissy watches Ben climb out of bed, and she clasps her hands together so she won't reach out to him. She's watched him become more independent this year, learning the hard way not to offer help unless he wants it. Sometimes, she slips up, like that time last month when he was trying to file some documents for Reggie. She doesn't know who was more embarrassed—him for her attempt to step in to help, or her when he snapped at her. They had a long talk that night, coming to the agreement that he would ask when he needs help. So far, they've both kept to the understanding.

As he begins to shuffle past her, Ben stops and leans in, resting his head on her shoulder for a minute. "Thanks, Mom," he whispers, and Chrissy gives him a quick hug before he continues toward the bathroom. Once she hears the door close, she gets to work changing the bedding. She shoves the used sheets in the laundry basket then prepares his breakfast. By the time he leaves the bathroom, his eyes are brighter and he's breathing through his nose.

"How do you feel?"

"Better." He sits down, his head propped on one hand. "Tired though."

"Have this and then you can go back to bed."

"Okay." Ben munches his toast while Chrissy sips her tea. "What did Reggie say?"

"She hopes you feel better. She'll call me later. She gave me tomorrow off, too, so you don't need to worry."

"You two seem closer."

"Ben." *He must be feeling better if he's back on this subject.* The problem with these conversations is how she becomes hopeful. It's dangerous for her. *What if I make my interest clear and she rebuffs my advances?* So far, all their flirting can be explained away. It's true they've toed the line more often over the last month, but she wants to be as sure as possible before she reveals her heart.

"Come on, Mom. You can't deny it. I saw you two yesterday at work. She was checking you out."

Shaking her head, Chrissy is quick to reject his words. "I doubt it. She's too professional to ever do something like that at work."

"She's also a human being who likes you. Have you seen any new jobs posted?"

"No, but Cathy mentioned a position might be opening up soon on her floor."

"That's great. You can apply and after you get it, you can ask Reggie out on a proper date."

"Whoa. Hold on there, kid. There's no guarantee I'll get the position, never mind the huge question mark of whether Reggie would date me."

"Mom, be brave." Ben stares at her with so much hope, Chrissy can't help but smile. "You know, she told me about the holiday party. Are you going?"

Dipping her head forward, Chrissy sighs. She wants to go—of course she does—but she doesn't want to leave Ben alone. That's why she missed the party last year. "I'm not sure."

"Why? It's at her house. Don't you want to see it?"

"You know I do, but I haven't made a decision, yet." Chrissy picks up his empty plate and places it in the sink. "Off to bed with you, sicko."

"At least tell me you've thought about my idea for her Christmas present."

"I have, and I like it. We'll start working on it next week, if you're feeling better."

"Yes!" Ben throws his fist in the air, a smile splitting his face. "All the big sales start next week. She'll love it."

"Of course, she will. Now..."

"Off to bed. I know." Ben leaves without any more stalling, his body slouched and his feet sliding over the floor. Chrissy barely keeps herself from following, knowing he'd rather she not hover. It's a near thing, though. He's still her little boy.

Chrissy uses the time to clean. Rolling up the sleeves of her red and black flannel shirt, she wipes down the counters and kitchen table then washes the few dirty dishes by hand. After everything is spotless, she empties the dishwasher and places all the kitchenware where they belong. It takes all of ten minutes to finish the kitchen. The bathroom's next.

The day passes second by snail second, but the apartment is sparkling by the time Ben drags himself out of bed in the early afternoon. Chrissy gives him some orange juice and scrambled eggs. He's not coughing, but his eyes are glazed. He still feels warm, too.

"How are you feeling?"

"I'm stuffed up, and my throat's sore. And my head's starting to hurt."

"Take this glass of water. I got you some cough drops and tissues. You might want to take another shower later so you can clear your head. The doctor said it was okay to give you some medicine." He makes a face, and she smiles. "I know. Only if you really need it. I want you to get more rest."

"Thanks, Mom." He trudges back in his room, the bed squeaking when he drops down on it. She frowns. This boy is never still, yet here he is, sleeping the day away. It worries her, even though she understands he'll get better. Not wanting to be too far from Ben, Chrissy settles in the kitchen to make a list of possible Christmas gifts.

A knock on the door breaks her concentration, and she hurries to open it. Peering through the peep-hole, she sees Reggie with two grocery bags, so Chrissy swings the door open. "Reggie." She can't hold back her smile of relief and leans forward to grab a bag. "Come in. What's all this?" When Reggie doesn't respond, she glances up. Reggie stands motionless, biting her lower lip. Her stare is so intense the hairs on Chrissy's arms stand at attention. "Reggie?"

"You, um, went jogging today?"

"What do you..." Chrissy stops talking as she looks down, catching sight of her clothes. She's still dressed in her jogging outfit. She hadn't seen any reason to change. Her black leggings fit like a second skin, as do her black T-shirt and open flannel shirt. "I was planning on it, but I didn't want to leave Ben alone for too long." She starts to remove the items from the bag and places them on the counter, doing her best to act as if Reggie's eyes aren't doing funny things to her. A few moments later, Reggie empties the contents of her bag, and Chrissy takes inventory once everything is on the counter. Carrots, celery, chicken stock, some fresh seasonings, pasta, and a rotisserie chicken, still warm.

"I'm cheating a bit since normally I would boil the chicken and use the stock. It will still taste good. Chicken soup is great for fighting the flu. We'll get Ben up and about in no time."

This time it's Chrissy's turn to stare, rendered mute by Reggie's actions.

"Christina?"

Blinking back her emotions, Chrissy says, "Reggie, this is incredible. You're incredible. I can't believe you did this. You...you're...thank you." She takes a deep breath, trying to settle herself. No one's ever done this for her before. No one. She looks down at the counter, doing her best to push back the tears lining her eyes. She feels Reggie's warmth next to her a moment before a hand squeezes her shoulder.

"I wrestled with whether this was a good idea. I'm always afraid I'll overstep. But that's not what this is." She applies enough pressure on Chrissy's shoulder to turn her away from the counter, and before Chrissy quite realizes what's happening, Reggie embraces her. Her voice softens. "I care about you and Ben. I wanted to do something to help."

Nodding, Chrissy hangs on, forehead resting on Reggie's shoulder, tears escaping her closed eyes.

"Tell me." Reggie's hand strokes her hair before resting at the nape of her neck, her thumb rubbing soothing circles on the side of her neck.

"I'm afraid." Chrissy pulls back enough to look Reggie in the eyes. "I don't trust people. I don't let them in. I don't depend on anyone. But here we are, and I want you here." It takes all her courage to say these words. Her biggest fear is being rejected again. The last time she was this vulnerable, she lost everything—her parents, her boyfriend, and her friends. Yet, Reggie makes her feel safe.

Reggie cups her cheek, and Chrissy sighs. "Don't be afraid." Reggie leans in, pressing her forehead against Chrissy's. "I don't know how I gained your trust, but I'm grateful."

Tiny puffs of air caress Chrissy's lips with every exhalation Reggie makes. She sinks into the comfort Reggie exudes, her body relaxing within Reggie's arms. Taking a few deep breaths, Chrissy squeezes Reggie before stepping back. "I'm the one who's grateful. So, how can I help?"

"Right. You can cut up the carrots and celery while I boil the noodles and shred the chicken."

They fall into a comfortable silence, and Chrissy revels in the simple domesticity. She can imagine a future filled with such teamwork, a natural extension of the connection they've forged through work. She wants that future, can taste it. Time passes in the blink of an eye, long enough to hear Ben moving around in his room. Long enough for the soup to be ready.

"The company holiday party will be here before you know it. Will you be able to come?" Reggie turns off the stove and shifts from one foot to the other.

Chrissy's heart sinks. She looks away. "I want to attend, but I don't want to leave Ben alone." Chrissy's dying to see Reggie's house, to understand more about her.

"Well, lucky for you I happen to know the host," Reggie says with a wink. "Bring him. We can set him up in the den. He's spent enough hours at the office for me to know he can keep himself occupied. And I'll make sure we have some food he'll enjoy. He can read, watch a movie, play games on my tablet. I'm sure he'll be fine, and you'll be able to attend."

Why Reggie's working so hard to solve Chrissy's problems is unfathomable. Nevertheless, Chrissy's ecstatic. Warmth floods her chest, and she's hard-pressed not to throw her arms around Reggie again. She settles on smiling broadly. She wants to go, and now she can. "That sounds perfect. Thank you, Reggie."

"You're welcome. Besides, I can assure you my motives are entirely selfish."

Their gazes intersect, and Chrissy's unable to stop from falling into Reggie's warm eyes. She gathers some bowls and spoons, standing close to Reggie as she doles out portions for everyone. Chrissy hums a Christmas tune under her breath, grinning when Reggie joins in. She can't wait to get a look at Reggie's home, her personal space, her brownstone on Beacon Hill. She knows Ben will be psyched for the same reason. For the first time in a long time, Chrissy's happy.

Chapter Eight

THOUGHTS RUN THROUGH CHRISSY'S mind as she walks up the steps to Reggie's home. *My colleagues are here. This is a work-related function. It will probably be boring. I'll talk to people I hardly know, eat what's sure to be delicious food, and leave before I make a fool of myself. I'll make sure not to drink, not to watch Reggie's every move, and not to declare my undying love. Simple.*

"You look pretty, Mom." Chrissy shoots Ben a grateful look. She's wearing a black slinky dress, a splurge purchase she made the week before. Reggie's reaction the last few times she's seen Chrissy in form-fitting clothes has given her the courage to wear a more revealing outfit.

"Thank you, honey. And you look handsome." He's dressed in a fir-green cable-knit sweater and black jeans. His hair is combed back for once, and he's wearing his Guardian Angel pendant. He wears it every day.

Pressing the doorbell, Chrissy rubs her hands together. She exhales a loud gush of air, watching a white plume of breath form in front of her. *It's too cold to stand around.* When the heavy wooden door swings inward, a blast of sound greets them. Chrissy smiles at Reggie, who opens the iron security gate.

"Christina, Ben, welcome to my home." The authentic smile, so different from the polite one she uses on her clients, is a balm to Chrissy's frayed nerves. Reggie's dressed in a fitted, maroon velvet dress with a plunging neckline. Chrissy has a hard time keeping her eyes from wandering.

After Reggie turns to the side so they can enter, Chrissy steps over the threshold into the atrium, awed by the intricate detail in the ceilings, walls, and floor. Everything is complex—a perfect reflection of the woman who lives here.

"Whoa," Ben mutters, and although Chrissy agrees, she says nothing.

Diagonally from them a magnificent fir tree is decorated with twinkling white lights and matching ornaments hanging from its branches. The distinctive smells of fir, cinnamon, and pumpkin tease Chrissy's nose. "You have a gorgeous home." Looking to the right, she sees the parlor full of people. Many are milling about, talking and laughing. Others are seated throughout the large room.

"I thought Ben might be most comfortable in my den. It's this way." Reggie gestures toward the staircase. They pass white columns and ascend the winding, marble staircase. Chrissy tries hard not to stare at Reggie's backside and fails beautifully. Garland and gold bows interspersed with red ribbon wrap around the banister, warm and festive. A statue of Athena stands in a small alcove halfway up the stairs, and several oil paintings are arranged on the walls.

After reaching the top of the stairs, they turn to the right and enter the second room on the left. Chrissy sucks in a breath. A grand walnut-paneled library, the room is furnished with overstuffed sofas and chairs set around a roaring fire. *They look comfortable enough to fall asleep on.* Floor-to-ceiling bookcases are filled with leather-bound books, and the ceiling has carved wooden panels. The drapes and furniture are light-colored, offsetting the dark wood.

Chrissy imagines spending hours in here, working, relaxing, dreaming. She can smell Reggie's perfume, and the familiar scent—a sweet and spicy blend of roses, patchouli, and muguet—brings a smile to Chrissy's lips. Their eyes connect, and something intimate passes between them.

"Beautiful." Chrissy realizes she's talking about Reggie as much as the room.

It doesn't take long to get Ben settled, and although she wants to explore the rest of Reggie's home, Chrissy doesn't dare ask for a tour. Instead, she follows Reggie down the stairs, the sway of her hips keeping Chrissy's attention.

"The bar's straight ahead, and food will be served in about twenty minutes."

Recognizing the dismissal, Chrissy says, "Great. Thanks." A hand on her arm stops her before she can enter the parlor.

"I'll catch up with you later." Reggie's tone is apologetic.

Feeling her spirits rise, Chrissy grins. "Sounds good."

She walks through the crowd, exchanging pleasantries with several coworkers. Once at the bar, she asks for a glass of ginger ale. Many will assume she's drinking alcohol, and that's fine with her. The parlor is connected to a large formal ballroom. *Who has that?*

"Chrissy. How are you?" Cathy asks, as she comes up beside her at the bar.

Leaning in, Chrissy hugs her. "I'm great. Ready for Christmas?"

"Oh, yes. David and I finished our shopping, and his parents are visiting from Rhode Island." She's wearing a green silk blouse and black slacks, her emerald drop earrings and matching pendant complementing the outfit well.

"I've never been. Maybe I'll have to take a road trip with the kid to visit the area this summer."

"Oh, let me know if you do. I can tell you all the great places to visit, and maybe David and I can even meet up with you."

Chrissy perks up at the suggestion. She tends to avoid taking trips since that means making all the arrangements. She's sure Cathy can give her all the information she needs so it'll be easy to plan. "That's a good idea. Once the weather gets warmer, we're there." Since Cathy already has a glass of wine in hand, they move toward the ballroom once Chrissy gets her beverage. A trio plays jazz in the corner while people mingle. It's starting to get crowded, the noise increasing as people fill the room.

"Hi, Chrissy." David wraps an arm around Cathy. "Going solo tonight?"

"I like to keep my options open," Chrissy says, feigning nonchalance.

"Ah, well your open option is staring at you right now." David's eyes twinkle, as he jerks his chin toward their right.

Her eyes connect with Reggie's, and heat crawls up Chrissy's neck.

"David!" Cathy swats him on the arm. "Don't embarrass her."

"What?" He rubs his arm, a pronounced pout making him look much younger. "I thought she'd want to know the interest isn't one-sided." He's wearing a maroon Oxford shirt open at the collar and black slacks. His outfit is festive but more relaxed than what he wears to work. He looks more like a first-year associate than a junior partner.

I never should have confided in Cathy. Chrissy sighs, but Reggie's dulcet voice announces the buffet's open.

"That's my cue," David says, taking Cathy's hand. "Shall we?"

Chrissy follows them, planning to fill a plate for Ben and then get herself settled.

"Christina, tell me what you want, and I'll take care of it while you get Ben's plate," Reggie says beside her.

Chrissy smiles. "Okay. Thanks." She looks at the display and rattles off less than what she would normally eat, not wanting to sound like too much of a glutton. Looking back at Reggie, she notices the raised eyebrows.

"What?"

"That's all you want? Really?"

"Um," Chrissy stalls. *How does she do that? How does she know me so well?*

"We've eaten together enough times for me to know you're trying to be polite."

"Well, the others have to eat, too." She preens when she hears Reggie's chuckle.

"Right. I'll figure it out." Reggie moves away, and Chrissy watches her while trying not to salivate.

"Good job, Romeo." David nudges her.

Chrissy rubs the back of her neck, doubts beginning to plague her with David's ribbing. *Maybe Reggie's being the consummate hostess by offering to organize my plate and I'm letting my desires run away from reality.* With a frown, Chrissy says, "Thanks. I'm so smooth, it's a wonder she didn't swoon at my feet."

"Don't sell yourself short. She's taking care of you. That's positive," Cathy says.

"True." Chrissy's spirits revive.

After filling a plate with lasagna, meatballs, ham, vegetables, fresh Italian bread, and the proper condiments, Chrissy snags a tall glass of water and makes her way to the den.

"That smells good." Ben's eyes widen when he sees the food.

"I bet it tastes good, too." Chrissy hands over the food. "Be careful. Don't get anything on the furniture or yourself. Are you doing okay? You're not too bored, are you?"

"I'm fine, Mom. Have fun, okay? And dance with her at least once." Ben turns his attention to the food, digging in.

"Dance with her. Right," Chrissy mumbles, as she makes her way to the dining room. She spots Reggie with an empty seat next to her. *She saved me a seat?* Chrissy's heart rate triples. Reggie looks up and smiles, as Chrissy reaches her.

"Thanks, Reggie." Chrissy sits down, and her eyes widen, much as Ben's eyes had. Reggie has loaded Chrissy's plate with a variety of food, and every single morsel is something Chrissy knows she'll love. "Oh, my God."

A husky chuckle catches her attention. "I hope you enjoy it. I spent all day cooking."

"You cooked all this?" Chrissy asks, her voice squeaking. The spread looks incredible. Without waiting any longer, Chrissy scoops up a forkful of lasagna and inhales it as if it's her last meal. Groaning, Chrissy is certain she's never eaten anything so melt-in-your-mouth, ambrosia-for-the-gods, perfect food in her entire life. It is heavenly. Orgasmic.

After swallowing her first bite, she turns to Reggie to tell her and pauses. Reggie's fork is frozen halfway to her mouth, staring at Chrissy as if she's the Holy Grail. The same look from when they shared dessert at Gino's months ago.

Chrissy holds herself back, barely, from leaning in to click Reggie's tempting mouth closed and covering it with her own. "Your cooking is exceptional. How did you learn to do it?" She loves being the center of Reggie's attention. She feels desirable. Powerful. Confident.

Nothing. Reggie says nothing. She continues to stare at Chrissy as if she is a meal, a meal she wants to consume. "Reggie? Are you all right?" Chrissy places her hand on Reggie's knee and squeezes.

"Y...yes. Sorry." Reggie clears her throat and shakes her head. "I got lost in thought. My father was an accomplished cook, and he taught me."

"He was an accomplished teacher, too." She doesn't like the melancholy underlying Reggie's words, but she doesn't know how to address it. With another squeeze, Chrissy removes her hand and returns her attention to the food.

"Yes, I miss him. He loved the holidays. When he died of a heart attack," Reggie shakes her head, "it was awful." A deep sadness crosses Reggie's brown eyes, staining them with grief. "It was unexpected. He and my mother had divorced. Oh, it was so nasty...and then mere months later, he died."

Chrissy wants to hug Reggie, remove the hurt. All she can do, though, is grab her hand and squeeze it before reluctantly releasing it. "I'm so sorry, Reggie. I'm sure you miss him greatly."

Reggie nods, eyes skittering away. "Thank you."

Chrissy ignores how her face heats and her body hums. All this touching is having a marked effect on her equilibrium.

"My father's name was Ben." It takes a moment for Chrissy to process the words before she grins brightly.

"Great name."

"Yes. It is." Reggie's lips curve up.

They eat in silence before another thought strikes Chrissy. "What are your plans for Christmas?"

"I'll be hosting the family dinner here."

Chrissy watches Reggie sip her wine, understanding what she has not said. She's not looking forward to Christmas dinner.

"And are you and your mother getting along?" Chrissy's hesitant to pry, but she's unable to ignore the obvious signs of her unhappiness.

"We're working on it. I was furious for what she did to my father." Reggie's laugh is bitter. "They split up years ago, but I still hate her for the hell she put him through. He refused to fight back. Said he'd always love her, even though she cheated on him with some younger, richer, slimy guy. That's why I refuse to handle divorce cases. They cause so much pain. And I probably still wouldn't be talking to my mother if my father hadn't died."

Chrissy raises her eyebrows. If it were her, she doubts she'd give her mother another chance.

"I might have continued to ignore my dear mother's entreaties that we talk if not for my sisters." Reggie's lips twist even as she shakes her head. "They are such busybodies. But they love me and my mother, and they want us all to spend Christmas together. I was able to get out of Thanksgiving dinner fairly early thanks to that case I settled last week, but I can't exactly escape from my own house. So, one large, uncomfortable Christmas dinner is what I have to look forward to."

"That sounds nice." Seeing Reggie's incredulous look, Chrissy hastens to add, "I mean, spending time with family. Even if it's uncomfortable, at least you have a family. I remember you mentioned your mom lives in Chestnut Hill. Are your sisters local?"

Reggie gives her a contemplative stare. "Pretty much. Newton and Winthrop. How about you?"

Chrissy's not sure what she's asking—how she's spending her Christmas or whether her family is local. It doesn't matter, though, because for once she doesn't mind opening up. At least not when it comes to Reggie.

"Ben and I usually buy a tree on Christmas Eve and trim it. We have all these ornaments we've made over the years. And I sew popcorn garland, which takes forever but looks great." She chews on a piece of bread, gathering her thoughts. "Our Christmas is pretty low-key. We open presents, make a big breakfast together, and watch some holiday movies. If there's a good movie playing in the theaters, we go. Now that I'm thinking about it, it's kinda lame."

Reggie's hand on Chrissy's bicep stops her from taking another bite of juicy ham. "No, Christina. That doesn't sound lame at all. It sounds relaxing."

They smile at each other before Chrissy clears her throat. "Yeah, well, we like it. It's me and Ben, and every year we plan what we want to do." She pops the piece of ham in her mouth.

"You're an amazing woman." It takes a moment for Chrissy to register Reggie's hand is still grasping her arm, her thumb rubbing small circles.

"I don't think so," Chrissy admits, her voice soft. She's becoming emotional, and it reminds her of why she never reveals her past to anyone. "I mean, my parents threw me out when I was seventeen for getting pregnant, and then my boyfriend dumped me and my friends stopped talking to me. Obviously, I wasn't worth keeping around. I wasn't worth the effort. So, I made the decision not to rely on anyone. I worry, though, that I'm not doing what's best for Ben. I try, but…" Chrissy shrugs. She doesn't feel hungry anymore, and she pushes the plate away.

Chrissy swallows the emotions fighting to get out. *This is not the time to lose it.* She'll be mortified if anyone notices the tears brimming in her eyes. The holidays are tough for her. The years of loneliness, the years she's spent with no gifts, love, or feeling of belonging, all trigger her. A soft finger wipes away the tears that escape despite her best effort.

"Christina," Reggie whispers, her concern obvious.

"I'm okay." Chrissy ducks her head and swipes at her face. *I can't believe I'm falling apart like this.* "I'm sorry, Reggie. I'm not usually like this."

"Don't apologize. Please, tell me what I can do."

The distress in Reggie's voice makes Chrissy feel worse. It's not like she can ask the woman to kiss her, hug her. No, she can't ask for those things, even though that's what she longs for. Sniffing, Chrissy looks up and tries to smile. "I'm fine. I promise. Let's change the subject. Okay?"

Chrissy withstands Reggie's discerning gaze for several seconds before Reggie nods. "Then tell me what you got Ben for Christmas."

"That I can do."

After dinner the music is turned up and part of the ballroom is cleared so people can dance. Reggie leaves to coordinate dessert and coffee, and Chrissy stands next to Cathy and David. Cathy bops to the beat, as Chrissy and David grin at her obvious wish to dance. No one's on the dance floor, yet, and Cathy's not the type to dance alone.

"How can no one be dancing to this song?" Cathy complains.

Chuckling, Chrissy says, "Go on, then. Others are probably thinking the same thing."

"Come on. I'll go with you." David swallows the last of his beer before handing the empty bottle to Chrissy. "Wish me luck." He grabs Cathy's hand and heads for the floor.

Chrissy places the bottle on a nearby table and watches them dance. People start to filter onto the floor, and she taps her foot in time with the pop music, recognizing the song as one of Ben's favorites. Once the next song begins, Cathy waves at Chrissy with a 'join us' motion. Although self-conscious, Chrissy steps onto the dance floor. She's always enjoyed music, and she's not bad at dancing. She likes to try new moves, and she indulges herself by twisting her body, twirling around. She laughs when Cathy and David cheer her on.

Twirling again, she finds herself peering into Reggie's amused dark eyes. Chrissy keeps dancing, backing up a bit so Reggie has space to join her. They dance through the rest of the song together, Chrissy breaking out some of her best moves. She's watching Reggie's body as it undulates to the beat, that's for damn sure.

The song ends, and a slow dance begins. Chrissy looks at Reggie, ready to exit the dance floor if she's uncomfortable, but Reggie simply gathers Chrissy in her arms. Chrissy smiles, heat suffusing her when she rests her fingers on the soft curves of her waist. Reggie links her hands around her neck in a loose hold, and when their eyes meet, she's surprised by how piercing Reggie's stare is. She's sure Reggie can see right into her heart.

After a few moments of gazing into each other's eyes, having a conversation Chrissy is afraid to misinterpret, Reggie says, "I noticed you've nursed the same drink all night. Non-alcoholic, I presume."

"Yeah. Since we do have to make our way home at some point, I don't want to drink." Chrissy's pleased by Reggie's words. It's another example of how much she cares.

"Or you could stay here."

"That's...tempting," Chrissy says, pulling Reggie a bit closer. *Am I romanticizing this or is she offering as a friend?*

"That or me?" Reggie whispers in her ear, making Chrissy shiver.

"I think you know the answer to that." Chrissy turns her head so their breath mingles. *Is Reggie offering what I dream about?* Misinterpreting this could make things between them extremely uncomfortable.

"I do, but I wonder whether you know how I feel." Fingers gently comb through Chrissy's unruly curls, distracting her. "Christina, your feelings are not one-sided."

"I, um, I can't make a mistake here. I really love my job." Chrissy catches her bottom lip between her teeth, daring to gaze into Reggie's eyes, willing her to understand what she's trying to say. "I need it to provide for Ben."

"And I love working with you. But I heard a paralegal position in Hawk's division will be opening up at the beginning of the year. It's yours if you want it."

The promise of what will happen once Chrissy changes jobs spurs another shiver up her spine. She has a hard time catching her breath, the full weight of Reggie's offer making her feel weak. "Are you sure?"

"Yes, so if you aren't, you'd better think about it before you give me your answer." Reggie's eyes are as serious as her voice.

"I'm sure. I'll move over to Hawk's division." The smile she receives knocks the breath from her. "God, you're so beautiful," Chrissy murmurs, her eyes widening, as she realizes what she's said.

Reggie's grin brightens, and she's so gorgeous Chrissy doesn't mind being vulnerable. Reggie knows how she feels and is making arrangements so they can explore their feelings.

"You make me happy, Christina. I've never felt as excited to get to work each day." Reggie chuckles. "But I'm selfish. I want more. Much more."

"Me, too."

Chrissy wonders how she's still standing upright. She's never seen that look in Reggie's eyes or felt those magical fingers massaging her neck, making her tremble with each caress. *I'm in over my head.*

"Will you stay over tonight?" Reggie asks, her lilting voice tempting Chrissy. She wants to say yes. She really does.

"No, but I hope you'll extend the offer again soon." She hopes Reggie can hear the regret in her voice.

Reggie nods. "We'll plan it. Not too long from now."

"Not too long," Chrissy repeats. *I need some time to get this through my thick head. Reggie wants me.*

The song ends, and they move to the side of the dance floor, standing close. People approach in an informal line, saying their goodbyes to Reggie, thanking her for opening her home to them. Chrissy starts to inch away, wanting to give her privacy, but Reggie casually winds her arm around her waist. Chrissy doesn't mind.

When Cathy and David join them, David wiggles his eyebrows,

making her laugh. "Cut it out, you nerd," Chrissy grouses.

Cathy leans in. "Does this mean what I think it means?"

"God, I hope so," Chrissy whispers back. "Otherwise I'm going to die of a broken heart."

"No one will be dying today," Reggie whispers at them both, causing them to laugh. Reggie shoots a teasing smile at Chrissy, and she falls in love even more.

They sit at a table, chatting about whatever comes to mind. It turns out Cathy knows everything about everyone at the firm. The entire time, Reggie holds Chrissy's hand in her lap, stroking it with her thumb. They sneak looks at each other. Chrissy's ecstatic.

Attorney Hawk strolls up to the table, his wife's hand securely tucked in the crook of his elbow. He's a tall, thin man with a hooked nose and freckles. His dark brown hair is sprinkled with white, and his eyes are an unusual bluish green. His wife is at least a half a foot shorter than him, with dark brown eyes and long black hair.

"Christina, have you met Afanc Hawk and his wife, Erin?" Reggie asks.

"No. It's nice to meet you both."

"This is your paralegal?" Seeing the gleam in Hawk's eyes, Chrissy wonders what he knows.

"Not for much longer," Reggie answers. Her eyes rest on Chrissy for a moment, and her smile softens.

Well, that answers that.

"Good. I shall see you on January second. Enjoy your holidays." He turns back to Reggie. "An excellent party, as always. The food was scrumptious. Most unfortunate." He pats his flat stomach.

"Oh, stop, you fool," Erin chastises before delivering a kiss to his cheek.

"Goodnight, all." Hawk waves as they move away.

"As much as I hate to say it, I should probably get Ben and leave soon." Chrissy rises, and she watches as Reggie's chin dips to her chest before she rises, too, lips pressed together. Chrissy wants to kiss the sad look away.

"We're going, too. Chrissy, we can drop you and Ben off on our way," Cathy says.

"You don't mind?"

"Not at all. It's cold out. And David can go heat up the car."

"Jeez, thanks. Reggie, this was an excellent party. Have a good weekend." Cathy stops David to deliver a chaste kiss before he walks away, whistling a tune Chrissy doesn't recognize.

"I'll wait for you and Ben near the door." She leans in to whisper to Chrissy, "And then you can tell me what Hawk meant." She winks then goes to gather their coats.

"Shall we?" Reggie says with a sigh.

Chrissy nods, sad they're leaving, second-guessing her decision.

They find Ben napping on the couch. As Chrissy goes to step in the room, Reggie blocks her way with a hand across the entryway. Tilting her head, Chrissy follows Reggie's eyes upward and spots the sprig of mistletoe. *Well, that's gotta be safer than staying the night. Why am I being so careful when she's gotten me a job in a different division and admitted she has feelings for me? She's taken a big risk. It's time I do, too.* A slow smile inches across Chrissy's face as she makes her decision, and heat unfurls in her belly. She turns toward Reggie and frames her cheeks with her hands, leaning in to capture plump, blood-red lips.

Delivering a chaste kiss against impossibly soft lips, Chrissy takes her time memorizing their texture. She kisses her again, arousal building at how perfect Reggie feels. After a third soft kiss, she hears Reggie growl and takes that as her cue to press their lips together more firmly. She moves a hand to the back of Reggie's head, sifting her fingers through silky locks as she nibbles on Reggie's lower lip, and Chrissy swallows the resulting moan, opening her mouth to welcome Reggie's tongue. Reggie's hands pull her closer, and their tongues wrestle.

I'm gonna pass out. She feels incredible. Tastes heavenly. Wine, chocolate, and mint. God, I'm lost. Chrissy whimpers, continuing to explore every inch of Reggie's addictive mouth. After several minutes, the kisses wind down. Chrissy withdraws, resting her forehead against Reggie's while trying to catch her breath.

"I've wanted to do that for so long. It was worth the wait." Reggie pulls back. "You are worth the wait, Christina Kramer."

"I don't know how I got lucky enough to capture your attention. I've always felt worthless. Like I don't matter to anyone. Ben's the only one who cared, and that's because I'm his mom." Chrissy shrugs.

"Well, you have me, and I'm not letting you go. It'll be hard enough to let you leave tonight."

They smile, an understanding settling between them. Chrissy pulls Reggie in for a hug, breathing in her signature perfume before letting her go and walking over to where Ben is reclining.

"Hey, kid." Chrissy shakes his shoulder. "It's time to go." He sits up while rubbing his eyes. Times like this remind her of when he was a little boy.

"Okay. I'm up." He sees Reggie and beams at her. "That food was awesome."

"I make wonderful breakfasts, too." Reggie sits on the arm of the couch and rubs Chrissy's back.

Chrissy sees the promise in her eyes and wants to change her answer. Things are going fast, though, and she really wants to plan for that eventuality. She wants it to be special. Reggie is worth it.

"I have no doubt about that. Ready, kid? Cathy and David are giving us a ride home."

"Cool. Yeah. I'm good." He gathers his belongings and leads the way out of the room.

Chrissy can't help but look up at the mistletoe as they exit, chuckling at Reggie's smirk and raised eyebrow. *Yeah, it really happened.* They made out under the mistletoe.

After layering up for the cold, Chrissy and Ben head for the door. Others are calling out to Reggie, ready to leave and wanting to say goodbye. Reggie holds up a finger, signifying she'll be a minute, and she turns to Cathy, Chrissy, and Ben.

"Thanks for a great party," Cathy says, stepping forward to deliver a quick hug.

Ben sticks out a hand to shake Reggie's hand, but she pulls him in for a hug, whispering something which makes him smile and the tips of his ears redden.

Chrissy hugs her. "I'll be dreaming of those kisses tonight."

"As will I. And you do matter, Christina. You matter to me."

As they pull back, Chrissy sees how genuine Reggie is. Swallowing the lump in her throat, Chrissy nods. Smiles. "Goodnight."

"Sweet dreams, Christina," Reggie says with a grin.

"You, too." Chrissy knows hers will be filled with those moments under the mistletoe. She can't wait for her head to hit the pillow.

After

Jazzy Mitchell

Chapter Nine

"WHERE'S BEN?" ARE THE first words out of Chrissy's mouth when she awakens.

"He's with David and Cathy getting some food." Reggie steps into view. Her lips tremble, and Chrissy wonders what's happened. "Is he okay? Did he get hurt?"

"He's fine." Reggie's eyes are puffy. She stands with her arms wrapped around herself, her clothes wrinkled.

"And you're okay? Hogan didn't get to you?"

"I'm okay." Reggie lays a hand on Chrissy's arm and squeezes before turning away.

Blinking several times, Chrissy rolls her head around to see if anyone else is in the room. She sees white walls, a television mounted across from where she's lying down in a bed, closed window blinds, some chairs near the far wall, and a closed door. It has a distinctive, sharp medicinal smell. *A hospital room. I'm in a hospital. Well, at least I'm still alive.* She's having trouble connecting the dots, though. Chrissy looks for Reggie and watches her stamp toward her.

"What the hell did you think you were doing?" Reggie demands, her hands balled into fists.

Who's Reggie talking to? Why is she glaring at me?

With no one else in the room, Chrissy deduces Reggie must be directing her ire at her. God, she hasn't heard such a tone of voice since that time a month into working for her when Chrissy forgot to record a court date change in the calendar. Reggie had returned from court and skewered her with a glower that made Chrissy sink into her chair. And then the verbal evisceration came. She never made that mistake again. She shakes her head, wondering whether she missed part of the conversation. Every thought, every motion she makes is couched in sand—soft, suffocating, shifting sand.

Reggie's body is quaking, her eyes flashing, and she's so passionate. Chrissy wants nothing more than to pull her into a hug. She feels sluggish, though, and heavy. Dried tears mar Reggie's beautiful face, her eyes red and swollen. *Why is Reggie so upset with me?*

"If that's your way of saying thank you, I'd rather you act ungrateful," Chrissy jokes, surprised by how weak her voice sounds.

"Thank you? You nearly got yourself killed. Where would I be without you? Where would Ben be? How could we be thankful then?" Reggie asks, her voice becoming louder with each question. A vein pops out on her temple, and Chrissy swallows.

"Because you're alive. You two are the most important people in my life. I will always try to protect you," Chrissy says as she rubs her eyes. She's tired. Sore. Confused. And her left side is numb. Looking down she sees an ice pack over her ribs. She shifts, and a sharp pain makes her yelp. She bites down on her lower lip and tastes copper. Squeezing her eyes shut, she swallows the urge to throw up, sucking on her bleeding lip. *Why is she so upset with me?*

"Christina, you're an idiot! Dying to save me is unacceptable. I need you in my life. I...I..." Losing steam, Reggie slumps down on the hospital bed, next to Chrissy's waist, looking lost.

"What?" Chrissy stretches her hand out and is reassured by how Reggie clasps it tight. Reggie remains quiet. "I know we've only shared one kiss, and I'm sorry if this is too much, but I love you. I love you with all my heart, and I can't live in a world without you in it. I had to do everything in my power to protect you."

"And I told you that your feelings are not one-sided." Reggie gazes at her, eyes bright.

It takes Chrissy some time to understand, truly understand, what Reggie is telling her. It's impossible. *How can Reggie love me? How can Reggie feel the same depth of emotion for me when I'm nothing, worthless, when even my own parents kicked me out?*

"If you'd died, I would've been left with these feelings I need to express. I've never fallen this fast or this hard." Reggie glares at her. "And even though it scares me, I need you. So, you see, you simply can't leave me. I need the opportunity," Chrissy is shocked to hear Reggie's voice break, "to love you."

Full of questions and doubts and hope and love, Chrissy's breath catches in her throat. In Reggie's eyes she sees the torment, the adoration, the hope, and Chrissy understands. *I'm sorry I frightened you. I know how I'd feel if our roles were reversed.* That's what Chrissy says in her head. It's what she means to say out loud. But she's exhausted. The pain is pulsing through her, and what comes out is, "When I feel better, I'm gonna kiss you 'til you pass out."

A burst of laughter erupts from Reggie, who covers her mouth. Tears stream down her cheeks, her long fingers trembling in front of her parted lips, and Chrissy wants to pull her in, comfort her, love her. Instead she squeezes the hand she holds. "It's okay. I'm okay."

They sit in silence, allowing themselves the time to accept what has occurred and the comfort of knowing they're together now.

"Are you in much pain?" Reggie asks, her eyes bouncing all over Chrissy, a crease marring her forehead.

"Yeah. What's wrong with me? Did the doctor tell you? And what time is it?" Chrissy has a terrible thought. "I didn't miss Christmas, did I?" She doesn't think she's been out of it for that long, but everything's so hazy.

"It's around nine at night on Friday. You haven't missed Christmas."

I've been out for about four hours then. Tomorrow's Christmas Eve. We can still get a tree and celebrate. Chrissy's relieved. She looks forward to spoiling Ben at Christmas.

Reggie runs her hand over Chrissy's cheek, giving her a small smile. "The doctor told me what's wrong with you, which reminds me...when did you have me named as your healthcare proxy? That's something you normally tell a person."

"Oh, um, yeah. I'm sorry, Reggie. I was talking to Cathy last week about the holidays, and she said it's a good idea to have my affairs in order since I'm a single mom. She drew up the paperwork, and I named you on everything...executor of the will, Ben's guardian, power of attorney, healthcare proxy, and the personal representative for the HIPAA release. I signed everything today while you were at court. I was going to tell you this afternoon. I don't have any family members I trust. I know we only got together last week, but I knew that if anything happened to me, you'd take care of Ben. And me." She stops when she sees Reggie's eyes tearing up. "I'm sorry, Reggie. I'll change them once I'm out of here."

"No, no. You misunderstand. I'm honored you trust me to such an extent." Reggie swipes at her eyes with her finger, smearing a small amount of eyeliner. "Although if I had known, I wouldn't have masqueraded as your wife."

"Wh...what?"

Reggie straightens up, tossing her hair back in an extremely confident, attractive, don't-fuck-with-me kind of way and scowls. "I needed to know how badly hurt you are."

Noticing Reggie's defiant stare, and in truth loving her arrogance,

Chrissy doesn't challenge her. *Nope, not worth worrying about.* "So, how bad am I?"

She feels a dull pounding in the back of her head, but she hasn't really tried to move around, afraid she might hurt herself. Reggie leans forward to deliver a sweet kiss before sighing with relief.

"Two fractured ribs on your left side, abrasions and contusions on your knees, shoulders, and arms. When you tackled him, he shot at you and missed. He hit the glass panels surrounding my door, and in the scuffle you were cut by some of the glass shards. Those will probably hurt for a bit, particularly the ones on your shoulder and calf. They used surgical glue on them." Reggie stops, her clinical voice falling away.

"Glue? Not stitches?"

"You're showing your age." Reggie smiles for a moment before her face becomes solemn once more. "You know, you're lucky to be alive. What you did was extremely brave...and stupid."

Chrissy nods. She is lucky. She inhales deeply and coughs. Pain slices through her, and she places a hand over her ribs, trying to stop her body from moving. Exhausted, Chrissy's eyes close against her will. She needs to rest a moment. Long fingers comb through her hair, and she smiles. *That feels good.*

When Chrissy wakes up, she notices a few things. Fingers still comb through her hair. Voices murmur. Her body feels heavy. Her throat is dry. And besides her ribs, she feels niggling pain sparking from her leg, arm, and shoulder. She's a mess. Lying still, Chrissy listens as the voices become clearer. She hears Ben. Reggie. Cathy. David. *And is that Attorney Hawk?* Finally ready, Chrissy opens her eyes.

"Who decided to have a party in here?" she asks, trying her best to sound light-hearted. She doesn't think she pulls it off. Reggie's fingers stall for a moment before sifting through her hair once more. Chrissy sighs, the fingers doing their magic and making her feel loved.

"Well, look who decided to wake up." Reggie is sitting up near her head, shoes off and legs under her, leaning over as she continues to run her fingers through Chrissy's messy hair. "How are you feeling?"

"Sore. Sorry I fell asleep. I don't feel as if I have cotton between my ears anymore, so that's an improvement."

"Mom?" Ben says from the foot of her bed, catching Chrissy's attention.

"Ben. Are you okay?" Chrissy asks, her anxiety ratcheting up as she takes in his red eyes and hunched body. "Come here." She extends her arm, needing to comfort him, and takes his hand, squeezing it. "Talk to me."

"I'm okay. But, Mom, you could have died." The pain is clear in his eyes.

"But I didn't. And neither did you or Reggie. I'd do the same thing a thousand times if it meant keeping you safe." She hates seeing Ben upset, but he needs to understand. He sniffles, barely holding it together. "I'm sorry I scared you, kid."

"I knew I'd be okay. I was wearing the pendant." He's trembling, and she knows he's trying hard to be strong, to not cry in front of anyone.

"Ben," Chrissy says. His shadowed eyes are weighed down by events he'd only seen in video games and movies. As preposterous and unbelievable as the shooting was, it happened, and now he knows how dangerous life can be and how desperate a person can become. Her heart aches. A part of his innocence has been stripped away. "It's okay to be afraid. A brave person acts even when afraid. And it's okay to cry. It means you feel deeply, and you should never be ashamed of that."

As if she's said the magic words, tears fall down his face, faster and faster. He burrows into the crook of her neck, and Chrissy holds him close as Reggie wraps her arms around them both.

Once his sobs lessen to sniffles, Chrissy's attention turns to the rest of the people in the room. Her eyes connect with Cathy, David, and Hawk.

"Well, well, looks like Sleeping Beauty has awakened," Hawk says lightly as he steps forward.

Taking a deep breath, Chrissy releases the two most important people in her world and shoots a smile at her future boss. "So I have." Noticing the blinds are raised and light is shining through the windows, she asks, "Is it Christmas Eve?"

Ben nods. She can tell he feels better, and she wonders whether he had let himself cry at all since the shooting.

"Oh, kid. I'm sorry. If they let me out of here today, I'm sure we can still find a tree. You'll have to do most of the decorating, though." Chrissy frowns. Over the years she's worked hard to make Christmas special for him.

Before he can say anything, the doctor enters the room. He's about six feet tall with closely cropped salt and pepper hair. He has bags under his eyes and dry skin. Chrissy wonders whether he ever smiles. Everyone steps out except Reggie. Ben wants to stay, but Chrissy's afraid whatever the doctor says might upset him. The doctor checks her, informing her of the various injuries and the expected recuperation time as he removes the IV.

"We used Dermabond on the deeper lacerations on your right shoulder and right calf. I'll want you back in seven days to check them. Also, you fractured two ribs on your left side. Although this may sound counterintuitive, some people prefer to lie on the same side as the broken ribs so as to prohibit movement while asleep. You'll want to do some deep breathing exercises to deter contracting any respiratory ailments. Ice your ribs every few hours for the next couple of days before spacing it out to three times a day. More if they're swollen. I'll prescribe some oral pain medication, and you're on bed rest for the week. It can take up to six weeks for ribs to completely heal, but you can return to work in three, provided you rest beforehand and avoid any strenuous activities. It's a good idea to have someone help you with getting around. You may not feel it, yet, but your body's experienced a traumatic event. You'll be tired, sore, and weak."

"I'll take responsibility for her and make sure she rests," Reggie volunteers, her fingers on the nape of Chrissy's neck, rubbing little circles. The doctor gives a brisk nod.

"I'll get the paperwork ready, including information on what to look for if the ribs shift, and the nurse will bring the documents in for signatures. It'll take about an hour." After he leaves, Reggie wraps an arm around Chrissy's shoulders. She drops her head against Reggie's side with a sigh. She feels safe and loved. Everyone returns to the room, and Chrissy does her best to look alert.

"Hey, champ. You're making all of us look like wimps, charging in and saving the day," David jokes, a hand on her knee.

"I'm sure others would have acted the same way I did. I was lucky to be in the right place at the right time."

"Lucky," Reggie sneers. Chrissy ignores it, knowing Reggie's dealing with how afraid she was for her.

"Well, we're glad you're okay." Cathy leans in, kissing her on her forehead.

"Thanks," Chrissy says, a slight smile on her face.

"Of course, you're on paid medical leave. Take the full six weeks, if needed. Rest, recover, and return when you're ready. Your job will be waiting for you," Hawk says.

"That's awfully kind of you, Mr. Hawk—" Chrissy begins.

"None of that," he interrupts, wagging his finger. "If you hadn't taken on the role of hero, who knows how many more that madman would have hurt. As it is, we have dozens who were injured and five people recovering from bullet wounds. You are the bravest person I've ever met, and I will make sure everyone is aware of that fact. Erin sends her best wishes for a speedy recovery." He pulls on his coat. "Reggie, I'll talk to you soon." With a nod toward the Freedmans, he leaves the room.

"Well, we'll let you get some rest. Please let me know if you need anything, anything at all," Cathy says. "And Merry Christmas, to all three of you. At least you'll be together."

"See you later, hero," David teases, nodding at Reggie and clapping his hand on Ben's shoulder before leaving.

A silence falls on them. It's comforting. She feels horrible for ruining Reggie's Christmas, though. "Reggie, you don't have to take care of me. I know you need to get ready for tomorrow's dinner, and all I need to do is rest."

Reggie shakes her head. "I want to. You and Ben don't need to be by yourselves. I have plenty of room, and you'll get the benefit of eating the feast I'm preparing." Not wanting to impose, Chrissy wrestles with whether to accept Reggie's offer.

"Mom, how can you say no to her cooking? Food's your greatest weakness. Besides, I'd feel better knowing someone will be helping us over the next few days." Ben is pulling out all the stops, puppy-dog eyes at their widest.

Sighing, Chrissy knows she'll give in. She wants to spend time with Reggie. On the other hand, she thought her next time at Reggie's brownstone would be after a date or as the result of a more sensual offer. She doesn't want to be a burden.

"Christina, please let me do this. I need to be able to see with my own eyes that you're okay. Safe. Recovering. It will give me peace of mind. And I want to spend the holidays with you and Ben. No one could compel me to do it if I were opposed."

Chrissy's heart warms. "Thank you, Reggie. We'll have to arrange to get the Christmas presents from my apartment." Remembering she'd brought Reggie's present to work, Chrissy asks Ben, "Do you have my purse?" She can see he understands what she's really asking.

"Yup. Nice and safe." He grins, and she returns it.

"I can go to your apartment with Ben now and get the presents and some clothes for you," Reggie volunteers. "Is there anything else you want from there? A stuffed bear? Fuzzy socks?"

Reggie's playing with her. "No, no. If I need some cuddle time, I have you." They beam at each other, and Chrissy loves the fact they've revealed their feelings for each other, loves having the privilege of expressing them. Last week, Chrissy told Ben about Reggie arranging for her to switch into Hawk's division so they can date. If the way he jumped around the apartment was any indication, he was happy to hear the news.

"We'll grab some food on the way back." Chrissy happily accepts the chaste kiss Reggie delivers before she moves to retrieve her coat and purse. "The police will probably be by soon to take your statement. I know they've been interviewing people since yesterday."

"Okay. Hopefully they'll come sooner rather than later so I can get it over with." Chrissy sighs. She's not looking forward to reliving yesterday's events.

"Do you want me to stay?" Reggie gives her a concerned look.

"No. I'll be fine. I promise."

As they move toward the door, Ben says, "I didn't think the hospital food was that bad." He shrugs and shoots a teasing look at Chrissy. "Of course, I'm used to Mom's cooking."

Guffawing, Chrissy ends up coughing and waving them away as they turn toward her. "Oh, jeez. That hurts. On so many levels. Get going, you two, so you can get back here quicker." Once they leave, Chrissy melts into the bed. Although she won't admit it, she's worn out from talking.

She closes her eyes and falls into a light sleep. Lethargic and achy, Chrissy hears the door open. An hour has passed. It takes a moment to focus on the two people standing by the door.

A middle-aged, slim man with a crew cut and chiseled features clears his throat. "We're sorry to intrude. I'm Officer Limner, and this is Detective Oliver. Is now a good time to take your statement concerning yesterday's events?"

"Yeah, sure," Chrissy answers, struggling to wake up. "Go ahead and ask your questions. I'm ready."

"So, Ms. Kramer, we've spoken to people at your firm, including Attorney Esposito, and we have a good idea of what happened. Please tell us what you saw and heard yesterday and how you reacted," says Detective Oliver, a short, stout man with a receding hairline and sharp eyes.

"Right. I was leaving the restroom when I heard screaming and gunshots. I saw Frank Hogan heading toward Reggie's office." Chrissy can hear the screams as if it was happening all over again, and her breathing picks up. She clutches at the blanket, staring at her white knuckles. *We're safe. I stopped him. It's okay.* She thinks those words several times before she continues. "I ran down a parallel hallway, pulled my son, who was spending time at the office while on winter break, into Reggie's office, and told them to hide under Reggie's desk. I turned off the lights, closed the door, and sat down at my desk as he reached me."

As that moment washes over her, Chrissy's chest tightens. She places her hand over her sternum and takes a deep breath. "He demanded to know where Reggie was, and I stalled him, offered to help him. He had that rifle in my face, and I tackled him before he shot me and went into Reggie's office. I aimed for his waist, and we bounced. I held on and pulled the rifle out of his hands, hitting him on the chin with the butt to knock him out. I was in a lot of pain, and I passed out after help arrived."

"All right. What exactly did he say once he reached you?" Officer Limner asks.

Struggling to recall the details, Chrissy repeats their brief conversation.

"Okay. Anything else you think will help?" Detective Oliver asks.

"His case ended last week. Reggie's been trying to find some legal grounds to appeal the decision. It was a pro bono case."

"Yes. Attorney Esposito mentioned that when we spoke to her last night. Here's my card. If you think of anything else, please feel free to contact me." The detective hands her his card and steps back.

"Thanks. Is he in jail now?" Chrissy asks, a chill making its way down her spine.

"Yes," Officer Limner says. "He was booked last night and will spend the weekend in jail before he's arraigned on Monday. We'll recommend that he not be released on bail since he's a danger to the public. He'll be charged with attempted murder, several counts of assault with a deadly weapon, assault and battery, possession of a large capacity firearm and feeding device, threats, and whatever else we can throw in there so he remains locked up."

Feeling better, Chrissy thanks them, and they leave. Remembering what the doctor said about breathing deeply, she breathes in, holds it, and exhales. Four more times she repeats the process, gritting her teeth at how sore her ribs feel. She adjusts the bed to sit up and, noticing her cell phone on the side table, twists to pick it up.

"Mother-fucker!" she shouts as a sharp pain overwhelms her.

Taking several shallow breaths, Chrissy keeps her eyes screwed shut. She holds her hand over her aching ribs, thankful she didn't have an audience for that stupid move.

Reggie and Ben's arrival takes her focus off her abused body, as does the food they carry with them. "We've got your favorite," Ben crows. He pulls out a cheesesteak from a paper bag, and her stomach rumbles.

"Great. Thanks. I didn't realize how hungry I am." The cell phone she worked so hard to get is resting next to her waist. She can look at it later. "Did you get my cell phone charger?"

"Yup. You're all set. We even brought the laptop." Ben places the food on a rolling table, the smell mouth-watering.

She seeks out Reggie's eyes and smiles, relieved when she receives a sweet grin in return. Reggie kisses her on the cheek, and Chrissy can't help but pout. She wants to taste Reggie's lips. Or maybe not. She hasn't even used the restroom since right before the attack occurred. She probably looks a mess. And her breath must reek.

"Here you go," Ben says as he guides the table across Chrissy's lap and pulls up a chair.

Reggie perches on the bed on the other side of the table so she can use it, too. It's intimate and homey eating this way, which is a minor miracle since they're in a hospital room on Christmas Eve. After they finish eating, Chrissy hobbles to the bathroom. Her calf is hurting like a bitch, and each step reminds her she needs to move slowly to avoid jostling her ribs. She insists she can take care of herself once in the bathroom. She doesn't want Reggie to see her in such a compromising position. Chrissy knows it's her pride talking, but she wants Reggie's first time seeing her without her pants on to be when they're about to make love.

Looking down at herself, she realizes she's wearing scrubs. It's a good thing she's leaving the hospital today, because these clothes aren't that comfortable or warm. She'll be glad to don some flannel pants and a thick sweatshirt. And socks—wool socks. Untying the drawstring, Chrissy allows the pants and her panties to pool around her ankles. *Now for the hard part.* She grasps the hand bars on either side of the toilet and lowers herself, groaning and squeezing her eyes shut as her abused ribs complain. She breathes in and out to the count of five, waiting for the pain to dissipate. Once she opens her eyes, they move to the surgical tape over the wound on her calf. Blood covers the area. Well, there's no way she can wash that off right now.

She nearly passes out from wiping herself. *This is ridiculous.* Biting back a groan, she pulls on her clothes again and stands, wincing from the pain and the realization she'll have to bend to flush the toilet. She looks at the door, tempted to call Reggie in to help. Shaking her head, she leans forward and flushes, moaning as a knifelike pain shoots through her.

"You okay in there?" Chrissy hears Ben's worried tone of voice and grimaces.

"Yeah. Still alive," she jokes. Hearing the loud silence, she realizes her poor joke. "I'll be out in a minute."

She moves in front of the sink, eyeing herself in the mirror. Pale. Dark circles under her eyes. Chapped lips. Matted hair. Smeared eye makeup. She's quite a fright. She grabs some tissues from the sink and wets them, washing her face clean. A brush is on the side, as well as a new toothbrush and toothpaste. Chrissy uses them all. She still looks like she's been through a battle, but she's cleaner. That makes her feel a bit better. She'll take it as a win.

She lifts her shirt to look at her ribs. Deep bruising is settling in, and the area is swollen. *I'll have to ice the area more.* With a frown, Chrissy recognizes this is the best she's going to look today. Opening the door, she meets concerned eyes. Chrissy smiles. At least she tries. Reggie must read something in her face, as she's over in a flash, wrapping her arm around Chrissy and guiding her back to bed.

"You should have asked for help," Reggie says.

"I'm pretty sure you didn't sign up for wiping my ass," Chrissy mutters, frustrated with how her body has betrayed her. She looks around to make sure Ben hasn't heard her. He has his earphones on, his foot tapping to the music he's listening to on his phone.

"Christina," Reggie whispers, her voice breaking. She doesn't say anything else until Chrissy is back in bed with the ice pack on her ribs. "I would never even think about that. The bending must be torturous. I'm so sorry."

"Please don't apologize." Chrissy regrets allowing her frustration to get the better of her. "I'm sorry for acting like a spoiled child. I've never learned to deal with feeling sick or helpless or in pain. I'm a horrible patient. And this isn't how I want you to see me."

A hand settles over hers, and Chrissy's frustration crests, tears forming. "Christina, please don't be so hard on yourself. Your body needs to heal. Give yourself some time. Let me take care of you."

It's hard to rely on someone after being independent for most of her life. With her autonomy compromised, she feels like a burden, even though she recognizes how irrational she's being. It doesn't help to know that she'll have to wait weeks before she can explore Reggie's body, worship it in the ways she's dreamed about all these months.

"I'm not going anywhere, Christina." Reggie's soft voice wraps around Chrissy like a soothing hug.

The promise in Reggie's eyes makes her breathless. Reggie squeezes her hand before she lets go and crosses to her purse. Chrissy watches her retrieve a pad of paper and pen, her forehead crinkling in an adorable way while she jots down her thoughts.

"Are you working?" Chrissy asks. "Can I help?"

Reggie looks up from her notes and shakes her head. "Not work. It's for when we get out of here. I'm afraid I'll forget." She grins. "It's hard getting old."

"Please. You are not old, and your mind is like a steel trap."

"Maybe, but I also prefer to jot down my thoughts whenever possible."

Chrissy nods, watching her write. She's pretty worn out, and she knows traveling to Reggie's home is going to take a lot of energy. She closes her eyes. It soothes her to visualize Reggie's warm brown eyes and sparkling smile.

***

"Are you sure, Reggie?" Chrissy stands in the doorway of the bedroom, taking in the queen-sized bed with navy sheets and a matching comforter. The walls are painted a cream color, the hardwood floors partially covered with an intricately designed rug. Near the windows are some cushioned upright chairs and a small coffee table with magazines spread across them. The art on the walls include photographs of castles, crashing waves against a lighthouse in the middle of a storm, and the sun shining on snowy Boston brownstones as children throw snowballs at each other. The room is rich and complex, a perfect reflection of Reggie.

"This room has an en suite. It will save you from having to walk too far." Reggie places the bag of Chrissy's clothes on a gray chaise lounge at the end of the bed. She takes Chrissy's hands. "Besides, I want to be near you, and if you stay in one of the guestrooms, I'll have to get up several times each night to check on you. You don't want me to have to walk through the cold, dark hallways throughout the night, do you?"

She pouts.

Sleeping in a bed with Reggie sounds like heaven. "No, of course not. I'd rather know you're close and safe."

"Good," Reggie says with a small smile. "Let's get you set up, shall we?" She bustles around the room, changing the bed sheets and bringing a few more pillows out from a closet. "Do you need me to help you change?"

"No. If you can bring my clothes into the bathroom, I'll manage."

Reggie looks like she's about to object, but she snaps her lips shut and nods. A moment later she returns with a pair of Chrissy's nightclothes—a navy fleece top and matching flannel sweatpants—and leads Chrissy to the bathroom. "Here you go." She leaves the clothes on top of the sink. "Let me know if you need help."

"Thanks." Chrissy's exhausted by the time she finishes changing. Once she returns to the bedroom, Reggie helps her into bed, propping her up with pillows. The afternoon flies by, and Chrissy fills the time by taking catnaps and reading a magazine Reggie gave her.

"What are you thinking?" Reggie asks from her seat next to the window. She's reviewing some legal documents, and the last thing Chrissy wants to do is distract her.

"Nothing important."

"I beg to differ." Reggie removes her reading glasses. "Tell me what's on your mind."

"It's just, I came so close to losing everyone I care for. Ben. You. And now I just want to pull both of you close and never let go." After a pause, she admits in a small voice, "It's entirely irrational, but I wish I could hold you."

"That sounds pretty important to me." Reggie smiles, rising from her seat.

"No, no. I don't want to interrupt, and you've already lost time from yesterday's events."

"Christina, please humor me." Reggie relocates to the bed, plumping up some pillows before leaning against them. "I lost time yesterday due to a madman who tried to kill me, not because you're hurt." She nestles into Chrissy's right side. "Let me know if this is too much."

"I will," Chrissy whispers. She's glad that Reggie is next to her, even if she's feeling rather needy. A knock on the door precedes Ben entering the room.

"Mind if I hang out here?" he asks.

"Not at all. Sit wherever," Chrissy replies.

His eyes wander the room before he shrugs and plops himself on his stomach at the end of the bed. Chrissy turns her head to catch Reggie's eyes, and they grin at each other. It feels good to have both of them close.

They while away the afternoon reading, working, and when a thought needs to be shared, chatting. It's comfortable, their past interactions the perfect foundation to get them to this point.

A kiss to her jaw captures Chrissy's attention, and she looks at Reggie, melting into her smile. "Hi," she whispers.

"Hi," Reggie whispers back, stroking Chrissy's arm. "Are you hungry?"

"Getting there."

Nodding, Reggie grabs a drink on the bedside table and hands it to Chrissy. "Drink this, and I'll have Ben bring you a refill." She takes the empty glass and rises from the bed. "Ben, how do you feel about helping me whip up some supper?"

He looks up with a smile. "Sure!"

"Do you need to use the bathroom?" Reggie asks.

"Yeah. That's a good idea." Chrissy holds her ribs while slowly swinging her feet off the bed onto the floor. She glares at her feet for a moment before wrapping her arm around Reggie's waist and rising. Once standing, she catches her breath. "Okay." They make their way to the en suite while the sun sets, the seasons change, and her hair turns gray. Chrissy's patience fades with each step.

"Do you need help?" Reggie asks, her voice soft, once they cross the threshold into the bathroom.

"No. Later, though, maybe tomorrow morning, I'd like to take a shower. I might need help then." Chrissy stares at the floor. Although she doesn't like Reggie seeing her this way, Chrissy doesn't want to make her injuries worse or the recuperation time longer by being stubborn.

"Whatever you need." Reggie's voice is soothing, and Chrissy knows it will be okay.

Taking her time in the bathroom, Chrissy lifts her right foot while she's seated to look at her bloody calf. Maybe she'll ask Reggie to help her clean it off. And her shoulder. She knows she won't be able to do it herself, and seeing the iodine and blood bothers her. Finishing up, Chrissy returns to the bedroom as Ben comes in. He holds a drink and a new ice pack.

"Thanks, Ben." She swallows some of the ginger ale, smiling at how Reggie remembers such small details, and Ben takes the glass, placing it on the bedside table. He helps her back into bed and places the ice carefully on her side. "What are you and Reggie cooking up?"

Ben's eyes light. "Something you'll love. Are you okay for now?"

"Yup. I'm good."

"Be back soon. It shouldn't take long." He practically skips out of the room.

While waiting for them, Chrissy turns on her cell phone and is surprised to see a number of missed calls, texts, and emails. Most are from the media, and she wonders how they got her contact information. It's probably better she's not at home.

Skipping through the voicemails, she listens to one from Cathy. She wants to come by tomorrow afternoon to say hello. David shouts in the background that he wants to come, too, and Chrissy laughs before she remembers it hurts to do so. They're good people. A couple of messages are from parents of Ben's friends, reaching out to see if she needs anything. She's surprised since she's had limited interactions with them. She sends several texts before setting the phone aside.

"Here we go," Reggie says as she enters the room with a tray. Ben walks in behind her with another tray. Both are laden with food. The aromas of toasted bread and tangy tomatoes are amazing.

"Oh, my God, that smells heavenly." Chrissy's stomach growls.

"You can call me Reggie, dear," Reggie teases as she sets the tray down. Ben chuckles. Chrissy ignores him. Her attention is focused solely on the food—garden salads, grilled cheese sandwiches, and tomato soup. Each looks a thousand times better than anything she's ever tasted.

"This looks great, Reggie." Chrissy emphasizes her name, flashing a quick smile, and they eat on the bed together.

Moaning as she chews the sandwich, Chrissy's eyes are captured by Reggie's intense stare. She watches as Reggie's pupils dilate, widening so much she can hardly see the brown irises. A flirty smile spreads across Reggie's face.

"I take it you're enjoying the food," Reggie says with a throaty voice.

"That's an understatement." How Reggie can make such simple fare taste orgasmic is beyond her understanding. But she's grateful. So grateful. And that smile. It hints at a passion Chrissy briefly tasted at the party.

"I told you the way to Mom's heart is through food," Ben says.

"So it seems," Reggie says, her amusement clear.

Chrissy blushes because it's true. Food is important to her, and Reggie is an awesome cook. It's another reason to love her.

"I realized that at the holiday party." Reggie picks up Chrissy's hand and kisses her knuckles. "Before then, I thought you might have a sweet tooth, or maybe a soft spot for tiramisu. Now I know better."

They grin at each other, and Chrissy wonders whether the mistletoe is still in the den.

"I took it down," Reggie whispers.

"Pity," Chrissy whispers back.

"I no longer need an excuse to kiss you, do I?"

"Not at all. I'm all yours," Chrissy says, and although they're flirting, she's serious.

Reggie cups her face with both hands and leans her forehead against Chrissy's. They remain that way for a few moments before Reggie pulls back. Her eyes assure Chrissy the feeling's mutual. They finish eating, and Ben leaves to shower and change for bed. It's still early, but he's tired. Chrissy is, too.

After piling the dirty plates on a tray, Reggie places it and the other tray on top of the bureau. Returning to Chrissy, she settles next to her. The kiss is unexpected. Chrissy moans, as Reggie's tongue swipes across her lower lip. Allowing entrance, Chrissy tilts her head to get closer, their tongues rubbing together. Reggie's fingers weave through Chrissy's hair, and Chrissy loses herself in the taste and texture of Reggie's addictive mouth.

Soft lips move down to her chin, sucking on it before butterfly kisses are delivered down her neck to her pulse point. Those magical lips stall and suck for several exquisite moments, and then Reggie's tongue and teeth join in, driving Chrissy crazy. Chrissy keeps her eyes closed, head leaning against her pillow, hands holding Reggie close. These feelings Reggie inspires overwhelm her, and she wouldn't have it any other way.

"I love you, Christina." Reggie takes Chrissy's earlobe between her teeth and sucks it. "And I intend to take every opportunity to show you. To make you feel my love."

"I do," Chrissy says breathlessly, trembling with the force of her desire. "I feel it. And I love you. So much."

"Good." Reggie pulls back and they beam at each other, hands clasped between them. "I know you're tired. I think we all are. I'm going to take care of the dishes and prepare some of the food for tomorrow. Don't feel you need to wait up for me."

"I don't think I'll be able to even if I try. Don't take too long."

"I won't. I plan on holding you all night long," Reggie promises.

Chrissy believes her.

Chapter Ten

THE BEDROOM IS QUIET, peaceful, and warm. Reggie's body is curled against her, arm around her waist, and fingers splayed on her belly underneath her T-shirt. She's glad she shed the sweatshirt for sleepwear. Reggie is a furnace. *Guess I'm the little spoon.* Not that she minds. Soft breasts press into her back, and toned thighs hug hers. It feels glorious.

She slept surprisingly well. Her ribs ache, but she's able to breathe deeper. Opening her eyes, Chrissy places her hand over Reggie's, stroking it with her thumb. She hears an inhalation, and Reggie's breath hits the back of her neck, stirring the little hairs at her nape. She shivers. Reggie's nose pushes aside her hair, and lips kiss the juncture of neck and shoulder before sucking. Chrissy hums.

"Merry Christmas, Christina," Reggie says, her hand turning over to capture Chrissy's fingers, intertwining them.

"Merry Christmas, Reggie."

"You feel wonderful in my arms. I can't remember the last time I slept so well." Reggie delivers several featherlike kisses to Chrissy's neck.

"Same here." Chrissy tilts her head, sighing with pleasure. *I can get used to this.*

"I'm going to make you the best breakfast you've ever tasted."

It's as if Reggie has declared she's going to make love to her until they can no longer move. Chrissy's body lights up, and she shudders. Reggie's knowing chuckle does nothing to help Chrissy calm down.

"I had envisioned the morning after a bit differently, or at least the night before," Chrissy murmurs.

"Don't worry, dear. We'll get there." Reggie nips Chrissy's earlobe before getting up. "If I stay in bed any longer I may end up doing something that might hurt you. I'm trying to keep my hands to myself." She rounds the bed and sinks down next to Chrissy while pushing one hand through her brunette hair, mussing it adorably. "You're quite irresistible, particularly looking like that in my bed."

Her words, although delivered with no small amount of frustration, reassure Chrissy. She squeezes the pillow she's been holding all night, wondering whether she might be able to spoon Reggie tonight. She hadn't felt Reggie move during the night, so she doubts she'll get an elbow to her ribs.

Lifting herself up, Chrissy swings her feet off the bed and sits. Reggie rises, too. Although sore, Chrissy does not feel any sharp pains. It's a good start to the day. Reggie helps her stand, and they remain in a loose embrace.

Sighing, Chrissy inhales the scent of Reggie's hair—lavender. "You smell good."

A soft kiss on her collarbone is Reggie's response. "I'm glad you're here. I've dreamt about having you closer, wanted this so much."

"I'm not going anywhere," Chrissy says. Reggie raises her head, and when their eyes connect, she nods.

With a small parting kiss, Chrissy makes her way to the bathroom while Reggie leaves to make breakfast. Chrissy brushes her teeth with care, not wanting to jostle her ribs. She finishes her ablutions as efficiently as she can while cutting herself some slack. She knows her injuries are temporary, and it could be much worse.

Walking back in the bedroom, she hears a knock on the door. Ben's awake. Smiling brightly, she beckons him to enter. His yellow and blue-striped pajamas are getting too small. The pants end mid-calf, while his button-down top barely reaches his hips. *I'll have to get him new ones soon. I don't even know what size he is anymore.* He shuffles toward the bed, a grin on his face.

"Merry Christmas, Ben." She extends her arms. They hug, Ben hesitant and gentle.

"Merry Christmas, Mom. Let me help you back into bed."

"Did you sleep well?" Chrissy stifles a groan as she slides under the covers. Her entire left side aches, a dull throbbing with every breath.

Ben fluffs up the pillows and helps her lean against them. "Yeah. The bed's really comfortable."

"I know, right. This bed is incredible. Reggie's making breakfast. Do you want to help her?"

"She said she didn't need any help. I was gonna get the presents so we can open them after we eat." Ben talks through a yawn, stretching his arms over his head, and arching his back.

"Right. Can you hand me my purse?" Once she receives it, she retrieves Reggie's gift and places the small jewelry box under the covers, near her hip. She had the store wrap the black box with festive gold and green paper. "Okay. Go get the rest of the presents, please." She runs a hand through her hair while a thousand butterflies flutter in her stomach. It's silly. Even if Reggie doesn't like the gift, she'll still accept it gracefully. Reggie will understand the emotions attached to it.

Mouthwatering smells make Chrissy's nose twitch, and Reggie enters with a large tray laden with plates, cutlery, juice, bacon, sausages, scrambled eggs, toast, and fruit. "I didn't want to make too much since you'll be eating a feast later on."

"This is what, a snack?" Chrissy jokes.

"Mmhmm. Yes. Like your kisses," Reggie whispers into Chrissy ear as she hands her a filled plate. Reggie's eyes sparkle. "A tasty snack. A hint of what's to come."

A trickle of perspiration rolls between Chrissy's shoulder blades, and she swallows, trying to add moisture to her suddenly dry mouth. *Did it get hot in here?* Chrissy pulls at the front of her shirt, her skin sensitive to the cotton against it.

"Um," Chrissy says, dazed.

Reggie is too sexy for her own good. *How am I supposed to function when she's whispering such provocative words, gazing at me like she's ravenous, touching me so lovingly?* Shaking her head, Chrissy hears Ben talking and realizes he's returned to the room with the presents. Reggie's hand on her knee reassures her, and when she lifts her eyes, Reggie greets them with an affectionate look.

"Aren't you hungry?" Ben asks.

His voice sounds concerned, but his eyes let her know that if she doesn't start eating soon, he's going to swipe what's on her plate. She shovels some eggs into her mouth. *How does she make scrambled eggs taste so light and creamy? And is that kick at the end chili flakes?*

"Reggie, this is heavenly," Chrissy mutters around her next forkful. "Thank you."

"You're welcome," Reggie replies with one of those special smiles that makes the day infinitely better.

They spend the next several minutes eating quietly. Once they finish, Reggie piles the used dishware on the tray and places it on the bureau.

"Time for presents?" Ben asks, excitement plain in his voice.

"Yup." Chrissy hopes Ben will always feel this exuberant about the holidays. It wasn't until he came along she even began to care about Christmas. "But Christmas pictures first." She turns to Reggie. "Every year we take individual and group pictures." She looks at Ben. "At least this year we'll have more than two in the group."

Noticing Reggie's dumbfounded look, Chrissy says, "Unless you don't want to be in the pictures. You don't have to, of course. It's not like you even expected us to be here or to be sharing the holidays with us. We've never had anyone else in them, so..."

"No, no," Reggie interjects, stopping Chrissy's nervous rambling. "I want to be in them." She smiles brightly, and Chrissy sighs with relief.Ben takes Chrissy's cell phone and points it at her. "Ready?"

"Oh, wait." Chrissy grimaces, knowing how horrible she looks. "Maybe we should take them after I take a shower. Or maybe I should wear a hat or something." Reggie's soft fingers comb through her hair, calming her.

"Let me tie it back, okay?" Reggie says. Chrissy nods. Reggie sits back down a moment later with a brush and hair tie. It only takes her a minute to finish, and Chrissy feels much better. She can't help the tightness of her eyes or the evidence of pain on her face, but her grin is real when Ben takes the picture. He takes Reggie's photo next, and her smile is breathtaking. Reggie takes the phone from Ben to take his picture, and his goofy smirk exudes happiness.

"Now, how are we going to take the group picture?" Chrissy asks.

"First let me take a picture of you two," Reggie says.

Chrissy looks at her. "You're not getting out of the group photo."

Chuckling, Reggie holds her hands up. "I'm not trying to." She takes their picture, Ben sitting next to Chrissy on the bed, before approaching them. "Let's see if we can all fit in the photo." She sits on Chrissy's other side, an arm around Chrissy's shoulders, and holds her hand out in front of them with the camera. It's a tight fit, but she takes the picture of them, their smiles filling up the screen.

"Cathy and David mentioned coming by later. Maybe they can take our picture, too."

"Are you insinuating that I am not a good picture-taker?" Reggie teases, a mock-scowl on her face.

"Insinuating is much too subtle for me," Chrissy says. After a moment, Reggie's scowl dissolves into a grin.

"Now is it time for presents?" Ben asks.

"Yes, absolutely." Chrissy fingers Reggie's gift under the covers.

"I'll be right back." Reggie leaves the room, the tray filled with dirty dishes in her hands.

Humming a Christmas tune, Chrissy grins at her son as he plunks the bag of presents on the bed. They had made a stocking for Reggie, Chrissy's barely-used sewing skills put to work last weekend to add Reggie's name on it. It's silly. She and Ben always filled stockings for each other with little things like candy and pens, socks and puzzles. They went shopping to fill Reggie's stocking, finding various items they hope she'll enjoy. Ben removes all three stockings from the bag and lays them out on the bed. He makes a big production of pulling out the wrapped gifts. Several are for him, including a large box containing a videogame system, something he's talked about for months.

Ben pulls out two thin presents and places one before Chrissy and the other next to Reggie's stocking. "Those are from me," he says unnecessarily.

"Thanks," Chrissy says. "I can't wait to open it." Ben's made her presents since kindergarten. Always thoughtful, for the last few years Ben has even created them without the guidance of schoolteachers. She knows he'll eventually begin buying them, but for now she treasures these gifts and the time he spends on them.

As Reggie enters, her hands full of presents, Chrissy admires her. The plum-colored button-down shirt and loose pajama pants complement her coffee-colored eyes and olive complexion. Reggie sets down a large box in front of Chrissy and a smaller one in front of Ben.

"It's funny. I didn't even think to bring these to work on Friday. I assumed I'd see you both this weekend." Reggie frowns. "I'd imagined under better circumstances."

"Well, yeah, Friday sucked, but it's all working out." Chrissy wants to pat Reggie's knee or rub her arm, but to do so Chrissy would have to bend. Right now, she doesn't want to show any discomfort. She doesn't want them to know how her ribs are aching and the wounds glued together are itching. She prefers for them to enjoy exchanging gifts without the constant reminder of why they're sitting on Reggie's bed on Christmas morning. *Who knows? Next year at this time we may all be sitting here like this.* She hopes. Seeing Ben eying the gifts, Chrissy shakes her finger. "Stockings first."

"Right." Ben's natural impatience melts away to happiness, and he pulls his stocking toward him.

"I know it's hokey, but it's made with love," Chrissy says as she indicates Reggie's stocking. "We have a tradition for Christmas stockings where we put small things in there." After a moment's hesitation she waves her hand over the stockings. "I guess we assumed we'd see you, too."

Reggie's wondrous smile flows over Chrissy, and she's glad they made the effort. Ben's exclamations as he finishes emptying his stocking are music to Chrissy's ears. She laughs at his enthusiasm and empties her own stocking. Inside are chocolate bars and mechanical pencils, mints and Sudoku, cherry lip balm and makeup wipes, and in the toe of the stocking, a jewelry box.

Flitting her eyes toward Ben, she notices he's watching her closely, and her eyebrows shoot up. Lifting the lid, Chrissy's eyes widen. Inside is a breathtaking glass ring, a unique mixture of gold, brown, blue, green, yellow, and red, swirling, weaving, and combining to form a dazzling design.

"It's Italian. What's it called, Reggie?"

"Murano. Ben has good taste." Reggie shares a smile with him.

"Reggie helped me pick it out. I wanted to give you something special this year." Ben's ears redden adorably.

"I love it, Ben. Thank you." She dons it, appreciating how it looks on her right ring finger. It's beautiful, and she loves how Ben and Reggie picked it out together. She's tempted to ask when they went shopping, but she lets that go. She trusts Reggie with Ben.

She checks to see whether Reggie has finished discovering what's in her stocking. They had so much fun finding things for her, walking through Faneuil Hall and checking out all the stalls. They filled it with little items like a scales of justice pencil sharpener and crosswords, red fuzzy socks and a *Star Wars* Death Star tea infuser, and homemade peppermint soap and a booklet of passes for movie nights, foot rubs, kisses, errands, and date nights. They stuffed the stocking, and Chrissy realizes they may have overdone it. Reggie's eyes tear and her face reddens. She squeezes the stress ball they gave her.

"Reggie?" Chrissy's heart tightens with the thought they've made her unhappy. But when those bright eyes look up at her, she's rendered speechless. The adoration is so prevalent they quiet Chrissy's fears. "We had a great time filling it."

"Yeah, we made some of the stuff," Ben adds. "Like the soap and the passes and the snow globe. That was cool. Oh! And the instant mocha mix. We know you love that stuff, even if you try to eat healthy."

A burst of laughter erupts from Reggie. "I love it. All of it. I've never felt so loved. Thank you."

"You're welcome. But next year you'll help me with Ben's stocking." Chrissy smirks at her.

"That works for me! Now to the presents." Ben grabs the gift

Reggie placed before him and rips off the beautiful navy and silver wrapping paper. The silver bow finds its way onto his shirt. He opens the gift box and breathes out. "Whoa."

"What is it?" Chrissy asks, barely refraining from leaning forward. She watches as he lifts out a handsome leather-bound journal. Her eyes widen. It's gorgeous. Obviously handmade, a strap wraps it closed around the middle of a chestnut-colored leather jacket. "BDK" is embossed on the bottom right of the cover. Now she understands why Reggie had asked about his name months ago. "Open it," Chrissy prompts Ben.

As soon as he does, she can see the paper is also handmade. A wooden pen with black and chrome accents hangs in its designated spot to the right of the paper. On the first page, Reggie's flowing penmanship can be seen. "Ben, in here you can write, draw, imagine, dare. Let yourself loose. Love, Reggie."

Ben smiles at Reggie. "Thanks. This is awesome. How did you know?"

"I've seen you take out a notebook at the firm, jotting down your thoughts before returning it to your backpack. At first, I thought you were doing homework, but I noticed you'd do it while playing a game on your phone or while reading one of those fantasy books you adore." Reggie shrugs. "You deserve a proper journal where you can get your thoughts down. And the paper is refillable, so don't hold back. When you get close to the end, let me know. And the same goes for the pen ink."

Ben's fingers run over the front of the journal, and Chrissy knows he will carry it everywhere. He's always had an active imagination, often acting out elaborate scenes where he's a knight, a prince, a hero. Over the last few years he's taken to writing down his stories, and his teachers have encouraged him to keep at it. A perfect gift.

"Christina, open yours next." Reggie's fingers brush the top of Chrissy's hand. Reggie lifts the large box, placing it carefully on Chrissy's lap. "Do you need help?"

Shaking her head, Chrissy admires the elegant red and gold wrapping paper. She sticks the bow on her head and slices through the tape at one corner with her thumbnail. She doesn't want to rip it.

"Mom, open it," Ben whines.

Even though Chrissy is curious, she takes her time removing the wrapping paper from the large box. Her breath catches as she spreads out a long, ebony trench-style suede coat with ebony-colored wool shearling cuffs and collar. It is soft and heavy and expensive. Chrissy runs her fingers over the coat, loving how it feels. Imprinted on the inside is "Pierotucci in Florence, Italy." She spots fur-lined, black leather gloves, a black woolen scarf, and a matching beanie hat in the box. Tears fill her eyes. She has never received anything so beautiful before. *It's too much.*

Reggie's hands cup her face, long fingers wiping away her tears. "Christina, if I could, I'd give you the world. You deserve it. I've never known anyone as selfless and loving."

Taking a few moments to gather herself, Chrissy sniffs and grins when Ben laughs. "Thank you, Reggie. These are gorgeous. Will you help me try the coat on?"

Smiling as Ben and Reggie move to support her, she rises, only groaning a little at the shooting pain. Perhaps after they finish with presents she'll take a pain pill. She doesn't like to rely on medicine, but her body needs to heal. After she cleans up in the bathroom, she can nap, too.

Chrissy holds out her arms as Reggie slides the coat over them. She makes her way to the full-length mirror to see how she looks.

"You look exquisite. As soon as I saw it, I knew it would be perfect. It will keep you warm during the winter months." She stands at Chrissy's side, one hand running down her arm.

"Thank you, Reggie. This coat is so warm and comfortable. I love it." Chrissy turns to Reggie and lifts a hand to brush her fingers down Reggie's cheek. "I love you. Not because of the gifts or you taking care of me while I'm healing or anything like that," Chrissy rambles, afraid of giving Reggie the wrong idea.

Reggie's hand captures Chrissy's and brings it to her lips to kiss. "We both know these feelings have been developing for a long time. I know what you mean, and you know I love you."

"Whoa," Ben says, capturing their attention. He flushes. "I...um...I didn't know you two had told each other. But that's good. Really good." His eyes bounce between Chrissy and Reggie. Reggie looks relieved at his acceptance of her.

"Yes, it's really good," Reggie says in a quiet voice.

"Then we're all in agreement," Chrissy says, clapping her hands and gritting her teeth when her ribs twinge. She views herself in the mirror for a few more moments. "Can you help me take this off?" She's roasting. As soon as it's removed, she moves back to the bed and carefully slides in. "Reggie, this is for you." She reaches under the covers to retrieve the jewelry box. Her fingers worry the blanket lying over her waist while she watches Reggie. She wants to know, really know, whether Reggie likes the gift. She spent weeks agonizing over what to give her.

With a big exhalation, Reggie opens the jewelry box and stares. Chrissy has no idea whether she likes it. *Oh, my God. I made a mistake. What a stupid idea. I'm an idiot. How corny and unsophisticated.*

"Christina," Reggie says, her voice strangled. Reggie's trembling, tears streaming over her cheeks. "This is...this is incredible..."

Chrissy doesn't know what to do to calm Reggie. She's still adjusting to seeing behind the veil, to witnessing how passionate Reggie is, how she feels so much. "You like it?"

"Like it?" Reggie repeats. "I love it. I love you." She looks over to Ben. "Both of you."

Chrissy and Ben beam. Any other time they'd be high-fiving.

"We picked out all the charms, and there's space to add more," Ben says, excitement lifting his voice.

Reggie fingers the gold charm bracelet and each charm. "God! I've cried more over the last few days than I have since I was a child," she grouses, mock-glaring at Chrissy as she wipes away more tears. They all laugh. "If anyone at the firm saw me, it'd ruin my reputation."

"This side of you is for us and a few select friends. After all, we don't want anyone to know what a complete mushball you truly are," Chrissy teases, happiness filling her. "So, the charms we got, they all mean something. The angel is me. The crown is you for your name—"

"I thought of that," Ben interrupts, and Reggie chuckles.

"Yeah. And the basketball is Ben, the rolling pin for your cooking skills, and the apple because you give me a run for my money when it comes to making the best apple pie in the world."

"Please tell me you're making one today," Ben says, his best puppy-dog face on display.

Reggie nods, laughing, and Chrissy joins her, ignoring the pain in her side.

"Yes!" Ben punches the air.

"The scales of justice charm are for you being an attorney, and the heart is, well, it represents..." Chrissy looks down, embarrassed.

"You have her heart," Ben says, and Chrissy's not sure whether to thank him or punch him in the arm. She shoots him a dirty look, and he has the good grace to look abashed. "Sorry," he mutters.

Fingers tangle with hers, and Chrissy sees Reggie's special, soul-lighting smile. "Thank you. I will always cherish it." They gaze lovingly at each other until Ben shifts on the bed. "Will you put it on me?" she asks, extending her arm.

"Sure." Chrissy finds the clasp and secures the bracelet on Reggie's delicate wrist. Reggie's pulse is racing, and she rubs the area to calm Reggie down. "It looks great." She's proud of herself. Proud she's given Reggie something meaningful.

"It does," Reggie says.

"So, here are my presents to you," Ben says while rolling his eyes, obviously done with all the sappiness, and pushes his presents toward Reggie and Chrissy.

Chrissy opens hers and finds a CD of songs Ben compiled. They're a mixture of songs they both enjoy. The last entry says, "Top Ten Reasons Why You're the Best Mom Ever."

"So, I made the last entry," Ben explains. "I did it last week. Otherwise I would have added hero."

She frowns, but she doesn't really care. She's still having trouble accepting how people believe she's a hero. *I bet this will be a hell of a list.* Reggie is also holding a CD. "Switch?" she asks, extending her arm with her CD. They swap, and Chrissy reviews the compilation list. It has a mixture of songs Ben likes and several they've heard Reggie hum over the last few months. She reads the last entry for Reggie's CD. It's titled, "Top Ten Reasons Why You're the Best Attorney Ever."

"Good job," Chrissy compliments Ben, and he smiles. "Thanks, Ben. I can't wait to listen to it."

"Me, too. Thank you for such a thoughtful gift," Reggie says. They swap back the CDs, and Chrissy urges Ben to open his other presents while Reggie moves to cuddle into Chrissy's side. They smirk and chuckle as Ben exclaims over his presents. It's a wonderful morning, and Chrissy has never felt so much love and comfort surrounding her. This is the best Christmas she's ever experienced, and she can tell by Ben's wide grin he feels the same way.

"Well," Reggie says apologetically as she rises from the bed. "I should get started on the food. I'll bring the ice pack up for you and a drink. Do you need anything else?"

"I was thinking of taking a shower. If you can help me up, I should be okay." She bites back her request for help in the shower, knowing Reggie will do it but not wanting to take up any more of her time. Being incapacitated sucks. She can handle the pain. What upsets her is how she has to rely on other people to help her. She doesn't want Ben or

Reggie to feel obligated.

Reggie's appraising gaze studies her for several seconds. "I don't feel comfortable leaving you alone. What if you slip in the shower or lose your balance?"

"I need to at least brush my teeth right now, but I can wait until later to take a shower." Chrissy hopes her seeming acquiescence will sound convincing. She looks away, fingers playing with some discarded wrapping paper.

"I don't believe you, M. Kramer," Reggie says, and Chrissy blushes, knowing she's caught. "So, here's what's going to happen. We're going to help you to the bathroom. While you are using it, I will go downstairs to pop a few items in the oven that I prepared last night, retrieve a drink for you, and return here, at which time I will knock on the bathroom door to let you know I am back. Then, I will help you with the shower. You will not give in to that stubborn, mule-headed thinking that you must take care of yourself every moment of every day. You will not take a shower while I'm downstairs. Understood?"

Chrissy blinks several times. "Okay," she says, properly cowed. She's heard Reggie use that tone of voice and formal language with her difficult clients. She doesn't want to be placed in that category.

"Christina," Reggie says, tenderness filling her voice now. "Let me help you. Please. I promise it won't change my feelings for you. I'm sorry if you're embarrassed, but it's more important to me that you're safe. I'll do my best not to make you feel uncomfortable."

With a large sigh, Chrissy nods. *I'm being ridiculous.* "I'm sorry, Reggie. Thank you for being so considerate."

Ben helps her up from the bed. "I get it, Mom, but don't worry so much," he whispers before kissing her cheek. He walks back to the bed and gathers his presents. "I'm gonna go get cleaned up, too." He exits as Reggie joins her, wrapping an arm around her waist.

They walk to the bathroom with slow steps, and Chrissy wants to rail at the world. This whole being hurt thing sucks royally.

"I'll be back in a few minutes. Don't do anything idiotic," Reggie says.

"Right," Chrissy mutters, going through the painful process of pulling down her pants and sitting on the toilet. "Ridiculous. Stupid. Pitiful." She's not sure whether she is complaining about how incapacitated she feels or her inability to accept the help freely offered.

After finishing her ablutions, Chrissy feels a thousand times better. At least her teeth don't feel like moss is growing over them. She hears

Reggie enter the bedroom and opens the bathroom door. She knows by the look in Reggie's eyes that she does not approve of the pain Chrissy's face must reflect. Although she'd felt pretty good when she first woke up, now she hurts all over.

"Oh, Chrissy," Reggie says, reaching forward to hug her. "Why do you insist on being so damn stubborn?"

Breathing in Reggie's scent, Chrissy rests her forehead against her shoulder and sighs. "I don't want you to see me like this," she whispers.

She knows she sounds like a broken record, but she's genuinely mortified at her weakness, at the ugly splashes of blood on her body, at the bruises and scratches and—*how can Reggie think of me as a possible lover while viewing me this way?* She doesn't realize she's crying until strong arms pull her in and gentle fingers comb through her snarled curls.

"Is it so hard to believe that I love you? That I want to help you? That it kills me to see you in pain? That my feelings will not diminish by viewing wounds you received while protecting Ben and me?"

Hearing the catch in Reggie's voice, Chrissy shakes her head. "I'm sorry. I've always had to be the strong one, and I'm unfamiliar with trusting anyone." Taking a deep breath, Chrissy looks up. "I do trust you. I swear. It's a hard adjustment, knowing I can let down my walls and be seen as weak."

"Weak? Christina Kramer, you are not weak. Far from it. And allowing yourself to be vulnerable shows great strength. I promise not to betray your trust." Reggie brushes soft lips across Chrissy's mouth, pulling a moan from deep within her. They kiss languidly, tongues slowly rubbing together, emotions high.

"Reggie," she whispers. Those delicious lips suck on her chin before sliding to her neck to lick her pulse point. "Oh, my God." She never understood the phrase 'toes curling.' Yet, hers do just that. What an incredibly erotic feeling.

"When you are feeling better, Christina Kramer, I am going to love you so well that you will always know," Reggie whispers in her ear. "You will always know that you're not alone. Will never be alone." Chrissy shivers, and Reggie nips her ear playfully before pulling back far enough so their eyes can connect. The love she sees shining through darkened eyes convinces her Reggie means every word. Chrissy finally allows herself to accept that Reggie really may love her.

Chrissy feels lightheaded, and it's only Reggie's firm grip which keeps her from falling to the floor. She burrows her head into the crook of Reggie's neck, breathing her in while she regains her equilibrium. The world shifts under her feet. *Reggie really loves me.*

"Are you okay?"

Pulling back, Chrissy smiles. "Yeah. I need some help getting my clothes off, but before that, I was wondering whether you'd be willing to wash off the blood and iodine from my shoulder and calf."

Reggie stares at her for a moment, and Chrissy wonders whether she's going to question her further. She knows she's acting weird. "Of course."

Chrissy sinks down on a stool near the large mirror, holding her side while Reggie fills the sink with warm water and gathers soap and a washcloth. "Calf first?" Chrissy nods and extends her leg. Reggie kneels before her and places the leg on her knee, pushing up the pant leg.

Focusing on Reggie's face, a bubble of emotion pushes against her chest—love so strong she fears she's going to burst into tears. *I'm so damn emotional!* Never has she felt this way, these waves of affection and respect and awe and gratefulness. The little furrow between Reggie's eyebrows which develops while she focuses on cleaning Chrissy's calf is nearly as attractive as the black glasses sliding down the bridge of her nose when she reads.

"All done." Reggie places Chrissy's leg on the ground. "Now the shoulder." She grabs a large, fluffy towel. "If you don't want me to see you, I understand. You can turn around so your back is to me, and wrap the towel around you once I help you remove your T-shirt."

"Reggie." Once she catches Reggie's gaze, she says, "It's not that I don't want you to see me. I mean it is, but not why you might think. I wanted the first time to be when we are, well, when we're ready to be closer physically. But I've been listening to you, and I believe you when you say that it won't change your feelings for me. So, I don't need this." She places her hand over Reggie's fisted one with the towel in it.

"Okay." Reggie looks blown away. And pleased.

So worth it.

"Okay," Reggie repeats. She places the towel back on the rack and slowly lifts the T-shirt up Chrissy's back and over her head, bunching the material over Chrissy's forearms. Chrissy allows it to slide completely off, feeling the cool air caress her sides, breasts, and shoulders. Reggie gasps.

"It's not that bad," Chrissy says, fighting not to cover herself. Looking down she can see how the bruising has intensified, black, blue, and purple covering most of her left side. "It looks worse than it feels."

She can hear the falseness of her words and watches Reggie frown.

"Regardless of how terrible those bruises appear, I have to admit you're stunning, and I can't wait to explore every inch of you. Slowly. And thoroughly." The look in Reggie's eyes matches the velvety sensuousness of her voice.

Chrissy barely keeps from swooning. She can't help but smirk. "That makes two of us."

They share a smile, and Chrissy turns on the seat so she's facing the mirror, allowing Reggie easier access to her shoulder. She watches her through the mirror, studying her look of concentration while she washes her shoulder.

"All done," Reggie says a few minutes later, her breath tickling the back of Chrissy's neck.

Goosebumps erupt on her arms, and her nipples tighten with Reggie's proximity. *This is not the time to get aroused*, she chastises herself. "Well, that didn't hurt nearly as much as I thought it would. Thanks." Reggie was so careful that she hardly felt any pressure, nothing more than a slight pain closest to the wounds.

"I hope you realize how much control I'm exercising right now." Reggie kisses behind Chrissy's ear before taking the unused towel and placing it closer to the shower with another one before turning the water on. After the temperature is set, Reggie looks at her, eyes dark and head tilted in that seductive way she has. "I think it will be safest if we shower together. I can make sure you don't twist suddenly or slip."

Before Chrissy can begin to feel self-conscious, Reggie unbuttons her pajama top, eyes burning into Chrissy's, daring her to say something, to stop her. Chrissy has no intention of doing either.

"Oh, God." The silk top slides off Reggie's torso to the floor, the whispering of the material stoking Chrissy's desire. "You're beautiful," she chokes out, glad she's able to say something, anything to express how breathtaking Reggie is.

"So are you, Christina." Reggie allows her pants to pool at her feet and steps out of them. "Let me help you." She pulls Chrissy into a standing position.

When Reggie's warm hands touch her around her waist, their breasts graze, and Chrissy squeezes her eyes closed, moaning Reggie's name. Reggie's gentle fingers rub circles on her lower back.

"Shh, dear. It's okay." Reggie rests her forehead on Chrissy's collarbone. "Let me feel you for a moment." They stand in each other's arms, bodies pressed together, breathing in sync, eyes closed.

A soft kiss above her left breast stirs Chrissy enough to open her eyes and meet an affectionate gaze. She allows her lips to curve up as she skims her hands over Reggie's toned arms. "If you were looking for a way to compel me to heal faster, you've found it."

Reggie's low chuckle washes over Chrissy. "Whatever works. Ready?" With Chrissy's nod, she wastes no time slipping her fingers inside the elastic band of her flannel pants and sliding them down, using her foot to push them to the floor. Reggie keeps a firm hold on Chrissy's hips to keep her steady while she steps out of them. When Reggie's eyes rake over her body a moment later, Chrissy feels it like a physical caress. "God, Christina. I want you so much."

"Me, too. Maybe if we're really careful..."

"Don't tempt me. I'd never forgive myself if you got hurt because of my inability to control my libido." Reggie huffs. "Come on. You in first."

Shuffling into the water stream, Chrissy makes sure the water is only hitting the front of her right side. She hopes taking a shower won't hurt too much, but having wounds all over the place pretty much guarantees this will not be pleasurable. She moves her right leg forward to get it out of the water, glad the spray isn't too forceful. The warm water feels good, although she'd prefer it to be steaming. She hisses as the water makes contact with some of the bruises sprinkled over her torso. Perhaps Reggie being with her in the shower isn't such a bad idea. Reggie's delicious curves crowd her, brushing against her back and buttocks, reminding her of how they'd cuddled throughout the night.

"Turn around." Reggie places her hands on Chrissy's shoulders, guiding her.

As soon as she turns, their bodies touch, only this time, their entire fronts meld together. Reggie turns Chrissy a bit more so the water isn't pounding down on the surgical tape and uses a hand under Chrissy's chin to guide her head under the water. She smells Reggie's lavender shampoo as strong fingers massage it through her hair. "I'll have to put new gauze on afterward. These won't continue to adhere to your skin after the water gets to them."

"Okay." Chrissy closes her eyes and hums as Reggie's fingers sift through her hair. "That feels wonderful." She leans against Reggie, reveling in the caring touches. Reggie rinses out the shampoo and suds up her hair again.

"You're gorgeous. I love feeling you against me," Reggie says, her hands lowering to the back of Chrissy's neck, her thumbs running behind her ears.

Gasping, Chrissy's eyes fly open and are caught by Reggie's vibrant chocolate ones, as Reggie pushes up on her toes to reach Chrissy's lips with her own. Chrissy tastes her desire, devotion, and restraint, and she loves Reggie all the more for it. Their lips open and tongues tangle. Chrissy reluctantly allows Reggie to withdraw, but she clutches to Reggie's hips while she finishes washing and conditioning Chrissy's hair.

"I wish I could return the favor," Chrissy says with regret.

"I'll hold you to that once you're more mobile." Reggie shampoos her own hair and rinses it, applying conditioner next while Chrissy leans against the tiled wall, outside of the water stream.

Reggie reaches for a loofah pad and applies shower gel to it. Chrissy can tell she's uncertain about what to do next, so she turns Reggie around and cups Reggie's face. "You can touch me. I know we aren't going to get too carried away, no matter how badly we want to do more, and I trust you." She kisses Reggie's cheeks, eyelids, and temples before placing her hand over Reggie's and guiding the loofah to her breastbone.

Reggie runs the sponge over her torso, neck, arms, legs, buttocks, and back with careful strokes, but then Reggie pauses. With a smirk, Chrissy widens her stance, the challenge clear. As expected, Reggie lifts her chin before zeroing in on the apex of her legs. Stepping forward, she directs the loofah to Chrissy's waist, inward over her curls, and finally through swollen folds. Chrissy cannot hold back a guttural moan as a spark of pleasure erupts, and if Reggie's other hand were not on her lower back, keeping her from wobbling, she wouldn't be able to remain standing.

Kisses are scattered over her chest and neck as Reggie continues to swipe through her weeping center, and it takes only a moment to realize Reggie has removed the loofah and is using her fingers. Chrissy whimpers. Fingers explore her so carefully, so gently.

"You feel incredible." Reggie's voice is low and shaky. It vibrates through Chrissy deliciously. With obvious reluctance, Reggie removes her fingers and turns Chrissy toward the water to rinse off the soap from her body.

Once Reggie places more soap on the loofah to clean her own body, Chrissy takes it from her. "Allow me," she breathes, wanting so badly to touch Reggie, to explore her wet, slippery skin.

A noise in the back of Reggie's throat makes Chrissy smile. She runs the loofah over Reggie's body, starting at her neck and stalling over her breasts, teasing her hardened nipples. She can see how aroused Reggie is, her body flushed. She holds her close as she moves the loofah over Reggie's shoulders and around to her back. Reggie's muscles flex, and Chrissy kisses the top of Reggie's wet tresses.

After washing Reggie's torso, Chrissy meets Reggie's intense stare and lowers her hand to the juncture of her legs. She can't bend to taste Reggie's breasts, can't bend to wash Reggie's legs, can't make love to her, but she can easily reach the place where Reggie's desire flows. Not bothering with any pretense, Chrissy slides her fingers through Reggie's folds, humming at the viscous fluid coating them. Her shoulder wound twinges when she moves her arm too much, and with a grimace, Chrissy pulls back.

"To be continued," she says.

Reggie smiles, her exhale shaky. She rinses and turns off the water, toweling herself before moving toward Chrissy with another towel. And if her hands stall over certain areas teasingly, Chrissy's not complaining. She changes the gauze on Chrissy's wounds before helping her dress in a pair of warm flannel pajamas, a matching set she's never seen before. "Where'd these come from?"

"I thought you might like them." Reggie buttons the top.

"Thank you." These little things Reggie does are so thoughtful. She's never had anyone besides Ben treat her this way, think of her comfort, her happiness.

"You're welcome." Reggie looks at Chrissy with a critical eye, and Chrissy's eyebrows rise. Before she can ask, Reggie says, "Let me dry your hair."

"Um, yeah, okay," Chrissy stutters. Reggie grabs the blow dryer, a comb, and a brush before leading her to an antique vanity in the bedroom and helping her sit. Chrissy's getting tired fast, and she leans against the back of the chair with a grateful sigh. The vanity's dark wood matches the hardwood floor, and the ornate carvings on it are elegant. Chrissy watches the play of emotions cross Reggie's face as her hands rifle through Chrissy's wet tresses. She wonders what she's thinking. *Does she regret what we did in the shower?*

As if Chrissy voiced her fears, Reggie's eyes, light and warm, connect with hers through the mirror, and gentle fingers massage Chrissy's neck. "That was the best shower I've ever experienced in my life," she says with a smirk. Chrissy grins, relieved.

It doesn't take long for Reggie to dry Chrissy's hair. She spends much more time brushing it to a luscious shine, curls bouncing around

Chrissy's face and on her shoulders. "I've never had anyone brush my hair before." Chrissy's eyes close while she enjoys the care infused in every stroke.

"Your hair is lovely. I've wanted to run my fingers through it for nearly as long as I've known you," Reggie says, kissing behind Chrissy's ear. "Let me help you back into bed. You look like you could do with a nap."

Without complaint, Chrissy accepts her drink and a pain pill. The shower brought out more of the bruises, and she aches. Not that she could ever regret taking that shower. Touching Reggie was magical.

Chrissy accepts the kiss Reggie delivers with a happy sigh. Their faces remain close together, eyes locked, and all Chrissy can do is trace every inch of Reggie's visage with her fingers, eyes, and moments later, lips. "I have a hard time believing that I'm kissing you, that I have the privilege of kissing you."

"Anytime you want," Reggie says, their lips meshing delightfully before she straightens up. "I'll get an ice pack for you. Get some rest, dear. Believe me...I would join you if I had the time."

Chrissy yawns. "Sorry."

"No need to apologize." Long fingers ghost down Chrissy's arm before grasping Chrissy's hand and squeezing. "You have bewitched me, Christina Kramer. Now, sleep."

"Mm, 'kay," Chrissy slurs, eyes closing. As she succumbs to sleep, she grins at the thought of dreaming about Reggie.

Chapter Eleven

A BUZZING FILLS CHRISSY'S ears. As consciousness returns to her, she A BUZZING FILLS CHRISSY'S ears. As consciousness returns to her, she becomes aware of female voices. Unfamiliar female voices. Remaining still with her eyes closed, Chrissy tries to make sense of what she's hearing.

"She's pretty."

"Nice chiseled facial features. Looks like she has muscles, too."

"Do you think she'll sleep all day?"

"I hope not. I need to know what she can possibly see in Reggie."

"Maybe it's a type of Stockholm's syndrome."

"That doesn't even make sense."

Hearing enough, Chrissy opens her eyes. Two women stare at her from the end of the bed. One is a tall, striking woman with short black hair and light eyes, and next to her is a brunette woman with dark eyes. They have the same cheekbones and forehead as Reggie. *Where's Reggie? Or Ben?*

"Ah, you're awake. We wondered whether you would continue to sleep away the hours." The taller woman smiles. "I'm Tracy. That's my sister, Maria. How are you feeling?"

"Sore. What has Reggie told you?" Every part of Chrissy hurts.

"You saved our sister's life. Went above and beyond what an employee normally would do for her boss, I must point out." Maria smirks.

"Well, she's worth saving," Chrissy mutters. She's propped up by several pillows and afraid to move. The last thing she wants to do is reveal her discomfort. It's hard enough overcoming her reservations to allow Reggie and Ben to see her vulnerable. She doesn't know these people.

"If you ever tell Reggie this, I'll deny it with my last breath, but I'm glad you were there to save her. She's lucky to have you," Tracy says, all humor gone from her expression.

"Yeah. That was brave," Maria adds.

"Not really. It wasn't even a choice...more like a necessary action, like breathing. Besides, her life's much more important than mine." She watches as they share a look of confusion.

"Don't let her hear you say that," Maria says. "Our sis is totally gaga over you, and she's not the type who falls in love every other week."

Tracy nods. "And she did everything she could for that guy. He's the one who decided to go psycho. I'd ask you what your intentions are, but throwing yourself in front of a crazy gunman makes it pretty obvious."

Chrissy stares at them, her lips quirking. *I like them. They have Reggie's back.*

"I should have known," Reggie growls from the doorway, marching into the room with a tray of food. Chrissy looks over with relief. The meat smells heavenly. She places it aside and comes over to the bed, leaning down to kiss Chrissy before removing the warm ice pack from her ribs. Chrissy forgets about everything except Reggie as she brushes back Chrissy's hair with gentle fingers. "How are you feeling?"

"Okay. I could use some more pain meds."

Reggie places the tray on her lap before handing her a pill and glass of water. Once Chrissy swallows the medication, Reggie places the glass on the bedside table.

"God, it's all so sickeningly sweet. The white knight saves the queen. The queen nurses her knight back to health," Tracy sneers, although her eyes sparkle with mirth.

"She does look rather at home in Reggie's bed." Maria tilts her head while studying Chrissy.

"Shut it, both of you. Do you need anything else, love?" Chrissy's brows shoot up with the endearment, and Reggie smirks.

"N...no. This looks delicious, but why don't I come downstairs and join everyone?"

"I'd rather you stay in bed—"

"I bet you do," Tracy says, and Reggie turns a nasty glower on her.

"The doctor wants you to rest the first few days and ice your ribs as often as possible." Reggie grabs the fresh ice pack from the tray and places it over Chrissy's ribs. "Please humor me. I know this is boring, but your body needs to recover before you start walking up and down the stairs."

With a sigh, Chrissy nods. She looks down at the bounty before her and decides to make the best of her situation. "Ben doing okay?"

"Yes. He's downstairs charming Mother, but he'll be coming up in a few minutes with dessert for both of you." Reggie grins. "If you want more of anything, send Ben down for it." Reggie leans in to deliver another kiss. She turns to her sisters. "All out. You'll have plenty of opportunities to see her in the future."

"When you're better we're all going out for drinks," Tracy says.

"Oh, I can hardly wait." Maria smirks, one similar to Reggie's well-loved one.

Chrissy wonders how much grilling she'll have to endure. Then again, she'll be able to ask questions about Reggie, too. She listens to their good-natured bickering fade. "They don't seem so bad."

"Give it more time and you'll change your mind. Trust me. They're insufferable." Reggie rises from the bed, a small smile on her face. "Eat your food so you can get stronger. I have plans for you." Her face turns sultry. "Big plans." She walks toward the door, hips swishing in a mesmerizing fashion. When she gets to it, she looks back over her shoulder and winks.

Smelling spiced meat, Chrissy redirects her attention to the food heaped on her plate. She digs in, appreciating the explosion of flavors each bite produces. The medium-rare beef tenderloin has a tangy, thick sauce on it. Whipped potatoes, fresh bread, and a broccoli dish with pecans and cranberries round it out, and Chrissy wishes she were well enough to show Reggie how appreciative she is of the Christmas meal. She wolfs it down quick enough that it's empty by the time Ben enters with two plates laden with desserts.

He hands her one with a lopsided grin and sits on the end of the bed. "How are you feeling?"

"Better than yesterday." Chrissy takes a bite of the apple pie and hums. Not that she'll ever say it, but it may be better than her own recipe. The flaky, buttery crust practically melts in her mouth. Chrissy scoops up a large dollop of whipped cream with the next forkful of pie and looks up to see Ben still grinning. "What?"

"Nothing. Reggie will be glad you like the pie."

"I do. What's her family like? I met her sisters when I woke up, but Reggie ran them off before I could say much."

Ben swipes some whipped cream off Chrissy's plate. "I was talking with Tracy's son, Ethan. He's eleven and plays the violin with the Boston Philharmonic Youth Orchestra. Reggie's other sister has two daughters. They both dance, I guess."

"Anyone else down there?"

"Well, yeah. Their husbands and Reggie's mom."

"What's she like?"

"Her mom? Stern. She frowns like she ate something sour. I could tell she was trying to be nice, but she's not good at it." He swallows the last of his pie and shrugs. "Really, she looks sad."

Chrissy places her empty plate on her lap. "I hear she warmed up to you."

"Well, I did get her to laugh." He puffs out his chest and gives her a cocky smirk.

"There's that Kramer charm. Can you hand me my cup?" She sips the water, wondering how long it will take before she can twist to pick up the glass from the bedside table without suffering a sharp pain. "Thanks." She hands the empty glass to him.

"Want some more water? Or something else? Do you want your computer?"

"Water sounds good and yeah. Might as well see what I've been sleeping through."

"Reggie said the articles on the shooting are examples of shoddy journalism, but some of them aren't bad. They don't have interviews with anyone important. I guess Mr. Hawk and the police gave official statements, but no one else." Ben takes the tray and places it on the dresser before giving her the laptop.

"That reminds me. I want to find out the names of the five people who were shot."

"That's in the articles. So is your name. Want me to pull them up?"

"No, I've got it." She boots up the computer after Ben leaves the room, surprised to see so many emails in her personal account. Several are from parents of Ben's friends and some from his teachers. Although she hasn't spoken to some of these people before, the school has an updated contact list with parents' information on it. She types out replies, touched they took the time to reach out. That reminds her that she wants to check her phone, too. She's sure some answered her texts.

The next email she opens makes her pause. It's from a journalist at *The Boston Globe*. He wants to interview her. Chrissy finds several other emails asking for interviews from radio, television, podcasts, blogs, newspapers, and magazines personalities. Every form of media wants to discuss what happened, and Chrissy's stomach churns. She's been a nobody all her life, and now everyone wants to talk to her. She closes her eyes and concentrates on her breathing. She doesn't want to deal with this, doesn't want to be interviewed, doesn't want to talk about

Frank Hogan or his dead-eyed stare or his bloodied pants or his goal to kill Reggie. She doesn't want to talk about what she did or what she felt while she threw herself at him or all the reasons why she isn't really a hero. She doesn't want to talk about the pain she's feeling or the insecurities she battles every day or the reasons why Reggie deserves better than what she can give her.

"Mom, are you okay?" The worry in Ben's voice matches the concern in his light eyes, and Chrissy automatically tries to soothe him.

"I'm fine. Really."

"Did one of the articles upset you?" He walks over to deliver the water before sitting down next to her hip.

"I haven't even gotten that far. I was reading my emails. Everyone wants an interview, and I just, I can't..." She shakes her head. "I don't want to think about it."

"Then don't. You don't have to talk to anyone. I mean the police, yeah, but no one else." He leans in to hug her, and Chrissy breathes in his scent. She smiles when she recognizes the smell as Reggie's shampoo.

"I know, but maybe I should grant one interview. Then it's done. Not TV. I don't want to be seen like this. Maybe for the newspaper, though. I'll talk to Reggie about it. I got some messages from some of your friends' parents. I wrote to let them know I'm okay."

"Who?"

"Leroy, Billy, Eileen, and Ryan. I got some texts, too." She lifts up the phone to take a look. "Mark and Sammy's moms asked if I needed anything." She stops talking when she hears familiar voices. Cocking her head, she recognizes them as Cathy and David right before they saunter into the room.

"Hey there, hero. How are you feeling?" David smiles, squeezing her blanket-covered foot. Before she can answer, Cathy swoops in to kiss her cheek.

"I'm sore, but I got to eat some fabulous food."

"I bet. We knew better than to try to compete with Reggie's holiday cooking. I made scones for breakfast instead. Cranberry and orange."

"That sounds great. Thanks." Chrissy takes a good look at the couple. "Those are good-looking sweaters you're wearing."

She hears Ben snicker, and Chrissy bites back her own chuckle. Cathy wears a green sweater with Rudolph on it. Around his antlers are a string of colored lights, and elves hang off him. David wears a cardigan with red and green stripes. Dancing gingerbread men and decorated Christmas trees are slotted between the stripes. They look ridiculous and quirky.

"Each year we pick out each other's Christmas sweater and donate the ones we wore the year before." David rubs the back of his neck, a chagrined look on his face. "It's hard for me to give them away. I really like them."

"Oh, honey. We want others to enjoy them, too." Cathy kisses him on the cheek.

"I'm sure everyone who sees them does," Reggie says. Chrissy looks over their shoulders to see Reggie leaning against the doorjamb, lips upturned. Although Reggie's voice reflects sarcasm, Cathy's face brightens.

"Of course, they do. They're so much fun, and that's what the holidays are all about."

"So, any leftovers?" David asks, rubbing his hands together.

"Yes. Ben, I'm sure you're ready for another round. Would you mind taking David down to the kitchen?" Reggie asks.

"Sure. Do you want anything else, Mom?"

"I'm good." Chrissy watches Ben lead David out of the room, smiling when Reggie takes his place on the bed. "Is everyone still downstairs?"

"No. There was a mass exodus once dessert was consumed. Now I can relax."

"Was your mother giving you a hard time again?" Cathy asks, her nose crinkling as if she's smelled something unpleasant.

Reggie's lips pucker and her eyes go distant before she shakes her head. "Not so bad this time. I think having Ben and Christina here gave her something else to focus on." She lays a hand over Chrissy's and squeezes it, eyes softening when their gazes connect. "Another way you've saved me."

"Afanc is going to the arraignment tomorrow morning. He's planning to talk to the DA to see what they need to make sure that guy isn't released," Cathy says.

"Is there a chance he will be?" Chrissy asks.

She remembers the hatred darkening Hogan's face, the blood, and she swallows several times. She can't hear anyone, can't see anyone, everything fades out except her heartbeat thundering in her ears. She tastes some of the food she ate, burning its way up the back of her throat, and coughs. A sharp pain rips through her, and Chrissy moves her hand to her ribs.

Hands cup her face, warm and soft and familiar. Chrissy tries to focus on Reggie, on the words she's saying. She can't hear her, though; her heartbeat is too loud. She stares and breathes and trembles and finally realizes she's crying when Reggie wipes away her tears.

"I'm sorry," Chrissy whispers.

"You have no reason to be sorry." Reggie kisses her, her movements slow and gentle. "What happened was terrifying, and I didn't even see what happened. I was hiding under a desk while you stared down a man bent on killing me. And you got hu...hurt."

Reggie's stutter surprises Chrissy. Pulling back, she loses her breath when she sees the tears streaming down Reggie's flushed cheeks.

"Don't cry. Please don't cry," Chrissy says. Cathy steps forward to rub Reggie's back with slow circles. "I'll heal. I'll get better. It's okay. I'm okay."

She pulls Reggie forward and tucks her under her chin, looking up at Cathy with wide eyes when Reggie starts to sob. Cathy grimaces and makes nonsensical noise while continuing to rub Reggie's back. Reggie's hands clutch at Chrissy's sides, and she does her best not to flinch in pain. She waits out the storm of Reggie's emotions.

When Reggie pulls back, eyes swollen and red, Chrissy says, "And it was so worth it, Reggie. I will always want to protect you. You and Ben. And if I lost either of you...I'd never heal." Chrissy waves a hand in front of her torso. "This is temporary. This is a nuisance. This will pass." She can't stand seeing Reggie so upset. She's recognizing how she's contributed to Reggie's sadness by caring so little about her own welfare. She was ready to die, thinking she wasn't nearly as important as Ben or Reggie, but now that she's accepted the truth of Reggie's affections, Chrissy's determined to do better. She's worth something in both their eyes and accepting that means taking better care of herself.

"Hey. Everyone okay?" David asks. He and Ben crowd around the bed, and Chrissy can see Reggie's embarrassed.

"Yeah. I got upset, and that got Reggie upset. We're a mess." Chrissy grimaces with exaggeration, rolling her eyes. She sneaks a look at Reggie and is glad to see her slight smile.

"Well, we're here for you. All of you," Cathy says.

"Are you worried he'll get out?" Ben asks, surprising Chrissy. He shrugs. "I know he'll be in court tomorrow. He won't, though, and even if he does, I'm here." He stands tall, eyes bright and chin jutted out.

"Kid, you're like a fire-breathing rubber ducky." Chrissy grins when the others laugh, their voices overriding Ben's squawk of outrage. "I love you, Ben, and you're right. We're safe."

"And we'll make sure you know what to expect every step of the way." David looks toward Cathy. "Did you ask..."

Cathy winces. "No."

"That's okay. Hey, Ben, want to play a game of chess?" He nods at a chess set on the other side of the room.

"Yeah. I've been learning all these new moves." He digs a hand into the front pocket of his jeans and pulls out a piece of paper. "I've been writing them down so I can practice."

"Cool. Maybe this old dog can learn some new tricks." They move away, and Chrissy looks at Cathy.

"We were wondering how you'd feel about having Ben sleep over during his break. Maybe toward the end of next week so he's more at ease about your recuperation. Todd will be staying with us while his parents are on a cruise. They don't usually leave him this long, but the cruise is a twentieth high school reunion event."

Chrissy's touched, both by the invitation and their tact with not discussing it in front of Ben. She nods. "That sounds great. I know he'll enjoy it. Feel free to talk to him about it."

"I'm glad. He and Todd seem to have hit it off."

Once Cathy joins David and Ben, Chrissy studies Reggie. Although beautiful, Reggie looks bedraggled, her hair mussed and eyes tired. "After they leave, how about an early night?"

"As long as I can sleep with you in my arms, I'll agree to just about anything."

"I'll be sure to remind you of that once I'm able to capitalize on it."

The way Reggie's tongue flicks out to wet her lips before she captures her bottom lip between her teeth mesmerizes Chrissy. "I certainly hope so."

***

"I don't know whether Ben brought this up with you, but I've received several messages from people wanting to interview me. I was thinking of talking to a reporter at *The Boston Globe*." Chrissy's sitting in one of the overstuffed chairs near the bedroom window, glad to be anywhere but in bed after several days of feeling like an invalid. Reggie's eyes flick up from the document she's studying, and Chrissy hurries to add, "I don't have to answer any questions I don't like, and I was thinking I could meet the person at their office. You can come, too."

"I'd rather have the reporter come here so you can be comfortable. I know you're feeling a bit better, but I can guarantee traveling across the city will take a toll on you."

With a nod, Chrissy realizes she's worried about overdoing it. "All right. If you don't mind, I can get set up in the downstairs parlor, and Ben can hang out in the den. I'll call back today to arrange it."

"I don't mind." Reggie's grin is rueful. "I hate sounding like a nagging Nellie, but I worry about you."

Warmth bubbles up in Chrissy's chest. "I love you. Thank you."

"Hi, Mom. How are you feeling?" Ben asks, crossing over to them. He leans over to deliver a gentle hug before plopping into a chair. His hair is still damp from his shower. He's wearing jeans and a blue-checkered flannel shirt.

"Better. How did you sleep?"

"Good. I talked to Todd. Is it okay if I sleep over David and Cathy's on Wednesday night?"

"That sounds fine. Listen. I'm going to agree to an interview for tomorrow. We'll set you up in the den, and—"

"What? No." Ben jumps up. "I want to be with you during it. I'll be quiet. I promise." His eyes plead with Chrissy to agree, but her mind's made up.

"That won't work. It's bad enough you've been reading all the articles on the internet. I don't know what I'll be asked, and I really don't want the reporter asking you anything."

"But that's why I have to be there. I have to protect you." His eyes well up. This isn't the first time he's expressed his desire to protect her.

Reggie tilts her head toward him, eyebrows lowered. "I'll be there. I'll make sure nothing happens to her. If I think the questions are too invasive, I'll step in."

Ben's face clears up. He gazes at Reggie, the two having a silent conversation. "Okay."

"Okay," Reggie echoes.

By the time the reporter arrives to interview Chrissy the next day, she's a nervous wreck. Chrissy sits in a cream-colored chair near the fireplace in the parlor. She has a handmade cinnamon-colored afghan covering her legs. Her ribs ache, but as long as she's cautious with her movements, she hopes to avoid any sharp pains. Her lacerations ache, but they're manageable. Reggie changed the gauzes that morning, and she said they didn't look as angry.

Detailed carvings over the mantel emphasize the realistic lion reliefs seated to each side of the fire, front paws crossed and mouths open to roar. Chrissy's restless gaze traces the animals' bodies while she listens to Reggie answer the front door. The reporter, a balding, slightly overweight man wearing a tan sweater and jeans, follows Reggie into the room. He has a jerky gait, as if he's pushing off the floor with each step. Reggie takes a seat on the fawn-colored sofa at the end farthest from Chrissy.

"Hi. I'm Lenny Morton." He shakes Chrissy's hand. "Thanks for agreeing to the interview. I promise not to take too much of your time." He sits down on the other end of the sofa, closer to Chrissy, and opens a notebook. "Is it okay if I record?" He looks up, a small recorder in his hand. Chrissy nods, and he places it on the table between them.

"Interview with Chrissy Kramer on December 27, 2016," he intones before looking up. "Chrissy, since I've done some preliminary work on this article, I'm going to jump right into it. Do you know the shooter?"

"Yes. He was a client of Reggie's."

Lenny looks down at some documents. "Frank Hogan. What was the case?"

"I believe you already have that information from the police report," Chrissy says. *Two questions in and already I'm getting a bad feeling about this guy. Why's he asking me about things he already knows?*

"Right. So, Chrissy, what were you thinking when you realized what was happening?"

"I needed to stop him. He was hurting people and heading toward Reggie's office."

"Where were you when you first saw him?"

"I was returning from the restroom." She twists her fingers in the blanket, her mind returning to December 23rd. She's done her best not to dwell, but the sight of Hogan striding through the law firm is one she will not forget.

"Had you ever spoken to Mr. Hogan before the day of the shooting?"

"Yes. He came into the office a few times to discuss his case with Reggie."

"So you were able to identify him as soon as you saw him."

"Yes."

"Weren't you afraid he would shoot you?"

"Of course. But I was more afraid he would kill Reggie." *What a stupid question. Who wouldn't be afraid?*

"Just Reggie?" Lenny rifles through some papers before reading it. "The police report states Ben Kramer was in the office, too. Isn't he your son?"

A spike of anger races through her, and she hesitates before answering. "I'd prefer you don't mention him by name in the paper. He's young."

He offers a small smile. "I understand. But, you were willing to place yourself in danger to protect him, too. Right?"

"Of course." The edge in her voice is unmistakable. *What the hell kind of question is that? What type of mother does he think I am?*

He hums, jotting down some notes. "Why was he there? It's an odd place for a teenager to hang out."

"What does that have to do with the shooting?" Chrissy glares at the guy. *He better not be insinuating I'm a bad mother for letting him visit me at work.*

"His being there motivated you to put your life in danger."

Chrissy nods, though she sees no reason to add she would have reacted the same way if only Reggie were in the office. "I would die for him."

He fiddles with his pen. "I find that although many people may make such a claim, few carry through when a loved one's in danger. It takes great courage. Which leads me to my next question: have you had any training for disarming a person?"

"No. I knew Hogan wasn't going to stop, though."

"And you needed to stop him because he wanted to kill your boss, and your son was with her. Did the alleged assailant know he was there?"

Chrissy shakes her head. "He was hiding in Reggie's office with her under the desk. I made them hide," she adds, not wanting this guy to get the wrong idea about Reggie. "I tried to talk to Hogan, but he became more agitated by the moment. So, I tackled him at the knees and got the rifle from him."

"Your son was on winter break?"

What the hell! Chrissy gives an explosive exhalation. "Why do you keep bringing him up? Yes, he's on break. Yes, he was there. It was Friday afternoon, and we were going to pick out a Christmas tree after work."

"Right. Sorry. I'm like a dog with a bone, sometimes." He looks around the room, and Chrissy's eyes also take in the area. The light gray walls bring a modern feel, while the overstuffed furniture, plush navy area rugs, and round side lamps lend comfort. "I'm curious. Why did we meet here instead of at the law firm or your home or at a coffee shop? Even my office?"

Not sure how to answer, Chrissy looks at Reggie, who gives her a reassuring smile. "She's allowing me to recuperate here."

"Oh. That's kind of you to help her," he says to Reggie with a fake smile. "Certainly more than what the typical boss would offer."

Seeing Reggie's eyes tighten and lips purse, Chrissy says, "Reggie's been great. She knew I'd have a hard time taking care of myself because of the broken ribs, and she offered to help me."

"I'm surprised you aren't staying with your family. Aren't they in Chelsea?"

Chrissy's eyes widen, her gut twisting. She rubs her hands together, wanting to dodge the question. Her eyes flitter around the room, finding Reggie's warm ones. Chrissy's stomach settles, and she redirects her gaze to the reporter. She offers a tight smile and remains silent. She has no intention of talking about her parents. They haven't been her family since they kicked her out.

"How has your family reacted to all this?" Lenny asks.

"I have a feeling you know more than I do." Chrissy does her best to maintain a genial expression, even though she wants to rail against this fool for asking questions she doesn't want to answer.

"They did mention they haven't spoken to you in a while."

Chrissy's eye twitches. She clasps her hands together, not wanting the reporter to see how they tremble. All this talk about her parents is upsetting. *What could they possibly have to say about me? Why is this guy talking to them about me? Why can't he stick to the shooting?* Chrissy stares at her hands, doing her best to control her anger. *First, he drags Ben into this, and now he's opening up my past like it's some sordid soap opera.*

"Right," Reggie says, clapping her hands together while jumping to her feet. "Thank you for coming. I'll show you out." She gives him a polite smile and extends her hand in the general direction of the front door.

The reporter turns off the recorder, gathers his notes, and nods at Chrissy. "It was nice to meet you. Thank you for your time." He pauses before exiting the parlor. "Happy New Year." He leaves before she can reply.

When Reggie returns, she leans over to deliver a soft kiss. "Are you okay?"

"Yeah. He just threw me for a loop when he mentioned Ben and then my parents. I don't understand why he was asking such personal questions." She shakes her head. "I thought this interview was about the shooting. Why was he asking about them?"

"He probably wants to make the article more interesting by inserting information about you. You may want to prepare Ben for it. And yourself." Reggie sits on the sofa and crosses her legs, hands smoothing over her black slacks. "He mentioned the article will appear in the Lifestyle Section on Thursday."

"Do you think he spoke to them? To my parents?"

"I do." Reggie stares at the table between them. Chrissy watches her rub her thumb and forefinger together in a circular motion while she's lost in thought. "Any idea what they might have told him?"

"Not really. I don't like to talk about them. After I became pregnant, they demanded I get married. Like all good Catholics do. When I refused, they threw me out."

"Don't feel you have to tell me..."

That makes Chrissy look up. "I want to tell you. I should have told you before now." She picks at the edge of the blanket. "They told me on several occasions I was an accident. A drunken mistake. They got married because they're Catholic, and their parents expected them to. Mom always complained I gave her heartburn during the pregnancy and it never went away. Dad worked long hours as a used car salesman. He used to let me clean the inside of the cars and keep any money I found." She frowns. "That's the best memory I have of Dad."

"Have you ever tried to contact them?"

"I did the first few years after Ben was born. I sent them pictures, begged them to meet their grandson, but I received no response. I knew they were ashamed of me. Angry, I only appeared at their home once." Chrissy shakes her head, weary. She always feels this way when she allows herself to think about the past. "They had company over. As soon as my mom opened the door, I knew she'd send me away. She told me to not return. I left the house key on the stoop and vowed never to talk to them again."

"I'm sorry. Ben's better off not being around them."

"I know, but he deserves better."

"You both do." Reggie moves over to Chrissy, kneeling before her and clasping their hands together. "I know it's not the same, but I'm grateful to have you in my life. I love you and Ben. You're not alone anymore, not for as long as you'll have me. And I know this is all new, but I feel like we've been dating for months."

"Well, I think we have been. You had me at Gino's."

Laughter bursts from Reggie like popcorn over a flame, making Chrissy smile. "Not at hello?"

"More like at tiramisu. Although, by then I'd already resigned myself to being head over heels in love with you."

Reggie squeezes Chrissy's hands. "When I started thinking of you while kissing Ashford, I knew I was in the best kind of trouble. That's when I began to let you in. I wanted to know everything about you. And please believe me when I say, I'm glad I took the chance."

It doesn't take much to make Chrissy believe Reggie means what she says. Reggie's words, her intense eyes and passionate voice, leave no doubt in Chrissy's mind that she's telling the truth. Besides, she wants to believe her. "Thank you." She rests her forehead against Reggie's, ignoring how her ribs twinge. "I love you."

Rising, Reggie extends her hands. "Let me help you up."

"That's okay." Chrissy places a hand on her ribs and rises. "I spoke to my doctor a bit earlier and made an appointment to see how my shoulder and calf are healing for Friday morning at ten."

"I'll take you to the appointment, if you don't mind." Reggie shifts from foot to foot.

Chrissy's forehead crinkles. "I'd like that," she says, watching Reggie straighten up, take a deep breath, and exhale slowly. Chrissy steps into Reggie's space and cups her jaw. "I think you're right. We've been dating for a long time, even if we didn't label it that way. I was afraid my feelings were one-sided, but you keep showing me how much you care." She delivers a chaste kiss, and when they part, she admires Reggie's upturned face and closed eyes. Unable to resist, she rests her hand on the back of Reggie's head, fingers sifting through silky brunette locks, and pulls her forward for another kiss.

I'll never get used to this. Chrissy moans when Reggie opens her mouth and runs her tongue over the seam of Chrissy's lips before slipping inside. Reggie's low growl chases fire through Chrissy's veins, and she squeezes her eyes tight. Their tongues rub together—long, focused strokes. She savors the sharp taste of mint and coffee and Reggie, her hunger increasing with each sound, each stroke, each stolen breath.

Reggie's hand runs up and down Chrissy's spine, her kisses turning less demanding. She slows, exploring Chrissy's mouth with a devotion which thrills Chrissy. Her breathing starts to slow, and Reggie sucks on her lower lip before pulling back.

Dropping her head, Chrissy keeps her eyes closed, panting. She can taste Reggie on her tongue, and she yearns for more. Fingers move through her hair, rubbing her skull before migrating to her neck. They stand together, Chrissy's arms loosely draped around Reggie's waist, as they calm down. Chrissy wishes she felt better, wishes she could take Reggie by the hand, lead her upstairs, and make love to her. She's too sore, though. Too bruised. Too achy. Too tired. "I want you so much."

"I'm not going anywhere. When you're feeling better, I promise I'm all yours."

"Okay." Chrissy loves the sultry smile Reggie aims at her. When it turns playful, Chrissy knows what's coming next.

"Now, how about some lunch?"

Jazzy Mitchell

Chapter Twelve

CHRISSY WATCHES REGGIE WORK on a legal file, happy to observe her. She'll miss these quiet moments, but she knows she and Ben will have to return to their apartment after the New Year. Ben will return to school on the second, and Reggie will need to return to work. Besides, Chrissy misses being surrounded by her belongings.

Ben enters the room with a smile. "Look what I have." He hands over *The Boston Globe*, and Chrissy wastes no time finding the article.

"Have you read it, yet?" she asks, glancing at Ben.

"Nope. I thought you should get first honors."

Reggie wanders over and slides on the bed next to her so their shoulders are touching. Chrissy shoots her a grin before focusing on the paper.

Meet Hero Who Stopped Shooter at Boston Law Firm

On Friday, December 23rd a disgruntled former client attempted to murder his attorney after being ordered by the court to pay more than $119,000 in damages. As reported last week, Frank Hogan lost a civil case for liability incurred when he tried to fix a furnace without professional help. The furnace caught fire at his duplex apartment, and the property was declared a total loss. Both Hogan and his tenants lost all their belongings, and the tenants sued him for damages.

The focus of the rampage was on Hogan's attorney, Isabel "Reggie" Esposito, a senior partner at Hawk, Esposito & Associates. She agreed to represent him pro bono after meeting him during the monthly Lawyer for the Day volunteer program at the Boston Municipal Court.

Hogan arrived at the law firm at approximately 4:05 PM and proceeded to shoot five people, none fatal, with a rifle and attached bump stock. When he arrived at Attorney Esposito's outer office, Christina Kramer, Esposito's paralegal, attempted to diffuse the situation by engaging Hogan in conversation.

What he did not know was how Kramer had warned Esposito of the danger moments before he arrived, urging Esposito and Kramer's fourteen-year-old son, who was visiting his mother, to hide under a desk. Kramer said when interviewed, "I made them hide. I tried to talk to him, but he was becoming more agitated by the moment. So, I tackled him and got the rifle from him."

According to Kramer, she has no formal training on how to disarm an assailant. That didn't stop her from placing her life in danger. When she tackled Hogan, his shot went wide, hitting the windows behind them. Kramer suffered two broken ribs when she hit the ground, deep lacerations from the shattered window panes, and numerous abrasions and bruises.

Senior partner Afanc Hawk issued a statement on the matter: "Chrissy Kramer is a hero. Not only did she save Reggie Esposito, but she also stopped the assailant from hurting anyone else. Without her courageous intervention, it is conceivable Mr. Hogan might have shot several others. We owe Chrissy a debt of gratitude and wish her a speedy recovery."

Ms. Kramer hails from Chelsea, where her parents still live. Mike and Lori Kramer admitted they were surprised to hear what happened. "I had no idea she's a paralegal in Boston. We haven't spoken to her in a while," Mrs. Kramer said. She described her daughter as a smart, independent woman and expressed relief when told she was recovering. "I'm glad she's okay." When asked whether she wanted to pass on a message to her daughter, Mrs. Kramer said, "I am so proud of her. Hopefully, we'll be able to reconnect soon." Kramer's father declined to comment.

Mr. Hogan was arraigned on Monday for multiple counts of felony assault and battery with a firearm, armed assault with intent to murder, possession of a large capacity feeding device, and several lesser charges. Judge Stark ordered a psychiatric evaluation to gauge both Hogan's ability to understand the proceedings against him and his criminal responsibility when the alleged crimes occurred.

Chrissy stares at the paper. Her heart's racing, and she wants to leave the room. She needs time to think. Time to herself. She doesn't know what to do, how to feel.

"Did it mention me?" Ben asks.

"Not by name. He did identify my parents and hometown, though." Chrissy taps the page with her finger.

"Can I read it?" he asks.

Chrissy nods. She hands him the paper and interlaces her fingers with Reggie's.

"Are you okay?" Reggie asks.

"Yeah. I'm just surprised my mom spoke to the reporter. And why is he getting a psych eval? He knew what he was doing."

"I'm sure his public defender petitioned for it. He won't get free. Those are serious charges lodged against him."

"I think the article is good. It lets people know what a hero you are. Can I keep it?" Ben looks at Chrissy and Reggie. They both nod. "Cool."

Chrissy rises from the bed, biting her lower lip when she turns too quickly. Although the shooting pain isn't as sharp, it still hurts enough to make her pause. Once she's standing, she looks back at Reggie and Ben, both sporting similar concerned looks. "I'm okay. Let me clean up and we can eat something. I was thinking of taking a walk today. It will be good to stretch my legs and breathe in some fresh air."

"Sounds good. I'll get dressed." Ben leaves the room, newspaper in hand.

Reggie still looks concerned, shifting from one foot to the other. "Not too long a walk?"

"I promise not to overdo it."

"All right. Do you need help getting dressed?"

"Let me try first. If it's too hard, I'll let you know." Reggie looks unhappy, but she nods. Before she enters the bathroom, Chrissy says, "I'll get to wear my new jacket today. In my book, that's a win." Satisfied by the upturn of Reggie's lips, Chrissy feels her spirits lifting as she gets ready for the day.

***

The murmur of the television doesn't keep Chrissy's attention while she reads her latest emails. Here it is exactly one week from the shooting, and this is the first time she's logged in to her work email. Most of it she deletes since Reggie's taken care of them. The remaining ones are from colleagues asking about her wellbeing, an internal memo welcoming her to Attorney Hawk's division, and notifications of messages on the work voicemail system. After responding to her colleagues, Chrissy calls in to the default voicemail center.

Most messages she forwards to Reggie's personal voicemail inbox since they're regarding her cases. When she hears her mother's voice, Chrissy gasps.

"Hi. This is Lori Kramer. I was told if I left a message, it would be forwarded to my daughter, Tina. Please give her my number and ask her to call me. Thank you."

Chrissy jots down the number and deletes the message. Her stomach cramps, and she wonders whether she's going to be sick. She hugs herself, her thoughts jumbled. *Should I call her? Do I want to call her? Why does she even want to talk to me? I still have a kid. I'm still single.*

The sinking of the cushion to her right and familiar perfume pulls a smile from Chrissy. Reggie's fingers travel across her forehead, as if to smooth away the proof of her concern. "Can I help?"

"My mother left a message on the company voicemail asking me to call her."

"Are you going to?"

She gazes at Reggie. This beautiful woman loves her. She doesn't have to deal with this alone. "What if I do, and she decides she doesn't want to see me again? I don't want to set myself up for more rejection."

"That is a distinct possibility, but do you think after all this time she would try to contact you only to turn away again?"

"Maybe." She clenches her fists on her lap. "If I contact her, I'm opening myself up. And what happens if Ben meets my parents? I want to protect him."

"Of course you do. If you do meet with her, you don't have to tell Ben ahead of time. You can see what she has to say."

"Kind of like a pretrial conference?"

With a chuckle, Reggie nods. "And if you need a mediator, I'm happy to go with you. You don't even have to divulge our relationship. We can meet her at the law firm."

"Let me think about it. I don't know that I'm ready to see her, but I think I'll call her."

"You're the bravest person I know. Even when something scares you, you keep stepping forward." Reggie's eyes fill with tears, her lower lip trembling.

Eyes widening, Chrissy says, "Come here." Reggie cuddles into her side, and Chrissy holds her as best she can while running her hand up and down her back. Reggie's hand rests on her stomach, the charm bracelet sparkling on her wrist. Chrissy lifts each charm, smiling as she studies them. When she gets to the heart, she looks over to see Reggie watching her.

"You know, it's easy to imagine the worst-case scenario, easy to give in to fear. But we're both here, together, and there's no sense in reliving what happened over and over." She feels Reggie's nod before she sits up.

"Can I see?" Reggie asks, hands poised over Chrissy's shirt hemline. Once Chrissy nods, Reggie lifts the T-shirt up her torso, revealing her bruised ribs. She runs her fingers over the area, causing Chrissy to hiss as pinpricks of sensation erupt wherever she touches. "They look a bit swollen. Let me get you an icepack." She's up and out of the den before Chrissy can say anything.

Studying her ribs, Chrissy frowns. The area has striated bands of bruising, a blend of dark reds, blues, and black. She takes a deep breath, ignoring the pain. She holds her breath for a count of five before releasing it to another count of five. She does this three more times. The last thing she wants is to deal with catching a cold. She feels weak enough. The walk they took yesterday reinforced how much of a beating her body took. It was a short walk, and she napped for a good two hours afterward.

"Here you go, dear." Reggie sits next to her, handing Chrissy an icepack which Chrissy rests on her ribs. "I was happy to hear your doctor say you're on the mend. Another week and your shoulder and calf won't bother you at all."

"They're not bad. Just itchy. And having to change the bandages after taking a shower is a pain. I'm more frustrated that I can't jog for another month at least."

"Well, if it's any consolation, you're the sexiest couch potato I've ever met."

"Gee, thanks." Chrissy can't keep her smile at bay, though. "What time is it?"

"About three. Ben should be home soon. I was going to cook some chicken for an early dinner."

"I can help. Make the salad."

"No, no. Soon enough you'll be back in the swing of things. I'd rather you take it easy." Reggie delivers a kiss on her cheek.

With a sigh, Chrissy lets it go. "Tomorrow's New Year's Eve. You can't tell me you haven't been invited to several parties. You should go to one." Chrissy looks at her hands while she talks, not liking the thought of Reggie having fun without her. It's a selfish sentiment, and she doesn't want Reggie to start the new year that way. She twists her fingers together. Reggie's hand guiding her chin up so their eyes connect surprises her. There's a soft look in Reggie's dark eyes, and

Chrissy's chest loosens.

"I want to start 2017 with you. We'll get to go to many parties in the future." She kisses Chrissy.

Relieved, Chrissy nods. "Well, then. We have some decisions to make. We have a tradition on New Year's Eve of watching the countdown on TV and eating Chinese food. I don't know which restaurants are good around here, though."

"Let me get my computer, and we can figure it out." Reggie hops up, and Chrissy watches her stroll across the room to her desk. Once she returns to Chrissy's side, it doesn't take long to find the information. "Do you want to see what Cathy and David are doing tomorrow night before we place an order?"

"Sure, I think while we're waiting for Ben, I'll call my mother."

"I'll give you your privacy," Reggie says, delivering another kiss. Chrissy doesn't think she'll ever tire of those plump lips pressing against hers. "I love you. No matter what she says or what you decide, you have me. You have Ben. You have David and Cathy and several others who care about you."

It's amazing to recognize the truth in Reggie's words. She's not alone. With that thought emboldening her, she dials the number, holding her breath until she hears a click.

"Hello?"

A sliver of fear runs through her. "Hi, Mom. I heard you called."

"Tina! Oh, my God. I didn't think you'd call. It's so good to hear your voice. How are you feeling?"

Pulling the phone away from her, Chrissy stares at it before raising it back to her ear. The last thing she expected was her mother sounding worried about her. "I'm healing."

"I read you broke some ribs. You're lucky you didn't get yourself killed."

"Yeah. Lucky." Her eyes travel along the bookcase, wanting to distract herself from the conversation even as she hangs on to every word. She doesn't know what to say after so much time. She sees the snow globe she and Ben made and grins. It's really cheesy. Inside is a polar bear wearing a red scarf and a judge's robe. He stands next to a Christmas tree with presents surrounding it. It took hours to decorate the tree with small, colorful beads, but the end result looks festive.

"Well, I was hoping we could meet for lunch somewhere. I know you're still recovering, but maybe next week?" At Chrissy's silence, her mother adds, "Or the following week?"

"I don't know, Mom. Why now?"

"Tina, I've tried to get in touch with you for years. There was no trace of you. It was like you dropped off the face of the earth. Your old friends had no idea where you were, and Jeff didn't—"

"You talked to Jeff?" Chrissy can't believe it. Jeff is Ben's father, and as far as Chrissy knew, he was living in California.

"He was in town for his father's funeral. I was surprised you didn't go, but then I thought maybe you didn't hear the news. He said he hasn't talked to you in fifteen years."

"He didn't want anything to do with Ben. He signed away his rights, and I never heard from him again." Chrissy hears the bitterness in her voice and takes a deep breath. This is old territory, something that happened long ago. She doesn't want to talk about it, certainly not with her mother.

"Ben? Is that your son's name?"

Chrissy curses under her breath. "Yes. If you bothered to open the letters I sent you with his pictures instead of sending them back, you'd know that. Look, Mom. I don't understand why you want to see me after all this time. What's changed?"

"You're my only child. I was talking to Father Michael a few years ago about you, and he helped me see I was wrong to turn you away."

A wash of emotion renders Chrissy mute. Her mouth twists as she clenches a fist. *Of course it was her priest who changed her mind. Missing me wouldn't have been enough reason to reach out. She had to have permission.* It was her religion that convinced her to reject Chrissy in the first place. "And what happens when you find out something else about me that doesn't fit in with your religious beliefs? I don't want Ben to get hurt." Nor does she want to be hurt. *What will Mom do when she finds out I love a woman?*

"Like what?"

Shaking her head, Chrissy's heard enough. She bites back the vitriol she wants to spew, clenching her jaw hard enough that it hurts. "How do you expect me to answer that?"

"It doesn't matter. Tina, that's not going to happen. I've missed you, and I've missed all these years getting to know you and my grandson."

"What about Dad?" Chrissy stares at the blanket while she picks some fuzz off it.

"He wants to see you both, too. Of course he does."

"I'm not ready to take that step. I'd prefer we talk more. Or email each other. We can get to know each other. I'd like to talk to Dad, too, sometime."

"You always were headstrong." The disapproval in her voice makes Chrissy shudder. It takes her back to when she was seventeen. "Fine. We'll do it your way. You'll call me next week?"

"Next week. Yes. Happy New Year, Mom." *This is a chance for Ben to have more family in his life. If they're ready to be in our lives, I need to give it a shot.*

"Happy New Year." After a pause, the call disconnects, and Chrissy places the phone next to her. She drums her fingers on the sofa. She struggled for years to make a good home for Ben, and now that she has Reggie and David and Cathy and other people in her life, she's afraid to risk her hard-won happiness by opening the door to the past. Yet, she needs to make the effort. They may have changed. She stares off into space, biting her lower lip while she runs the conversation through her mind. *Will Mom ever approve of me? Is this worth the effort? Maybe I'm a sucker for punishment. Maybe I should leave the past alone and not look back.*

"You okay?" Reggie is seated beside her, forehead crinkled and head tilted.

Chrissy looks up, wondering how long Reggie's been in the room. "Yeah. I said I'd call her next week. She wants to meet, but I'm not ready for that."

Reggie runs her hand up and down Chrissy's arm. "I'm proud of you. Go at your own pace. If she's sincere, I'm sure she'll wait for you to be ready."

"Yeah. I guess we'll see."

"I got a text from Cathy. They're on their way here."

"Oh, good." She reaches out for Reggie's hand. Bracing herself, Chrissy rises, holding the warm icepack. "Maybe another walk later? We can see if I can get farther than one block."

"And if you don't, it's okay." Reggie takes the pack. "As long as you're moving forward, it's not as important how many steps you take." Her words take on a different meaning for Chrissy. *One step at a time. I can do that.*

***

"Are you listening to yourself? How can you believe I'm going behind your back like that?" Chrissy says, her voice rising as outrage washes through her. Last night they shared a wonderful New Year's Eve together. They ate Chinese food, watched the ball drop, declared their resolutions, and kissed. Chrissy felt hopeful and happy. All that seems like a distant memory now.

Reggie frowns. "What am I supposed to think? All of a sudden you're going back to your apartment. You're back in touch with your family and who knows who else. I was here when you needed someone, but now that you're feeling stronger, you're leaving me."

Chrissy slams her glass on the counter. "What has gotten into you? Ben has to go back to school on Tuesday. Like I said this morning, I want to get him settled and back into a routine. We love it here, but…"

"But it's not your home." Reggie's voice is flat, and she crosses her arms. They're standing in the kitchen, dinner dishes forgotten. Reggie became quieter throughout the day, communication nonexistent. It was as if Chrissy were watching a thunderstorm roll in. And now the storm has hit.

"I want to sit on my worn couch and put my feet up on the coffee table and surf the channels."

"I get it. You don't feel at home here." Reggie turns toward the sink and runs water over the dishes before stacking the dishwasher.

Chrissy watches, not sure how to calm her down. "Reggie, you've taken such good care of me, but I'm your guest. Don't you want to be able to do whatever you want without worrying about me?"

"No. I want you and Ben here. I want to hear you talking while I cook us a meal. I want to find you napping on the sofa. I want to hold you throughout the night. I thought you wanted those things, too."

Chrissy places a hand on her shoulder, waiting for her to switch the water faucet off before turning her around. "Reggie, I love you. That hasn't changed. It's going to be hard to leave here."

"Then don't," Reggie whispers. Her dark brown eyes plead with her to agree.

Chrissy shakes her head. "You know it's too soon for that, but this doesn't mean we'll never see each other."

Reggie's eyes flash, and she turns away to slam the dishwasher closed. "How will that work exactly? Will you fit me in on the nights Ben's father isn't available?" Her chin juts out, voice chilly. "I'm nobody's booty call."

Bewildered, Chrissy tries to understand why Reggie's so upset. *Did I do something to make her think that's all she is to me? Why is she bringing Ben's father up?* "What are you talking about? I haven't seen him since before Ben was born."

"Don't lie to me," Reggie yells, eyes wild. "I know you've talked to him. He left a message two days ago on the office voicemail, and it was already picked up. Not telling me about it proves my point. The only reason I can think of for you keeping it a secret is that you want to see whether you have a shot at being with him again before breaking up with me."

Chrissy's jaw slackens as she listens to Reggie's accusations. She had no idea Jeff left a message. "I didn't hear the message."

Reggie scoffs, and from the way her eyes burn, Chrissy hardly recognizes her. "He said he got the number from your mother."

"You know, I don't know what's worse. Your belief I'll dump you as soon as I get a better offer or your belief I'd keep something like this from you. You really don't think much of me, do you? Not to mention I deserve the opportunity to decide for myself what to do. You should have brought it up when you heard the message, and I should have a choice on whether I want to contact him." *How can she think I'd go behind her back? She's supposed to believe in me.* Sadness and anger vie for attention, and anger's winning.

"Like the choice you gave me of hiding under a desk while you put your life on the line?"

"You'd rather Hogan shot you in the heart?"

"What do you think you're doing to me right now?" Reggie slaps her hands on the kitchen counter.

"I don't deserve this. I've done nothing to lead you to believe I'd betray you." Chrissy turns away, back stiff and mind set. Tears burn at the back of her throat as she walks away. They're leaving. Now. She can't stay in Reggie's house for another minute. She thought they were building a future, but that takes trust.

"Where are you going? We're not finished!" Reggie yells after her. Chrissy doesn't bother answering.

Making it up the stairs, Chrissy pokes her head in the den, where Ben is listening to music. She waves to gain his attention. Once he turns off the music, she says, "Ben, gather your things. We're leaving in ten minutes."

"What? Why? I thought we were staying until tomorrow."

"It's easier to do it now. Hurry up." Chrissy returns to Reggie's room. She finds her bag and fills it with her belongings. After deliberating, she dons the coat Reggie bought her and slings the bag strap over her neck to rest on her left shoulder so the bulky bag rests at her right hip. Although she's able to avoid hitting the large lacerations and broken ribs, she can't avoid various smaller bruises. She ignores the sparks of pain while scanning the room to make sure she hasn't forgotten anything. *Nope. The only thing I'm leaving behind is my heart.*

Ben appears in the door, backpack hanging off his shoulder. When they get downstairs, he goes into the kitchen to say goodbye to Reggie. Chrissy stands near the front door. She feels sick, and she can taste acid in the back of her mouth. She swallows, pushes down her doubts and despair. Finally, Ben comes out of the kitchen and takes her bag without a word.

"Let's go, kid." Her voice sounds hoarse, and she knows Ben is worried. As she opens the door, she feels Reggie's eyes on her. She doesn't look back.

"Mom?" Ben's voice is high. Chrissy realizes she's crying, and she sniffs, wiping her eyes. "Why did we leave? Reggie was crying, too."

"Everyone knew we'd have to return to our apartment. That doesn't make it easier."

"But we'll be seeing her this week, won't we?"

Shaking her head as they enter the subway stop, Chrissy mutters, "Come on, Ben. We'll talk at home."

She grits her teeth as they make their way downstairs to the platform, ignoring her body's aches and pains. Ben doesn't try to talk to her again until they're in their apartment. Chrissy makes some mint tea and sinks into the couch, not bothering to push away her melancholy thoughts. Now that they're home, Chrissy's anger has dissipated, replaced by sorrow. She sips the tea, and Ben sits beside her, arms around his gangly legs and chin propped on his knees.

"What happened, Mom?"

"I've never hidden what happened with my parents and your dad before you were born. I've always answered your questions. You know that, right?"

"Yeah. Did something happen?"

"My mother left a message at the law firm a few days ago, and I talked to her."

"You did?"

Chrissy nods. "I did. She wants to see us, but I'm not sure whether that's a good idea. I don't want either of us to get hurt."

"Maybe she's changed. Maybe she's sorry for what she did."

"Maybe. I'm going to talk to her again, and we'll see how it goes. Even if she's gotten over my being pregnant out of wedlock, I don't know how she'd feel about Reggie." Chrissy blanches, remembering Reggie may no longer be a factor. "The thing is, I'm not sure whether I want her or my dad in our lives at all. I grieved them for years. It was as if they died. Letting them back in means giving them the ability to hurt me again. To judge me. And I don't want you to be around people like that."

"People judge all the time, Mom. It doesn't matter what they say about you. I know how great you are."

"There's another person who's trying to get in touch. Your father." Ben's mouth drops open, but she pushes on. "I haven't called him back. I haven't actually listened to the message, yet. It was left at work."

"Did Reggie hear it?" She nods, and his somber look informs her he's guessed the rest. "She must know you love her."

"I don't know what she's thinking, other than that you, me, and your father are going to become a happy, little family." She sighs. "If after the week we shared she believes that, there isn't anything I can do. She has to trust me."

"Give her time, Mom."

Chrissy admits, "What she said hurt me. Her accusations were unfair. Maybe a little distance will help. I don't know what I'm going to do as far as your father goes. What are your thoughts?"

"I don't know. I mean, we've been fine without him." He pulls on a small hole over his knee, widening it. Chrissy wants to swat his hand away from his jeans, but she refrains. It's more important she doesn't interrupt him while he's sharing his thoughts. "Have I wondered about him? Yeah, but I've never felt like I needed him."

"You never had the opportunity before. Aren't you curious? Don't you have questions for him?" Chrissy reaches out to pat his back.

"Sure, but right now he doesn't mean anything to me. I mean, I don't know him. What if I get to know him and he doesn't want me again?"

He glances over, and she can see his eyes filling up. She hates that he's hurting. "The thing is, it's fifteen years later, and a lot has changed. You've grown into a wonderful young man, and I've turned my life around. It's possible he's changed, too. I won't know unless I talk to him. I think that even if it seems like he has changed, I won't allow him to meet with us right away."

"Like with your parents?"

"Yeah." Chrissy takes another sip of her tea before passing the mug to Ben. "Can you place that on the table?" Once he does, she opens her arms wide, not having to wait long before he moves in for a hug. "We've had a lot of changes happen in a short amount of time. If you want to talk about anything, we can."

"Just, give Reggie a chance. People fight. This is your first one. I mean, we've had some big ones over the years." The way he looks at her, eyes pleading and face flushed, reminds Chrissy of when he was a little boy begging to stay longer at the park. Not that he needs to work too hard to get her to agree. Now that some time has passed, Chrissy's realized Reggie jumped to conclusions due to fear. Talking to Ben about all the changes they've experienced in a short time has highlighted the fact that Reggie has also gone through some huge changes in her life, too.

"True. I'll try not to give up hope. But if Jeff has changed and we let him be a part of our lives, Reggie's going to have to be all right with it. These things can get complicated, and if she doesn't trust me, our relationship won't last. I get that she feels threatened, and I'll admit I didn't react too well when Ashford started sniffing around again a couple of months ago, but if I say nothing's happening, she needs to believe me."

"Mom, if you saw her face when I said goodbye. She was so sad."

"Me, too." She forces a smile. "And in the meantime, we have one more day of goofing off before you go back to school. Think about what you might like to do tomorrow."

"I will. Love you, Mom."

"Love you, too." She accepts another hug, heart heavy, before he rises from the couch. She wants to believe her fight with Reggie is merely a small hiccup, but that teenage girl inside of her whispers she's not worth the effort. Shaking her head, Chrissy rejects that voice. She knows Reggie loves her. *Reggie will realize she jumped to conclusions, and when she comes to her senses, I'll be here waiting with open arms.*

Chapter Thirteen

IT'S BEEN A WEEK. A week without talking to Reggie. Chrissy feels more alone as each day passes. Ben is back at school, and she does her best to act normal when he's around. *Normal. Whatever the hell that means. How does someone who doesn't have a broken heart act?* She knew last week, but now she can't remember.

She hasn't called Jeff and doesn't know whether she will. She needs to get her life back into some semblance of order before she invites more changes. She's curious to hear what he has to say. He may have some questions, but that doesn't mean he'll become a part of their lives.

Chrissy has gotten into a routine. She's too uncomfortable to return to work, but she takes a walk each day, continues the deep breathing exercises, and ices her ribs. The hardest part is walking up and down her apartment stairs. No, the hardest part is getting in and out of bed. Strike that. The worst part is sleeping without Reggie next to her. Maybe it's her waning hope that she'll ever see Reggie again. Her pride won't allow her to reach out to her. It took a long time for Chrissy to believe she's worthy of love. *What type of message would I be giving if I reached out first? I was so sure she'd come to her senses.*

A knock on her door interrupts her spiraling thoughts. *It must be a neighbor.* A few have stopped by to comment on the newspaper article. She opens the door and blinks, not sure what to do. Reggie stands before her, face flushed and eyes shining. Her hair looks windblown, and her heavy black wool coat is buttoned up to her chin. "May I come in? Please?"

Chrissy wants to say no. She wants to tell her to go to hell and slam the door. She wants to say something cutting, make her hurt the way she's been hurting for the last week. She's missed Reggie, and as each day passed, her heart hurt more. Even though she's angry that it's taken Reggie this long to show up, though, she's also relieved to see her. With a sigh, Chrissy moves away from the open door. She hears it close while she fills a pot with water and places it on the stove to heat. When she turns back, Reggie has placed a bag on the counter and is unbuttoning her coat. She stares at Reggie, biting her lower lip as she takes in Reggie's navy pantsuit and crisp white shirt.

"I brought lunch from Gino's."

"Shouldn't you be working?" Chrissy shifts from one foot to the other. She's wearing loose green sweatpants and a black sweatshirt. She wishes she had jeans on so she could slip her hands into the front pockets, but she settles for interlacing her fingers, allowing her sleeves to hide her clasped hands. *Am I weak for wanting to eat the food Reggie brought? Or for wanting to kiss that frown off her face? Or for wanting to forget about the stupid fight?*

"I was at work, training my new paralegal, and I was miserable." Reggie moves around the small kitchen with ease, gathering what's needed before placing the filled plates on the table. "I kept wondering how I could make this right. I accused you of things I know you would never do, all due to my insecurities. My belief that you're too good to be true." She gives a mirthless chuckle, switching off the stove and filling two cups for tea. She sets the mugs down and takes a seat. "And my greatest fear is that I've lost you."

With slow steps, Chrissy joins her at the table. "You treated me like what I was saying didn't matter. Like I wasn't worth the effort to even listen." Chrissy sighs, cutting up her piece of chicken, not sure she'll be able to eat but needing something to do. "I dealt with that my entire childhood, and when I was on my own, I promised myself I wouldn't let anyone treat me that way again."

"I understand that now. When you got hurt at the firm, I didn't. You said you didn't matter, and I thought you meant compared to Ben or maybe even me, but that wasn't it." She places a hand on Chrissy's forearm. "You had a shitty childhood with neglectful parents, the people who should have loved you, protected you, supported you no matter what. Ben's father did the same thing to you. And then I became the worst perpetrator."

Chrissy doesn't understand. "What do you mean?"

"I told you that you matter to me, but at the first opportunity to really prove it, I failed. I know you don't trust people. You don't let people in. Your love is a gift, and I didn't take care of it the way I should have. I'm sorry. I should have believed you. I promise I won't doubt you again."

She can see Reggie means every word. She can see the conviction, the regret, the yearning, all reflected through Reggie's expressive eyes.

Witnessing her remorse blunts the edge of Chrissy's anger. It may have taken Reggie some time to reach out, but she's here now.

"I'm afraid." Chrissy blinks, surprised by her admission. Nevertheless, what she's let slip is true. *What if I give Reggie another chance and she hurts me again? But I'm miserable without her. Isn't life better with Reggie in it, even with the possibility of getting hurt again?* She's never felt as happy as she was while in Reggie's arms, even with the broken ribs and battered body. Chrissy knows she's not perfect, and it's unfair to hold Reggie to a higher standard. After all, Reggie showing up at her door and admitting she was wrong is another example of her strength of character.

"Me, too. But I'm more afraid of what my life would be like without you in it."

For the first time in a week, Chrissy relaxes. She hadn't realized how stiff her shoulders were or how tight her jaw felt. With a deep, cleansing breath, a giant weight lifts from her chest, and as she gazes at Reggie, she allows herself a small smile. "Okay."

Reggie's reaction is unexpected. She drops her fork and covers her face with her hands, shoulders starting to shake.

Chrissy pulls Reggie into her arms, fingers sifting through her hair. She's only seen Reggie cry a handful of times, but the catalyst seems to be relief after a scare. It reassures Chrissy in a way Reggie's apology can't by showing her how strong Reggie's feelings are for her. "We're okay."

Reggie's arms wrap around her waist, her head burrowing into her chest, as she calms down. Soon Chrissy hears her sniffling, and she pulls away enough to capture Reggie's reddened eyes.

"I know you're sorry. I believe you when you say you trust me." Chrissy delivers a kiss on Reggie's head before sitting. Her ribs ache, and now that they've cleared the air, Chrissy finds the food's aroma much more enticing. She takes a mouthful of the chicken, closing her eyes, as she enjoys the warm spices. She opens her eyes to find Reggie's hungry gaze focused on her, and Chrissy feels a familiar heat in her belly.

"How are your ribs?" Reggie drinks her tea, her hand trembling.

"Better. They're still sore, but I'm getting stronger each day. I've been taking daily walks and resting." She takes another bite, but it's Reggie's dilated pupils which capture her attention. "Thanks for bringing the food. You know how much I love it."

"I figured I had a better shot at getting you to let me through the door if I brought it."

Chrissy doesn't know whether to feel insulted, but Reggie's smile softens the barb. They finish their meal and move to the couch, sinking into each other as if they've done so a thousand times before. Reggie plays with Chrissy's fingers, outlining each one. After a few minutes, she interlaces their fingers and rests them on her lap.

"The house isn't the same without you."

Nodding, Chrissy has to admit she misses being there. "I've missed having you close by. I'm betting that working in Hawk's division is going to be a tough transition."

"When are you thinking of going back?"

Chrissy stares at their hands. "Maybe the week after next, if I can navigate stairs without feeling any pain. The subway steps are the worst." She doesn't say more, not wanting to point out when she last traversed them.

"Well, we'll figure out when we can see each other at work. Maybe we can meet for lunch a few times a week." She hesitates, and Chrissy can see she's choosing her words with care. "Can I see you again this week? I'm on trial starting Thursday, but maybe we can go out for dinner on Friday or Saturday night? Ben's invited, too, if he's around."

"I'd like that."

Reggie beams at her, and Chrissy basks in her happiness, glad they're moving forward. Reggie's smile fades, replaced by a pensive look. "Jeff called the firm today. He said he hadn't heard from you and wanted to make sure you received the original message. He's in town for a few more days, and he wanted to meet with you, if possible."

"Oh." Chrissy's mind begins to race. *Did Reggie come here only because she realized I was telling the truth? Would she be here if she didn't speak to Jeff today? This is like my mom getting validation from her priest. Is she able to trust me now only because Jeff confirmed I didn't contact him?*

"I can see you're thinking the worst. I promise you, I was planning on coming here today. Gino's isn't open for lunch. I called Bruno last night to ask him to make an exception. You can speak to him to confirm, if it makes you feel better."

Feeling contrite, Chrissy nods. "I'm sorry. Here you've promised to trust me, yet I've immediately jumped to conclusions." She runs her hand through her hair, ignoring the slight pain in her ribs for the moment. "I'm going to call Jeff. I hope you can understand. I want to know why he's trying to talk to me after all this time. That doesn't mean it will go any further. Ben's not sure he wants to meet him, and I'm not sure I want to, either."

"I'd be lying if I said I wasn't concerned. Will you please keep me in the loop? I'll support whatever decision you make." Reggie keeps her eyes on their clasped hands, rubbing Chrissy's knuckles with her thumb. She looks up when Chrissy squeezes her hand.

"I want to be able to talk about it with you. And that's unusual for me. I haven't really confided in anyone before." The soft smile Chrissy receives makes the risk of being vulnerable worth it.

Reggie pushes some of Chrissy's curls behind her ear, stalling on her cheek. "You're a sight for sore eyes."

"Come here," Chrissy says, pulling her forward. Reggie leans in, tilting her head so their lips can touch. Chrissy sighs. She's missed this. Her eyes flutter closed, all thoughts blanking out as sensation overtakes her. Reggie is careful with her, soft and slow, and Chrissy feels cherished. Reggie pulls back to rest an ear over Chrissy's racing heart, one arm sliding around her lower back. Chrissy runs her fingers through Reggie's hair. She can imagine a future with these types of intimacies, can imagine the casual touches and companionable silences and chaste kisses. She wants it, can taste it, needs it.

"I wish I didn't have to return to the office. This week has been difficult. It looks like nothing happened, but every time I see my office, I remember the shooting." Reggie shivers, and she tightens her hold. "And on top of that, you're not there, and I was afraid we wouldn't get past this."

"It was just a fight. One of many, I'm sure. We're navigating a totally different relationship, and we're bound to make mistakes." Chrissy looks into Reggie's upturned face. "Please promise me you'll talk to me when you're feeling unsure of us. I promise I'll do my best to communicate better."

"I promise. I love you."

Chrissy smiles. "I love you, too." Their lips meet once more. "Once I'm working again, I'll come to your office so we can replace my last time there with better memories. Okay?"

"Okay."

***

For the next three weeks Chrissy and Reggie talk each day, and they're able to see each other several times for lunch and dinner. Today Chrissy is finally able to return to work, and she's nervous and excited.

She makes her way to the forty-third floor, where Hawk's division is housed, eyes darting around as she follows the main hallway. It has several small offices branching off before leading into a large atrium. Although the setup is similar to Reggie's division, the paralegal's desk is against the right wall, closer to his office. On the left side are two levels of lateral file cabinets, a workstation with office supplies and a printer, and an industrial free-standing copier. Against the far wall are visitor chairs and side tables where several magazines are available. A red-haired man in jeans and a black pin-striped Oxford shirt exits Hawk's office, files in his hands.

He stops when he notices Chrissy, and a smile lights up his face. "Are you Chrissy?"

"Yes." Chrissy pauses at the empty desk in front of Hawk's office. "I'm sorry. I don't know you."

"Oh." He shifts the files to his left hand and sticks out his right one. "I'm Jerry Taylor. It's a pleasure to meet you. I do some title rundown stuff for Mr. Hawk. He mentioned you'd be starting today. How are you feeling?"

Raising her eyebrows at his steady stream of words, Chrissy shakes his hand. "I'm much better. Thanks. Sounds like I'll be seeing you around."

"Yup. Glad you're feeling better. What you did was incredible. I hear the guy's in lockdown for a ninety-day psych eval. That's normal for these types of things. Anyway, I have a friend who works there, and she says the guy knew what he was doing, so he'll get put away for a good long time. See ya around." He saunters off.

Chrissy watches him leave, wondering what just happened.

"I see you've met our whirlwind title researcher. He's always like that," Hawk says, walking over. He's wearing an olive-colored three-piece suit with shiny black shoes. He stares at her, and Chrissy gets the distinct impression he's evaluating her. She's glad she wore one of her dressier outfits—a slate-gray skirt suit with a maroon blouse. "Ready to start your new adventure?"

"Yes. I'm looking forward to it."

"Good. You'll be sitting here." He waves toward the paralegal desk nearby. "Get settled. I'm sure you'll be on the phone with IT most of the morning switching over your permissions to this division and to the printers and scanners and whatever else you need. Let me know if you need anything from me. Phaedra left some helpful lists in the top drawer. I'm thinking we can go over my active files this afternoon."

"Sounds like a plan." Chrissy grins. She's looking forward to getting up to speed. Hawk is a real estate attorney, specializing in commercial transactions. He was part of Chinatown's redistricting zones and the sale of several Copley Place businesses. She has a steep learning curve ahead of her, but it doesn't scare her. She has a feeling Hawk will do his best to mentor her.

Once seated at her new desk, Chrissy takes inventory. The top drawers have various supplies for taking notes and organizing files. The bottom file drawers have empty hanging folders Chrissy's sure she'll be filling up soon. She has some office procedural files at her old desk she'll want to transfer over—manuals on how to navigate the telephone system and the computer servers. She also has several self-made lists of contacts for services needed within the legal industry. Although her digital lists will transfer over once she can get online, she also uses hardcopies. She's glad to see the list Hawk mentioned, filled with contact information for real estate services.

Chrissy spends the morning getting set up. It isn't until a bag is plopped in front of her that she realizes she's missed lunch. Looking up, she's thrilled to see Reggie's smiling face.

"I knew you'd forget to take a break. Are you in the middle of something?"

"Nope. I finished right before you arrived. Good timing." Reggie pulls up a chair and unpacks the bag. She hands a to-go container over, and Chrissy realizes how hungry she is when she smells the cheesesteak. "Thank you."

"You're welcome." They eat in companionable silence, and Chrissy welcomes the time to decompress. "I see Ben has a game Wednesday night. I'm hoping to go, if that's okay."

"Of course. Ben will be thrilled. We can go together from here." She loves how Reggie continues to take an interest in his life. "I'll let him know tonight."

"I have to get ready for court," Reggie says a few minutes later. She squeezes Chrissy's hand. "I'll talk to you later."

"Okay. Thanks for lunch. What's the name of your new paralegal?" Chrissy clears the lunch detritus from her desk and rises to throw it in a nearby trash barrel.

"Marie."

"Please let her know I'm going to be swinging by to get the files I had in the desk."

"I will." With that Reggie leaves, her sweet perfume lingering in the air.

A young woman with long, dark hair and large, square eyeglasses approaches. "Hi. My name's Eileen. I work on the fortieth floor." *Reggie's floor.* "I wanted to thank you for what you did. I was so scared. If you weren't there, he might have shot me. You're a hero, and I want you to know we all think so."

Chrissy shakes her head. "I'm no hero. I was stupid to get in his way, and I'm lucky to still be alive. I'm glad you're okay, though."

"You can downplay it all you want, but you saved a lot of people and got hurt in the process. Anyway, I'll see you around."

"Yeah. It was nice to meet you, Eileen. See you." Chrissy watches the woman walk away, nonplussed.

By the time Friday afternoon arrives, Chrissy is embarrassed by the number of coworkers who have approached her with similar messages. She isn't sure how to deal with her newfound popularity. Her desk phone rings, and Chrissy see's Reggie's extension flashing. "Hello, Attorney Esposito. How may I help you?" She hears that husky chuckle she loves.

"I can think of several ways."

She shivers, taking a quick peek behind her. Hawk is on his phone. "Is that so? Care to elaborate?"

Reggie hums. "I will as soon as I get you alone. In the meantime, are you ready to leave?"

"I'm logging off now. Meet you at the entrance to the parking garage?"

"See you soon." Reggie hangs up, and Chrissy gathers her belongings, including a small overnight bag, before donning her coat.

She catches Hawk's eye and waves. After one week of working for him, she feels like she's completed a crash course in real estate law. She's taken copious notes on the process of working a real estate transaction. This week they've worked on residential transactions, and Chrissy is astounded by all the details involved. Next week, Hawk's going to show her what a commercial file entails.

Once the elevator arrives, Chrissy moves inside, her heart speeding up at the thought of seeing Reggie. She exits the elevator and sees her leaning against the wall, eyes on her phone, scrolling. Chrissy walks over, a smile blooming as her beloved mocha eyes light up.

"Hi." Chrissy kisses Reggie's cheek.

"Hi, yourself." Reggie tucks her phone in her pocket and turns toward the parked cars. "Ready?"

"I am. If you don't mind, I'd like to call Ben from the car. Make sure he got to Ryan's okay."

"I don't mind. He did great at Wednesday's game." Reggie unlocks the car, and they get settled before she begins to navigate the parking garage.

"I know. He was surprised he got to play at all. He's finally putting all that extra energy he has to good use." Chrissy calls Ben. He picks up on the second ring. "Hey, kid. You get there okay?"

"Yup. His dad's bringing home some pizzas. We're hanging out."

"Good. Reggie and I are going to dinner. If you need anything, call me."

"I'll be fine. Have fun. You deserve it." A sound in the background precedes Ben saying, "Pizza's here."

"Try to leave some for them. Love you."

"Love you, too. And Reggie. Bye."

"He sends his love," Chrissy says. "Where are we going?"

"To Revere. There's a teppanyaki place I think you'll enjoy. They cook the food in front of you."

"Yum." Chrissy moves her hand over to cover Reggie's resting on the console between them. "I've been looking forward to tonight."

With Ben over at Ryan's house, she can stay with Reggie, can feel her arms holding her throughout the night. They haven't slept together since New Year's Eve, an entire month, and Chrissy is desperate for the closeness. Even more exciting is the possibility of their making love. Her ribs have healed enough for her to begin jogging again, and the bruising has faded to a small cluster of yellow and green.

Once they arrive, Reggie turns in her seat, holding Chrissy's hand. "I'm tempted to whisk you back home so I can have you all to myself, but I also want you well-fed." She smirks, eyes making a slow progression down Chrissy's form before returning to her eyes.

"Why do I feel like I'm dinner?" Chrissy can see the promise in Reggie's eyes, and Chrissy's thoughts jump to the first time she saw her beautiful nude form when they showered together at Christmas.

"More like the best dessert I'll ever eat." With a wolfish smile, Reggie delivers a hard kiss, taking advantage of Chrissy's gasp to enter her mouth and explore it for several glorious moments. By the time she breaks the kiss and pulls out her lipstick, Chrissy's sitting with a dazed smile, doing her best to regulate her breathing. Reggie finishes applying a new coat of lipstick before turning to Chrissy, her eyes softening. She reaches out to wipe off some lipstick from Chrissy's lips. "Come on, dear. I'm starving."

"Me, too," Chrissy murmurs. Reggie's chuckle stirs her, and she pulls herself together enough to follow.

"You don't play fair, lady," Chrissy says once she catches up. She guides Reggie forward, one hand on her lower back, and once they're led to seats at one of the hibachi stations, helps her remove her coat. Three other couples are already seated, and a server takes their order before the cook rolls a rack of ingredients over to them. Chrissy gets the Hibachi shrimp, while Reggie orders the Teriyaki chicken. They are given salads with ginger dressing and bowls of miso soup.

"How are things going with your parents?"

"Okay. Mom gets pushy sometimes about meeting Ben, but that's to be expected, I guess. She told me Dad may be retiring this year. Also, she may have to switch to a different real estate brokerage since the one she's at may be closing." She found out through their conversations that her mom became an office manager at a local brokerage about ten years ago.

"Are you talking to your father?"

Chrissy takes a sip of her white wine. "I talked to him last night. It was tough. He's never been a big talker, and with everything that's happened, I wasn't sure what to say. He asked about Ben and work." Chrissy shrugs.

"How are you feeling about all this?" Reggie chews some of her salad.

"I want to reconcile with them, but it's hard to know whether I can trust them. And I have no idea how they'll react when I tell them about you." Chrissy leans in. "If it's a choice between them and you, I'd rather not have them in my life."

"You shouldn't have to make that choice." Reggie's gaze softens.

"I know, but it's a possibility. That's one of the reasons I haven't let them meet Ben. I need to know what their reactions are to you, to us, before I introduce them." Chrissy eats more of her salad, her mind turning over all her interactions with her parents since they got back in touch. "I'm planning on bringing you up soon. We've talked about you a few times in relation to work and the shooting, but not about our relationship." She takes a deep breath and exhales. "I'm scared because if they act anywhere near the way they did when they found out I was pregnant, then that will be the end of our relationship."

"Maybe you can wait on it."

"No. That's sweet of you to say, but no." The chef starts to cook, and Chrissy sits back to watch. She smiles at Reggie, glad they're together.

Reggie leans over, capturing Chrissy's attention again. "What about Ben's father? Have you contacted him?"

Chrissy shakes her head. "No, and before you ask why, I don't have a good reason. I mean, I believe Ben has a right to get to know him, but I want to protect him, too."

"You know nothing can happen without your approval. A conversation with him will reveal what he wants, if anything." Reggie rests her hand on Chrissy's knee. "And if you're afraid he'll somehow steal Ben away from you, I can assure you it won't happen. Ben adores you."

It doesn't surprise her Reggie's guessed her biggest fear. "Yeah. I know. Sometimes I let my insecurities get the better of me. Maybe I'll call him this weekend. The longer I put it off, the harder it is."

By the time they finish dinner, Chrissy's pleasantly full. The stress of the past week has fallen away, replaced by Reggie's smiling eyes and affectionate words. It isn't until they enter Reggie's home that a sense of expectation takes hold. Excitement thrums through her, and she flushes when Reggie takes her coat, fingers skimming down her arm.

Reggie hangs it up and returns to her, a gleam in her eyes. "Would you like something to drink?"

Chrissy clears her throat. "Sure."

She's wearing a form-fitting camel-colored pantsuit, and although she may not have the curves Reggie does, the way Reggie's dark eyes run over Chrissy's body lets her know she likes how the suit showcases her toned frame. She follows Reggie up the stairs to the den, sinking into the leather sofa while Reggie uncorks a bottle of red wine. She brings over two glasses and sits close enough that their knees touch.

"To us." Chrissy taps her glass to Reggie's before sipping the wine. She sighs as the fruity taste bursts in her mouth. "Is it weird that I'm nervous?"

Taking Chrissy's glass, Reggie places their drinks on the coffee table and leans in to deliver a short kiss. "Not at all. I'm anxious, too." She rests a hand on Chrissy's collarbone. "I'm also dying to touch you."

I shouldn't be nervous. This is Reggie, the woman I love. "I want to touch you, too. I've wanted to for a long time." A pleased expression travels over Reggie's face like the rising sun, and Chrissy's lips quirk in response.

"Is that right?" Reggie moves to straddle her, her skirt riding up her thighs, providing an enticing view. It's nearly as mesmerizing as the low-cut, blood-red blouse. Her eyes catch sight of a lacy red bra, and Chrissy groans. "I've relived that day in the shower too many times to count." She twirls one of Chrissy's curls around her finger and grazes her lips up the column of Chrissy's throat, stalling to suck under her jaw before taking her earlobe in her mouth. It feels exquisite.

Making a small noise in the back of her throat, Chrissy pulls Reggie closer, wrapping an arm around her lower back while cupping Reggie's head. Reggie continues to suck on her earlobe, flicking it with her tongue then moving to tongue Chrissy's ear canal. Chrissy concentrates on every sensation Reggie evokes—as the wet tongue fills her ear, she imagines that tongue filling other places. Heat crawls up her belly and spreads, and her eyes close as a long, needy moan is ripped from her soul.

"I want to explore every inch of you," Reggie whispers. "I want to taste and suck and lick and nibble until you can't remember your name." She pulls back, and Chrissy gasps at eyes so dilated she can only see a tiny rim of brown. "I'm going to love you so well you'll never doubt how much I love you, how much I need you, how much you matter to me." When she swoops in to deliver another devastating kiss, Chrissy can do nothing but capitulate to her passion.

Chrissy's hands slide up Reggie's thighs, stalling on the garters before continuing to shapely hips. She feels lace under her fingers and toys with the edge of the material. Reggie's gasp is swallowed, their tongues rubbing against each other. Chrissy's thumb traces the seam of Reggie's sex through her panties, groaning at the wetness. Reggie jolts against her, and Chrissy continues to move her thumb in whimsical patterns.

"Shit. You're driving me crazy," Reggie mutters, her trembling fingers unbuttoning Chrissy's shirt. Chrissy slips her hand inside Reggie's panties and poses two fingers at Reggie's entrance. "Yes," Reggie hisses, and Chrissy enters her, mewling at the delicious sensation of sinking into wet heat.

Reggie finishes unbuttoning Chrissy's shirt and pushes the cups of her bra up so she can suck on a nipple. Chrissy feels the edge of teeth, the dichotomy of pleasure and pain driving her higher. Reggie switches to the other breast, and Chrissy whines when she squeezes the abandoned nipple with her fingers.

Their bodies are close and hot and gyrating, and Chrissy pushes with her hips while entering Reggie again. She hooks her fingers inside her, loving the sounds it pulls from Reggie each time she meets Chrissy's thrusting fingers. She needs to make Reggie gasp and moan and whimper.

"You're so sexy. I love listening to you." All Chrissy can focus on is how her fingers are being swallowed, slickness making the most obscene, addictive sounds. Reggie's body moves faster, jerking each time Chrissy's fingers connect with her G-spot.

"I want to touch you," Reggie says. "I need to."

"Baby, we have all night. Concentrate on you." Chrissy tries to unbutton Reggie's shirt with one hand and growls with frustration. "Unless you don't mind having your shirt ripped, I suggest you take it off."

With a dirty chuckle that pushes Chrissy's arousal higher, Reggie parts her shirt and unclasps the front of her bra. Chrissy angles her head and sucks on Reggie's breast, running her tongue around the hard point of her nipple. She speeds up her movements and rubs her thumb over Reggie's clit, knowing this will push her over the edge. With a shout, Reggie's body jerks, her back curving and eyes closing as she bears down on Chrissy's fingers. Reggie looks glorious with her flushed cheeks, the peaks and valleys of her body begging Chrissy to explore. Chrissy's fingers feel the pull of inner walls squeezing, and as Reggie slows to a sensual roll, Chrissy rubs her thumb over the extended clit with slow strokes to prolong her pleasure.

Chrissy's body is like a live wire, but she ignores it, keeping her attention on Reggie. Reggie rests her head on Chrissy's shoulder, panting. Her hair is a just-been-fucked mess, and Chrissy loves it. She kisses the side of Reggie's neck and runs her tongue over the same path, enjoying the slightly salty taste.

"You have entirely derailed my plans." Reggie sits up, hands resting on Chrissy's shoulders. "I had every intention of ravishing you." She shifts, and Chrissy takes the hint to remove her fingers. "Come with me. I want to spread you out and take my time." Reggie removes her skirt and blouse before retrieving their wine and sashaying out the door in her lingerie. Chrissy doesn't hesitate to follow.

Chapter Fourteen

STANDING NEXT TO HER bedroom window, Chrissy shivers as coldness seeps into her. Her bare feet are freezing against the hardwood floor. Peering outside, she can barely make out a blanket of snow covering the street, unsullied by footprints or tires or plows. It's dark outside. Sleet hits the window pane, and it looks bad enough for school to be cancelled. *No way will Ben have school.* Her room is filled with shadows, making her wonder what time it is. Grabbing her charging cell phone, she reads 4:36 AM. They've known about the incoming Nor'easter for days, and Hawk suggested yesterday for her to make it a long weekend if the storm didn't blow out to sea.

It's too early for the news outlets to read the list of cancellations, but information may be posted on the school's website. When she was in school, she had to wait for the radio or television announcers to read the list. She'd never heard of half the towns, but she learned pretty quickly when to pay special attention. She always perked up after hearing Cambridge, knowing her city would be mentioned soon.

Hopping from foot to foot while searching in the sock drawer, she's quick to don heavy wool socks before grabbing a sweatshirt and shuffling into the living room. Without bothering to turn on any lights, Chrissy makes her way to the kitchen and turns on the coffeemaker, a large yawn cracking her jaw. Then, she sinks onto the couch and boots up her laptop, logging on. *No school.* With a sigh she pulls a blanket over her lap, tucks her feet into it, and leans against the arm of the couch. She wishes she was the type of person who can go back to sleep after waking. Unless she's awakened by her amorous girlfriend for a round of lovemaking. Then she's able to fall into a deep sleep afterward.

They've only managed to have sleepovers a few times since Chrissy's ribs healed, but each time is a memory she cherishes. Pulling out her phone, she types out a text to Reggie. *Happy Friday. I won't be going to the firm today. Ben has no school.* She's surprised when her phone rings. "Morning," she answers, her face breaking into a smile.

"Good morning, love. I'm staying home, too. I'm surprised you're awake so early."

"Maybe my bed is too cold and lonely."

"That sounds like my bed, and the reason why I'm awake." Reggie's words comfort Chrissy. Reggie takes care to let her know how much she loves her as often as possible. Chrissy still struggles to believe it, but she's trying. "Perhaps once the roads clear I can come over."

"I'd love that. I went food shopping yesterday, so we won't starve." The day's looking better by the minute.

"Great. I'll let you know when I'm ready to come over."

"Okay. Talk to you soon." Once Reggie disconnects the call, Chrissy rests her cell phone on the coffee table and turns the television on with the volume at a low hum. Rising to pour her first coffee of the day, Chrissy resituates herself on the couch and allows her thoughts to turn to two days ago when she called Jeff. It wasn't as terrible as she feared. She chose to call him when Ben wasn't home.

"I'm glad you called. After I saw the article on the shooting, I wanted to reconnect." Jeff's voice sounds different, deeper than it was on the voicemail.

"Yeah, well, I was surprised to get your messages. I was out of the office, and it's taken some time to get back into a regular schedule."

"I read you got hurt. I'm glad you're okay. And I read that, um, our son was there. Ben, is it?" Chrissy wonders how he knows Ben's name, but before she can question it, he hurries on. "I'm glad he didn't get hurt. You were really brave, but that doesn't surprise me. You were always a daredevil."

"It had nothing to do with being a daredevil. I had to protect them."

"I just mean you were a badass, and it's no surprise you still are. Anyway, I bumped into your mom at my dad's funeral, and I was shocked you hadn't kept in touch with your parents. You were always such a homebody."

"Homebody. What do you mean?"

"You know. You preferred to stay home instead of going out. So, when I saw your mom, of course I asked about you."

Chrissy remembers how he used to complain when she didn't want to go to drinking parties late at night. She'd never seen the attraction of getting drunk or high, though. Even though it feels like he's criticizing her, she takes a deep breath and lets it go. "I'm sorry about your dad." She doesn't remember much about his parents, other than that they encouraged Jeff to go away to college, even after they learned Chrissy was pregnant.

"Thanks. So, I got to thinking. I was hoping we could meet up the

next time I'm in town. I'm a mechanical engineer, and I'm going to be working on a project in Boston. I'd love to meet Ben, but if you want to meet with me first, that's fine."

"I'm not sure. It's been fifteen years. I don't know whether it's such a good idea for me or Ben." Five minutes on the phone, and he's already getting on her nerves.

"Come on, Tina. Let's just talk." That hasn't changed. He always used to wheedle her into doing things she didn't really want to do. "We can meet for lunch or a quick drink after work. Whatever's easier. And if that works out, maybe I can meet Ben."

"I don't know."

"Look. I'll be in town March twenty-second through the twenty-sixth. I'll contact you then. Okay?"

Chrissy sighs. "I guess."

"Talk to you then. Bye."

Between that conversation and her mother's increasing pressure to meet, Chrissy is overwhelmed and conflicted. It took a long time to rebuild her life. Once she was thrown out of her home, she went straight to Jeff, but he broke up with her when she told him she was pregnant, and he ignored her whenever she tried to reach out. It became easier for him to ignore her once she began to show and had to enroll in online schooling. He no longer had to worry about seeing her in the halls. It's easier to ignore someone you never see.

She convinced herself it was better not to be at school. She needed to make more money to save for baby expenses, and management at her part-time Marshalls job offered to convert her to full-time status so she could have health insurance. Her work family even gave her a baby shower. Standing for hours was problematic later in the pregnancy, but overall the job was steady. She was able to save enough money to rent a studio apartment after two months of couch-surfing at her best friend's house.

She lost touch with Crystal once she started college, and they eventually drifted apart. That was pretty much the story for all her high school friendships. They didn't have a baby, and she wasn't applying to colleges or figuring out what job to get after graduation. Conversations became stilted. Chrissy didn't want to spend money on movies or fast food. She needed to provide for Ben. She saw the divide become wider with each interaction, but she was helpless to build any bridges to cross it. So she stopped trying.

Hearing Ben's door open, Chrissy looks over the back of the couch and shoots a smile at him. He drags himself over and plops down beside her. "No school?"

"No school." She runs her hand through his messy mop of hair, and he tilts onto her shoulder, cuddling into her side. "You can go back to bed."

"Here's good."

She nods, focusing on the television. The weatherman is on, and she reaches for the remote, jostling Ben, who groans. "Sorry." She turns up the volume, watching the meteorologist point at the graphics on the screen.

"The storm is winding down, as you can see from the numbers." The screen switches to the news anchor. "Boston has declared a snow emergency, so don't forget to get your car off the major roads. Otherwise, they'll be ticketed and towed. If you need a list of parking lots and garages with discounted parking, take a look at our website for details."

She looks down at Ben, whose eyes are closed. "Are you hungry?" He grunts. "I can make us some eggs, if you let me up."

"Not yet." He curls into her more, making Chrissy chuckle. He acts much younger in these moments. She wraps an arm around him and sighs, changing the channel to an old movie she hasn't seen in years.

"Mom?"

It takes a moment for Chrissy to understand what's happening. Ben's voice sounds far away, but she feels him shaking her shoulder. Her eyes flutter open, and she sees Ben with her phone in his hand. "What?"

"Your phone. Reggie's calling."

"Oh." She takes it and answers the call. "Hi."

"Were you sleeping?"

"Do I sound that bad? I must have dozed off while we watched a movie." Chrissy sits up, shooting a smile at Ben. He gets up and stretches, his arms wide. Once he wanders off, she turns off the television. The room is much brighter. Glancing at her computer, she's surprised by the time. It's nearly ten.

"You sound sexy as hell, and I can't wait to see you."

"Me, too." Chrissy strolls to the window and parts the curtains to look outside. "Looks like they've cleared the roads, but the parking ban may still be in effect."

"I'm going to take the T. I'll see you in about an hour, ready to have you warm me up."

"Can't wait." Chrissy takes a quick shower and tidies up the apartment while she waits for Reggie to arrive. She looks around her bedroom, stalling on the newest framed photographs she hung on the walls. A picture of her with Ben and Reggie taken at the Freedmans' house last month brings a smile to her face. It's hard to believe she has a wonderful girlfriend, loving son, and close friends. *How did I create this life?*

It's been a long time coming. It's as if she's finally living her life instead of merely doing her best to get through each day. She has love and laughter and a feeling of belonging now. Pride in her job. Anticipation of what will happen next. Even her fractured relationship with her parents has potential. She walks out of her room in jeans and a light blue cable-knit sweater.

"Mom, can I go ice skating with Billy at Frog Pond?"

"Reggie's going to be here. When were you thinking?"

"Not for at least another hour. He has to finish shoveling."

"Bet you're glad we rent now, huh?" Chrissy jokes. "Sure. Make sure you bring your cell so I can reach you."

"Okay. Thanks." He looks down at his phone while typing furiously.

She puts some water on the stove. *Reggie will want something warm.* She hears her cell phone ping and pulls it from her back pocket.

Reggie has sent a text. *I'm getting off the T now.*

"I'll be right back," Chrissy says, slipping on her boots. "Turn off the water if it starts to boil."

She grabs her coat and keys, jogging down the stairs and exiting the building. The instant wall of cold takes her breath away. She zips up her coat, fingers fumbling. *It's fucking freezing.* She shivers, pulling her hat out of her pocket and donning it on her head before pulling on her gloves. The wind gusts are strong enough to make the wind chill feel like ten below zero. She bends over as she walks in a futile attempt to avoid the worst of the wind. By the time Chrissy spots Reggie, she makes a good impression of an icicle.

"Hey." She reaches out for one of her bags. "I can't believe Ben wants to go skating in this." She falls into step with Reggie. "I love you even more for walking through this crap to come over."

"Well, your promise to warm me up was quite the incentive."

Chrissy catches Reggie's smile and nearly trips on a block of ice sticking out from a snow bank. Reggie's hand shoots out to grasp her arm. "Thanks," Chrissy mutters. Reggie nods while linking their arms together. Once they're in the apartment, they shed their outerwear as Ben rises to give Reggie a hug.

"Want some tea?" Chrissy asks after hanging up their coats.

"I do." Reggie's throaty voice makes Chrissy pause for a moment, her hand holding a teabag while she glances over her shoulder. "Need any help?"

Shaking her head, Chrissy finishes the tea and brings them to the table. She reaches out to entwine their fingers in a loose grasp, smiling when Reggie rubs her thumb over the top of her hand. It's a familiar gesture, one which reminds her how much Reggie cares for her.

Leaning forward, Chrissy cradles Reggie's face in her hands and kisses her. "I love you."

Arms surround them, and Ben says in a high-pitched voice, "I love you, too." They laugh, as Chrissy pokes him in the side and he pulls away. His phone pings, and his eyes flickers to the text that came in. "Gotta go." He pulls on his coat while sliding into his boots. "Bye, Mom. Bye, Reggie." He swoops in and delivers a kiss on both of their cheeks. "See you later."

"Be careful. Check in with me later."

"I will." He's like a hurricane, blowing out the door and leaving a vacuum of silence.

Glancing over at Reggie, Chrissy grins. "Just you and me, baby. Your legs must be tired because you've been running through my mind all day."

"That's weak." Reggie pouts.

"I bet if you were a spider, you'd be a mommy long legs."

Reggie shakes her head, tutting. "I sense a theme here."

Chrissy goes through her mental catalogue of horrible pick up lines. It's a game they've played in the past, one she enjoys. "On a scale of one to America, how free are you tonight?" She earns a chuckle for that one. "I must be a snowflake, because I've fallen for you."

"Nice one." Reggie kisses her.

Chrissy tries another one. "Treat me like a pirate and give me that booty." Reggie groans.

"Oh, come on. At least I'm trying. But you know, this is so us. Me doing all the talking, and you just sitting there looking sexy." Reggie's guffaw validates Chrissy's latest attempt, and Chrissy rises to clean up the kitchen. Reggie's arms wrap around her from behind, pulling her into well-known curves.

"I love you more than all the grains of sand found on all the beaches in the world. More than all the stars shining in the Milky Way. More than all the drops of water in all the oceans." Reggie's voice is tender, her hands holding Chrissy close as her lips brush against Chrissy's ear. She tilts her head, glad when Reggie takes the invitation and slides her lips down the column of her neck. "And what's astounding is how this love grows more and more each day." She turns Chrissy in her arms, and their eyes connect.

Her eyes are so dark and rich and earnest, it takes Chrissy's breath away. To be that loved, it's scary. Reggie makes her feel cherished and worthy. Makes her want to forget she was the one her parents threw out of their home, and the one Jeff broke up with when things became complicated. The one her friends forgot about as she struggled to provide for her son. And even though those events happened long ago, they molded her, influencing her sense of worth. Yet in Reggie's eyes, she can believe she's worth more.

Reggie delivers a kiss, nibbling on Chrissy's bottom lip until she whimpers. She guides Chrissy while peppering her with kisses, navigating them into her bedroom and on the bed.

Chrissy's stomach does a little flip as she watches Reggie remove her clothes. It's sensual and enticing, and all she wants to do is touch every inch revealed. Something in her expression must give her thoughts away, since Reggie puts her hands on her hips and glares at her.

"You are not to distract me. I have specific plans for you. Got it?"

Chrissy swallows, imagining it to be the loudest sound ever, and nods. Reggie's smirk is all the warning she gets before her hands are everywhere, removing Chrissy's clothes, exploring collarbones and ribs and knees and ankles. Her body quivers, each touch burning a trail of fire. She feels as if she's drowning in honey—thick and sweet—all part of a secret recipe Reggie's intent on following. Reggie tastes her, stirring in love and passion and affection. She hums and growls while feasting on Chrissy from head to toe. It drives Chrissy insane. Her intensity demands Chrissy believe in her feelings, believe she is the center of Reggie's world. It's addictive.

By the time they rest, both sated and exhausted, Chrissy wants nothing more than to lie in this bubble of love and never leave. "I love you so much," she whispers while Reggie's fingers combed through her hair.

"You're the best thing that's ever happened to me. I love you, too." Reggie's arms wrap around her, and in that moment she feels secure in a way she's never experienced before.

***

Entering the cafeteria, Chrissy's eyes search for Cathy, David, and Reggie. She finds them and makes a beeline toward their table. Squeezing Reggie's shoulder, Chrissy sat next to her. "Sorry I'm late." She shoots a smile at everyone, glad to have a break.

"Hawk working you too hard?" Reggie's brows lower.

"Oh, no. It's not that. End of the month means more real estate transactions. I was trying to finish funding a file before I came. I only have two more this afternoon, and I'll have help."

"End of the month is busier?" David asks, taking a bite of his sandwich.

Feeling a plate being nudged into her arm, Chrissy notices the salad Reggie got her. "Thanks, Reggie." She picks up a fork. "People prefer closing at the end of the month so they're paying less interest on their loans, not to mention other expenses like taxes, impounds, stuff like that." She takes a bite of the Caesar salad, moaning at how good it is. Looking up, she notices their amused glances. "What?"

"I've never seen someone enjoy food as much as you do." Cathy chuckles. "It's cute."

"Well, if you ever want to try out a new recipe, I'm glad to be your taste-tester." Chrissy smirks.

"They were wondering whether we're available for dinner tomorrow night." Reggie grins.

Chrissy glances at Reggie and tilts her head. Ben's going to be at Leroy's house, and they'd planned to spend the night together at Reggie's. Dinner with their friends first will be fun.

She nods. "Sounds fun. Have you already discussed where?"

"I was thinking Top of the Hub for dinner and maybe the Oak Room for drinks afterward. A celebration of sorts," David says.

"We're happy you're both together, and we want to celebrate it with you."

"You're together?" a male voice asks. Looking up, Chrissy sees her parents. It takes her a moment to recognize the man next to them, Jeff. She sits back, eyes widening. She had rebuffed their attempts to see her, but evidently they decided to take that decision away from her. Jeff has black hair and hazel eyes. He no longer wears bangs, and he's let himself go over the years. He stands with his arms held out awkwardly, as if he wants to put his hands somewhere, like in his pockets. Instead, he crosses his arms and pops his chest out.

"What are you doing here?" Chrissy's heartbeat speeds up and her hands begin to tremble. She balls her fists and hides them under the table. A moment later Reggie takes one of her hands. When she glances over, Reggie nods.

"We knew you'd keep delaying a meeting, so we decided to come here to see you. Security was happy to let us in when we identified ourselves as your parents," her mother says. Her curly brunette hair is filled with gray, brushing her collarbones with uneven, stringy strands. Her light brown eyes are focused on Chrissy, an air of disapproval making Chrissy cringe.

"You're talking to each other?"

Although she directed the question to her mom, Jeff answers. "Since my dad's funeral, we've kept in touch. Not you, though. You left the neighborhood and never looked back. Everyone's talking about you now. They want to know about our son, and I have nothing to tell them. It's embarrassing."

Rage rolls through her. "Embarrasses you? Are you for real?" She can see Cathy and David across from her, concerned looks on their faces. Reggie's glowering at them. She squeezes Reggie's hand while shooting a withering glare at Jeff. "Yes, we are together. And I don't give a damn about how embarrassed you might feel for not knowing anything about my son. You gave up the right to know a God-damn thing when you signed away your rights. Now, please leave."

"Don't be absurd," Chrissy's father answers. "This nonsense has gone on long enough. I told your mother we should have tracked you down years ago. Well, we made that mistake, but we're here now, and we're not leaving until we know when we're going to see you again." Chrissy's father is a tall, broad man with sandy hair closely cropped over his ears and forearms the size of bowling pins. His blue eyes hold an impatience Chrissy well-remembers.

"Tina," her mother implores, hands held up in a placating gesture. "We just want to meet Ben. He's our grandson. And we want to spend time with you both. Jeff wants to be the father he should have been. Is that so wrong?"

Reggie clears her throat. "What's wrong is your refusal to wait for Christina to be comfortable with discussing this. What's wrong is how you've forced the issue in a public forum. What's wrong is how you're ganging up on her." Reggie holds Chrissy's hand in a tight grip, and it provides her with the strength she needs to get through this conversation.

Chrissy's mom glares at Reggie with disgust. "You don't get to talk to us about her life. If it weren't for the way you've twisted our daughter into thinking she harbors some type of deviant feelings for you, she wouldn't have gotten hurt."

Chrissy jumps up and stands in front of the table. "No. You don't get to talk to her that way. I love her. I'm with her. You know this. We discussed it." She's shaking, her anger palpable. *How dare they come here against my wishes.* Reggie's hand on her lower back calms her.

"It's just a phase. Now that Jeff's back in the picture, you three can be a true family. Ben deserves to have his father in his life. I don't expect this to happen overnight, of course, but give your real family a chance."

With each word her mother utters, Chrissy feels sicker to her stomach. She shakes her head, not wanting to hear anymore. "That's never going to happen. Even if we got to a place where I felt comfortable having Ben meet any of you," she glares at Jeff, "we're never getting back together."

"Come on, Tina," Jeff whines.

"Stop calling me Tina." Chrissy's mortified by this entire conversation, and she wants it to end. Tears burn her eyes. *I was stupid to think they'd changed.*

Chrissy's dad reaches out to grab her arm, and several things happen at once. She hears more than sees Reggie, David, and Cathy stand quickly enough that their chairs clatter against the linoleum floor, the racket making him pause. The room quiets, and as she looks around, several colleagues move to stand in front of her. Security arrives and orders her parents and Jeff to leave.

Seeing Reggie's concerned brown eyes, Chrissy lets out a sob. "I'm so sorry, Reggie. Please don't leave me." She shakes her head. This is her worst nightmare come true. Her family has decided there's something wrong with her, rejecting her true feelings. *What if Reggie believes them?* Even after all these months of Reggie telling her how wonderful she is, Chrissy allows her insecurities to get the better of her. She's once again that lost, lonely, seventeen-year-old pregnant girl.

Another voice overrides her panicked thoughts, a stronger one. *No. I'm different now. I'm a grown woman with a son, friends, and someone who makes my heart sing. I'm worthy of their love, and if my parents can't see that, they don't deserve to be a part of my life.*

Murmurs of conversation begin to sprout up, and Chrissy lets out a shaky breath, feeling woozy. She raises a hand to her head and lowers herself into a chair. When she looks up, she realizes Eileen and several other employees who sought her out to thank her when she first began working for Hawk surround her. They all sport troubled expressions, and she tries to smile.

"Thank you for your help. I'm sorry for interrupting your lunches."

"Don't worry about it," Eileen says. "You had our back. We have yours." Chrissy notes several people nodding, and her smile becomes more genuine. Eileen rubs Chrissy's shoulder. "Are you okay?"

"Yeah. Thank you. All of you." She looks around at the small group. Several of them nod, while others offer words of comfort. They wander off, and Chrissy takes a few deep breathes.

"Are you really okay?" David asks while righting their chairs, her three companions watching her. She nods.

"Yeah. That was horrible. Turns out my mom hasn't changed at all. I had no idea she was planning to get me and Jeff together, but it makes sense." She drops her face in her hands and groans. Ben's going to be disappointed. *How can I trust them with my son?*

"Everything's going to be all right. We have your back, too," Cathy says, her voice light.

"And what a lovely back it is," Reggie murmurs in her ear. She's kneeling next to Chrissy's chair, a hand rubbing slow circles on her back. Chrissy lifts her head and smiles. "I love you, and I'm not going anywhere." Reggie's face is solemn, her voice steady, and Chrissy believes her. She takes another deep breath and straightens.

"I know. I'm okay." Seeing the time, she rises. "I have to get back to work. Sorry for the drama." She looks at Cathy and David. "Tomorrow sounds great." Reggie pulls her into a hug, and she burrows into Reggie's body for a long moment before pulling away. "I'll see you after work."

"Are you sure you're okay?" Reggie asks.

Chrissy wants to brush it off, but the truth is she's shaken. "I think concentrating on work is the best thing for me right now. I can fall apart later."

"And I'll be here to put you back together."

"I'm counting on it." They share a smile, and Chrissy feels better already. *I may have lost my parents, but I've gained so much more.* With a wave, she walks away, knowing several people are watching her back. It's a new feeling. A good one.

Jazzy Mitchell

Chapter Fifteen

BY THE TIME THEY return from a night of indulging in fabulous food and decadent desserts, Chrissy's feeling much better. She and Reggie talked the night before about what happened in the cafeteria and how her fears of Reggie leaving her were unfounded. Their relationship is strong, thanks to the pains they've taken to discuss everything. Waking up in Reggie's arms this morning was a balm to her soul. Although they slept at Chrissy's house the night before, tonight they're staying at Reggie's.

"How about some wine?" Reggie removes her high heels after hanging up her coat. She wears a flattering black A-line dress which falls gracefully to below her knees. Black lace covers her arms, and she suspects Reggie's wearing matching lingerie.

"Sounds perfect."

They've fallen into a rhythm when together. At Reggie's home, they tend to relax in the den, sinking into the leather sofa and cuddling while talking. She follows Reggie up the stairs and veers off to the bedroom to deposit her overnight bag. Reggie keeps urging her to leave some clothes. Chrissy's been afraid to do it, afraid she'll jinx what they have, but the way Reggie shows her love every single day urges Chrissy to believe it's okay to trust her.

They snuggle on the sofa while sipping wine, treasuring the quiet moments. Chrissy's mind wanders to the events of the last week. She imagines if she were dealing with her parents and Jeff a year ago, she may have reacted differently. She would have done whatever they asked, eager to have them back in her life. She would have ignored her growing feelings for Reggie, missing the opportunity to build a future with an incredible woman. She would have allowed herself to be brainwashed, believing it was best for Ben. *Reggie's love has helped me become a stronger person.* Another reason to be thankful that Reggie's in her life.

"How do you feel about taking a bath with me?" Reggie asks.

"That sounds incredible."

They enter the master bathroom, and Reggie sets about preparing the bath, using her favorite bathing oils. Soon the air fills with the mingled scents of orange, sandalwood, pine, rose, and lemon. Chrissy removes Reggie's dress, lips moving over her smooth shoulders and down her spine once the material is removed. Her bra and panties are, as Chrissy suspected, black lace and silk, and she admires the contrast between the dark color and Reggie's olive skin. She runs her hands around Reggie's waist before sliding them up her back and stalling at the bra clasp. She removes Reggie's bra and watches as she steps out of her panties to stand in front of Chrissy, her natural femininity on display.

"Like something you see?" Reggie smirks, twirling some of her brunette locks around her finger.

"You take my breath away." Chrissy can smell Reggie's arousal, and her mouth waters.

"Your turn, Ms Kramer." Reggie's eyes shine like diamonds.

Chrissy shivers as she feels Reggie's fingers against her skin, slipping under her shirt and pushing it over her head. She unzips Chrissy's slacks and slips her hands down the back of them to cup her ass before pushing both pants and panties down her legs. Reggie's fingers make little circles at the base of her spine before moving in front of her and removing Chrissy's bra. She steps out of her slacks and stands before Reggie. She reminds herself not to hide from Reggie's ravenous stare, knowing she's loved and desired and wanted.

Reggie's gaze softens. "Christina, you must know you're beautiful. You have nothing to worry about. I adore you." She rests her hands on Chrissy's hips, her grip strong. Yet, Reggie trembles.

"Are you okay?" Chrissy asks.

"Yes." Reggie exhales. "With everything that happened yesterday…" She shakes her head. "I think of how fragile life is, how easily I can lose you. I can't imagine life without you."

Chrissy wants nothing more than to give her everything. "You tether me, keep me anchored. Any time I'm afraid or feel like I don't matter, I think of you." She takes one of Reggie's hands and pulls her to the bath.

The spacious marble bathroom contains a large cast iron, clawfoot tub next to a gas fireplace encased in glass through which one can see the bedroom suite. Chrissy never got to use the tub before, due to her injuries, and she's excited to sink into it. On the other side of the tub is a glass shower, and to its left, a double sink. The toilet is positioned in a small alcove behind a door on the far side of the room to afford privacy. The ambiance created through the cozy fire and romantic, candlelit tub area is undeniable. She takes a deep breath of the aromatic bath oils, the scent soothing.

Reggie looks at her over her shoulder with a smirk and a raised eyebrow as she bends over the tub, testing the water temperature. "Ready?"

"Yes. Let me get in first, so you can rest against me." Chrissy approaches the tub, delivering a chaste kiss before climbing in the warm water. Once she's comfortable, she holds out her arms. "Come here."

"Are you sure your ribs are healed enough?"

"I'm sure. I've been jogging with no pain." A slow smile crawls across Reggie's face before she steps in the tub and lies back. Closing her eyes at the sensation of Reggie's body sinking into hers, of feeling her weight, her skin, her presence, Chrissy rests her cheek on Reggie's head and sighs. Humming, Chrissy links her hands around Reggie and rests them on Reggie's belly.

When Chrissy feels how tight Reggie's muscles are, she silently curses. Even though they enjoyed a fun night with Cathy and David, yesterday's events must have rattled Reggie more than she let on. She's relieved when Reggie relaxes little by little, as they sit in a comfortable silence.

"Reggie, you know there was no chance I would break up with you so I could get back into my parents' good graces. Right?" When Reggie stiffens up, Chrissy sighs. "I'm sorry you felt I might. That's on me. I don't tell you enough how important you are to me."

Reggie turns her head as she sits up so their eyes can connect. "I was afraid I'd lose you, and I feel bad about it. I should have trusted you. You've told me how much I mean to you. Please don't feel like you haven't. But having an opportunity to reconcile with your parents...that's attractive for any child."

"Not to me, not under those terms. So, you don't need to worry. I love you. I'm with you." She leans forward to kiss her.

Reggie turns back around and sinks into Chrissy's welcoming arms once again. Chrissy moves Reggie's hair away so her lips can explore the area. She loves how sensitive Reggie's neck is. Hearing her breathless moans inspires Chrissy to continue delivering open-mouthed kisses down her neck, licking at the base before sucking on the pulse point. Reggie's heart's beating rapidly under her lips.

"I love feeling you move against me," Chrissy admits, as she nudges

Reggie's neck in the other direction and begins lavishing attention to that side. "You fit perfectly." She allows her hands to wander up Reggie's sides, cupping the underside of perfect breasts. Reggie becomes restless, her body tensing with arousal. Each time Reggie shifts, her tight backside rubs against Chrissy. "Let's get out."

Reggie steps out, extending a hand to help Chrissy. They grab towels and dry off before moving to the bed. Reggie lies down, and Chrissy crawls over her, nibbling on her collarbone. She covers Reggie's breast with her hand, brushing her thumb against a tight nipple. Reggie's whimpers spur Chrissy to lower her hand to Reggie's thigh, stroking her from hip to knee.

"Please, Christina. I need you."

"You've got me," Chrissy says, allowing her fingers to explore between Reggie's legs. Her fingers move through viscous fluid, and Chrissy focuses on Reggie's responses. Resting her hand on Reggie's trembling lower belly, she rubs her quivering, stiff clitoris, circling it before turning her attention to Reggie's opening. She enters, stimulating the nerves by rotating her finger. With each shallow thrust, Chrissy allows more of her finger to enter until she's sheathed it entirely within Reggie.

"More, darling, I need more."

Chrissy adds another finger, thrusting more forcefully as Reggie gyrates against her. Chrissy moves her thumb to play with the bundle of nerves, pulsating, as Reggie gets closer to climax. She moves around, brushing over the sensitive bud every so often while continuing to fill Reggie at an increasingly demanding pace. Reggie keens, her inner walls tightening, her body shaking, and her hands latching on to Chrissy's mane of curls. Chrissy watches in awe as her back bows and she screeches out a loud, sustained shout. Reggie's inner muscles grasp at her fingers, and Chrissy keeps thrusting into her, hitting her G-spot and pulling delicious sounds out of Reggie. Her body quakes, and with an animalistic howl, Reggie falls over the precipice into her second climax. Chrissy gentles her movements, guiding Reggie through the aftershocks while delivering small kisses to her flushed chest.

"You're breathtaking. I love how you fall apart in my arms," Chrissy says, running her hand over Reggie's legs, sides, stomach. Reggie lies spent, her eyes hooded, while she catches her breath.

"That was…that was incredible." Reggie pants. "You really do bring your A game to the bedroom, don't you?"

Reggie looks up through lowered lashes, a smirk on her face, and

Chrissy doesn't try to hold back her laughter. "Well, I wouldn't want you to get bored with me."

"No chance of that," Reggie murmurs, the satisfied glint in her eyes entrancing. She delivers an intense kiss, one that means Chrissy's about to experience the incredible privilege of having Reggie make love to her.

After another round of lovemaking, Reggie's cell phone rings, rending the peacefulness and stirring Chrissy from a light sleep. She listens to Reggie's side of the conversation, becoming concerned.

"How could that happen?" Reggie's eyebrows scrunch up. "Why am I finding out a day later? Right. Thank you." She places her phone on the bedside table and squeezes the bridge of her nose.

"What's going on?"

"That was Detective Oliver. Frank escaped yesterday while he was waiting to be transported back to jail. The authorities are on high alert, and they believe he's fled the state. Just in case, they're assigning a patrol car to sit out front and another at the law firm."

A chill runs through Chrissy. "How could he escape?" Chrissy makes her way to the window and looks outside. She spots the patrol car, but it doesn't make her feel any better. Reggie comes to stand next to her and slides an arm around her waist. "Should we go somewhere else?" She remembers the hate in his eyes, his drive to cut everyone down between him and Reggie. Knowing he's loose makes Chrissy wish they were far away from Boston.

"No. I doubt he knows where I live, and even if he does, we have protection."

"Still. He came after you once." *He'll come after her again. Why else escape? This is his only goal. Nothing else matters to him anymore.*

"I know what you're thinking, but if he meant to attack me, he could have done it yesterday after work. I doubt he stuck around."

Rocking back and forth, Chrissy tries to fight back the fear threatening to consume her. She wraps her arms around herself, shivering. "We don't know that, though. He could be waiting for the perfect chance to attack."

"We're okay." Reggie squeezes her. "The detective said he'd keep us updated. Let's get some sleep. You'll see. By tomorrow, they'll have him back in custody."

Although it takes some time after they return to the bed and Chrissy sinks into Reggie's arms, she eventually falls into a deep sleep. When she wakes up with a jolt, Chrissy holds her breath, peering around the dark bedroom, listening hard. She lifts her head, trying to figure out what woke her. Reggie is wrapped around her, arm over her waist and leg resting between hers. She knows as soon as she gets up, Reggie will awaken. Silence greets her, so Chrissy rests her head back on the pillow, deciding whatever woke her is nothing to worry about. Then she hears it—movement in the kitchen, like a drawer being opened. She recognizes the sound since usually it signifies food is being prepared. Reggie claims she's worse than a dog with the way she trots into the kitchen to see what's cooking.

Although Chrissy worries she's hearing phantom noises, she can't take a chance while Hogan's on the loose. "Reggie." She pats her arm while sitting up.

Reggie's eyes blink open, a hand rising to rub one as she focuses on Chrissy. "What's the matter?"

"I heard something. Throw some clothes on." Chrissy gets up and pulls jeans and a sweatshirt from her overnight bag, listening for more noises. She breaks out in a cold sweat, fingers fumbling while she tries to button her jeans. *This can't be happening again.* She freezes when she hears a step squeak. "Someone's coming." She moves to the door and closes it, locking it. Turning around, she sees Reggie is dressed, eyes wide and cell phone in her hand. "Good idea. Call the cops."

While Reggie talks to the emergency operator, Chrissy drags an overstuffed chair across the room and jams it under the doorknob. The doorknob turns.

"Whoever you are, leave. The police are on their way." Her voice comes out in a yelp, fear crushing her lungs.

A banging on the door makes Chrissy jump back, and she pulls Reggie to the other side of the room, near the windows. Chrissy takes a quick peek outside. Two police officers are getting out of the patrol car, readying their guns while approaching the home.

"The police are coming inside," she murmurs in Reggie's ear. "We'll be okay." Reggie's gripping the phone, listening to the operator while staring at the door. Her face is pale, lips pulled into a straight line.

Two shots rip through the silence, the wood of the bedroom door splintering. Chrissy screams. All her bravado from the last time Hogan attacked has deserted her. Chrissy's eyes dart around the room, looking for something she can use as a weapon.

"I'm going to kill you, Reggie Esposito. You don't get to be happy after ruining my life. By the time the police get here, you'll be dead," Hogan yells while banging on the door.

The door is buckling under his assault, and Chrissy is frozen. The hair on her arms stands on end. She gasps, not able to catch her breath. Hogan pushes his hand through the wrecked door and shoves the chair out of the way. His eyes glow in the dark, the rest of his form in shadow.

"I see you." He raises his gun and aims.

Before Chrissy can pull Reggie behind her, Reggie throws her down to the ground so they can hide behind the bed. Three bullets lodge into the thick, wooden baseboard, and Chrissy screeches. Near her is a free-standing lamp, and she grabs it, pulling the cord from the socket and launching it at Hogan. It hits him in the head.

"Fuck! You cunt. You'll pay for that." He stalks toward them, giving them a maniacal smile, blood running down his forehead.

Several shots are fired, and Chrissy waits for the pain to envelop her. Hogan's face turns from victorious to confused to pained. He drops to the ground, his gun beside him, and two police officers run into the room. Looking down at Hogan, Chrissy watches a pool of blood begin to spread underneath him, staining the area rug.

Hands touch her, and a frantic voice buzzes around her head. She can't focus on anything other than the dead man in front of her. It isn't until hands frame her face, until a well-loved voice breaks through her shock, that Chrissy realizes Reggie is talking to her. She blinks several times and swallows back bile as she concentrates on Reggie, the woman who's crying and pleading and shaking before her.

"I'm okay." She examines Reggie for any wounds and is reassured she isn't hurt. Next, she takes stock of her own body and is surprised to find she isn't hurt, either. "He didn't shoot me."

She pulls Reggie into a tight embrace, closing her eyes as the last several minutes overwhelm her. She begins to tremble, tears escaping her eyes. Reggie pulls her closer and whispers a steady stream of comforting words as she fights to regain control.

"I'm sorry, but we're going to need to cordon off this room so we can process the crime scene," a female officer about her age says.

"Okay. Can I take my phone? It's on the bedside table." Chrissy points to it on the other side of the bed.

"Let me make sure they took pictures over there and that they don't need it. In the meantime, let's get you both downstairs." She extends her hand toward the door, and Chrissy makes a wide berth around Hogan, Reggie maintaining an arm around her waist as they leave the room.

The next few hours are a blur. They give statements and wait in the parlor while talking to Ben and Cathy and even Reggie's mother. Reggie has finally closed her eyes for an impromptu nap, but Chrissy's too wired to rest. It's about six in the morning. This whole ordeal in what-the-fuckedness is finally over. Reggie's safe, and Chrissy thinks she might be able to accept that her being with Reggie made a difference.

***

Gentle kisses on her cheek wake Chrissy in the best possible way. Humming, she places her hand over Reggie's warm, wandering fingers, lifting them to her lips to suck each one while relishing the whimpers breathed into her hair. Tongue, lips, and teeth attack behind her ear, in the crook of her neck, over her pulse point, and she revels in Reggie's power to reduce her into a weak, trembling mess.

"Merry Christmas, Christina," Reggie says, pulling Chrissy's hips into her body and grinding against her backside. Her hands cup Chrissy's breasts, drawing out a needy moan.

"Merry Christmas, Reggie." Chrissy pants as Reggie continues to tweak her nipples between her thumbs and forefingers and push into Chrissy's body again and again. Not able to take anymore, Chrissy rolls over and draws Reggie into her arms, holding her close as she kisses smiling lips.

"I love waking up with you. And I particularly love waking up with you naked."

Reggie puffs out a surprised laugh that turns into a needy mewl when Chrissy takes one of her breasts into her mouth, flicking the hardened nub with her tongue. She rolls Reggie on her back, placing her hands on either side of Reggie's shoulders, as Reggie's legs wrap around her hips. Chrissy switches to the other breast, chewing on it gently, knowing how much Reggie enjoys it. Fingers weave through her hair, pulling lightly at her roots, before one hand cups her chin and pulls upward. Chrissy follows Reggie's directive and leans up to meet her lips.

Their kiss is fire and desire and love. Chrissy can't get enough. Never believes she will get enough. Doesn't want to get enough. No. She always wants to feel this way, always wants to be held by Reggie, always wants to be the only one who receives these looks and kisses and hands wandering over her body and making her forget everything but Reggie.

When the kiss breaks, she moves back. They smile at each other. "You make me so happy," Chrissy whispers, suddenly shy. She rests her head on Reggie's collarbone, distracting herself from her fears.

It's not like they don't express their feelings. Even after two years of being together, they tell each other all the time, and their actions reinforce those words. Chrissy still has trouble believing Reggie loves her, but she won't voice such insecurities to Reggie. She'd never want Reggie to believe she isn't doing enough to reassure her.

During these darkest hours, fears invade her mind. And she wonders. She wonders whether their being together might be due to Hogan's attempts to kill Reggie, whether her gratefulness when Chrissy saved her morphed into their being together. She wonders whether Reggie ever regrets that.

But she knows better. While she used to think of herself as weak and unworthy of love, Reggie's taught her how to be brave. How to voice her insecurities and listen. More than that, to accept. And although she sometimes falls back into those feelings of unworthiness, she will never let them persuade her into walking away from this relationship. Because Reggie is her water. Her sustenance. A precious elixir she'll always want to drink.

"Christina," Reggie says, and her tone of voice holds a question. Chrissy kisses her collarbone in apology and concentrates on making Reggie feel her love.

Squeaking in surprise, Chrissy finds herself on her back, Reggie smiling down on her. "What's bothering you?" she asks, tilting her head to catch Chrissy's eyes as she runs a finger down her cheek.

"I don't know. Remembering two years ago around this time." Chrissy shrugs.

Reggie's face becomes somber. "I was glad to have you with me, although not under those circumstances. And my sisters were such asses."

Chrissy can't help but grin. Her mind returns to Christmas Day two years ago
when she had awakened to both Reggie's sisters in front of her bed. "They weren't that bad," Chrissy says, releasing the memory.

"They like you. They say you humanize me," Reggie says. "You've even impressed Mother." Her distaste for her mother makes it sound as if she's eaten something sour. They're still at odds, and Chrissy knows today will be challenging for Reggie.

"You've always been warm and giving. I don't know how they can be serious. They were probably trying to rile you up." While she babbles, her hands rub up and down Reggie's back. The feel of Reggie's flexing muscles reminds her of how she woke up, of how they're naked, of how their bodies are pressed together. "Enough of that," she mutters and tangles her hand in glorious, silky locks to pull her in for a sizzling kiss.

It's as if Reggie has also remembered what they were doing, her hands running down Chrissy's sides. One hand stalls on Chrissy's healed ribs, fingers spread over them, while her other hand ends up grasping Chrissy's right shoulder blade, directly over her scar. They keep kissing, Reggie taking control, her tongue chasing Chrissy's into her mouth. Arousal courses through her veins. She feels alive and alert and loved and loveable. Whether she's worthy or not, she will never turn away from this.

They move against each other, undulating to a song their hearts sing together. Reggie sighs, her hand stroking Chrissy's ribs, her abdomen, her curls. She leans on one arm while playing in Chrissy's wetness, stroking gently as she takes Chrissy's breast in her mouth.

"I love how you respond to me," she says. "I love you."

Her words slay Chrissy's insecurities. As Reggie enters her with two fingers, Chrissy arches her back. "I love you. So much." She closes her eyes, overwhelmed by the physical stimulation, by the feelings flowing through her, by the strength of her love, Reggie's love, their love.

"Look at me," Reggie pleads. Chrissy opens her eyes, allowing Reggie to see her soul and gasping as Reggie's fingers pump, demanding she be entirely present as they make love.

"God." Chrissy moans, her voice thick, her climax approaching. She pulls Reggie into her, needing the contact, needing to be as close as possible. Reggie moves her hips in time with each stroke, pushing against her hand, perspiration forming along her hairline. She's gorgeous and fierce. Chrissy loves being the center of her attention. She moves her hand down Reggie's side, hip, thigh, before finally finding Reggie's warm, wet center. Chrissy groans. "You feel so good."

They pick up the pace, staring into each other's eyes, breathing each other's air. Their bodies tremble and shudder and break apart, eyes squeezing tight and inner muscles pulling fingers further inside, not wanting to let go. And as they slow down, they lie in an exhausted heap with wide smiles. This is heaven. Miraculous. Perfect.

The next time Chrissy wakes up, Reggie remains tucked tightly into her side, their legs entangled. She runs her fingers through Reggie's brunette locks, watching coffee-colored eyes flutter open. Her fuzzy gaze sharpens as she becomes aware of her surroundings, and Chrissy watches those eyes she loves darkening to a beautiful chocolate hue.

"Hi," Chrissy says. "I think it snowed."

Reggie's smile is as breathtaking as the first time she gifted it to Chrissy after they'd shared their first kiss. "I'm going to make you the best breakfast you've ever tasted."

Their kisses are unhurried, and Chrissy falls more in love. She fights her feelings of inadequacy, not wanting to dwell on all the reasons why Reggie could do so much better, deserves so much more. As time has passed, she's found it easier to convince herself that this is where she belongs.

"Before Ben gets up, I want to talk to you about something," Reggie says as she sits up, pulling the covers over her chest and interlacing their fingers together. She glances at Chrissy with a nervous smile, a trait uncommon enough that Chrissy's chest tightens.

"Did I do something wrong?" Chrissy asks.

"I want you and Ben to move in with me."

"Wh...what?" Chrissy asks, dazed.

"I love when you're both here. I want to share my life with you, Christina. If I didn't think you'd freak out, I'd be asking for more than this," Reggie says, one hand reaching out to cup Chrissy's cheek. "Please say yes. I love you. I made a promise I intend to keep. I want to show you how much you mean to me, how much I need you, how much I love you. I want you to feel my love every day. And it will be so much better with us all in one place."

Overwhelmed, Chrissy pulls Reggie toward her and kisses her with all the love, all the passion, all the trust she has for this incredible woman. "You know," Chrissy whispers. "What you were saying, the words you used, they kind of sounded like a marriage proposal."

Reggie leans back, her eyes searching Chrissy's for several moments, and Chrissy feels something settle within her. She does belong with Reggie–to Reggie. And even though at the beginning of their relationship, she was convinced she wasn't worthy of Reggie's affections, even though at times she still feels like a sham, a fraud, expendable, now she knows that's not true. More importantly, Reggie reassures her with her words, her actions, and her love every day.

"And how do you feel about that possibility?" Reggie asks carefully.

Chrissy knows this is important. Her next words can affect their future. If she's ever going to stop being that unwanted teen, that worthless loner, that damaged girl, then she needs to accept how, in Reggie's eyes and mind and heart, she is worthy.

"I love you with all my heart, and I can't live in a world without you in it," Chrissy says, repeating words she uttered to Reggie while in the hospital two years ago. "I'm yours in any way you want. Including as your wife." Chrissy exhales, glad she's said the words. Made the leap. Given Reggie everything she has. Excitement bubbles through her at the possibility of being with Reggie for the rest of their lives.

Reggie jumps up from the bed and hurries to her bureau, rummaging around before rejoining Chrissy. Her eyes widen when Reggie opens a jewelry box in front of her and removes a ring. Her mouth drops open.

Reggie takes her left hand, slides the ring on her finger, and kisses it. "My savior, my hero, my love. Marry me, Christina."

Tears flow down her cheeks, and Chrissy nods as she reaches for her fiancée. "Yes. Of course. I'd be honored to be your wife." She pulls Reggie forward, and they kiss while laughing and crying and hugging.

"You guys awake?" Ben yells through the door. "I'm starving out here."

They break apart and rush to put clothes on. Chrissy wraps Reggie in a tight hug and kisses her again. "The ring is beautiful. Ben's gonna flip."

Reggie's eyes sparkle. "He helped me pick it out. I asked for his blessing a while ago."

"You asked for his blessing?" Chrissy asks, stunned. *How romantic is that?* "God, I love you!"

Grinning, Reggie says, "Call me Reggie." And as they move to join Ben, Reggie says, "I'm going to spend the rest of our lives loving you. Because you matter, Christina Kramer."

And finally, finally, while gazing into eyes filled with adoration and earnestness, Chrissy realizes she believes her. Wholeheartedly. Without reservation.

It's the best gift of all.

About Jazzy Mitchell

Jazzy Mitchell loves to tell stories, one word at a time. She has taught in some capacity for over thirty years—English, real estate law, ethics, even energy work. She knows words are powerful, and she loves to connect them in different ways.

Jazzy lives in Oregon with her wife, three children, and two dogs, capturing the essence of life's journey in all its wonderful forms.

Connect with Jazzy ...

Email: jazzymitchell@jazwriter.com
Facebook: Jazzy Mitchell Author
Website: http://jazwriter.com/

Note to Readers:

Thank you for reading a book from Desert Palm Press. We have made every effort to edit this book. However, typos do slip in. If you find an error in the text, please email lee@desertpalmpress.com so the issue can be corrected.

We appreciate you as a reader and want to ensure you enjoy the reading process. We would like you to consider posting a review on your preferred media sites and/or your blog or website.

For more information on upcoming releases, author interviews, contest, giveaways and more, please sign up for our newsletter and visit us as at Desert Palm Press: www.desertpalmpress.com and "Like" us on Facebook: Desert Palm Press.

Bright Blessings

59841009R00119

Made in the USA
Columbia, SC
09 June 2019